MA
SURFER

21X12/12

MAHU SURFER

A Hawaiian Mystery

NEIL S. PLAKCY

alyson books
NEW YORK

© 2007 by Neil S. Plakcy

Manufactured in the United States of America

This trade paperback original is published by Alyson Books
245 West 17th Street, New York, NY 10011
Distribution in the United Kingdom by Turnaround Publisher Services Ltd.
Unit 3, Olympia Trading Estate, Coburg Road, Wood Green
London N22 6TZ England

First Edition: August 2007

07 08 09 10 11 a 10 9 8 7 6 5 4 3 2 1

ISBN: 1-59350-007-6
ISBN -13: 978-1-59350-007-8

Library of Congress Cataloging-in-Publication data are on file.

Cover design by Victor Mingovits
Interior design by Jane Raese

I met Sharon Sakson at a picnic table at a Bread Loaf writers' conference reunion, and we immediately clicked. That connection has resulted in a long friendship and a book together, *Paws and Reflect: Exploring the Bond Between Gay Men and Their Dogs*. Thanks for everything, Sharon.

Acknowledgments

Thanks to Les Standiford and the members of the summer 2004 graduate fiction workshop, where this manuscript had its beginnings, as well as all the FIU creative writing faculty.

My Hawaiian *ohana,* Cindy Chow and Ken Sentner, helped Kimo's voice sound more like that of a *kama'aina* and less like a *malihini.* I'll remember that there are no squirrels or seagulls in Hawaii.

My colleagues in the English department at Broward Community College's South Campus have been so supportive of my creative work.

The staff at Alyson Books—Dale Cunningham, Joe Pittman, Jeff Theis, Richard Fumosa, and Anthony La Sasso—have been great to work with.

Thanks go to fellow mystery writers Anthony Bidulka, P.A. Brown, and Christine Kling, the South Florida chapter of Mystery Writers of America, and all those writers and fans I've met at Sleuthfest, Bouchercon, and other conferences.

I appreciate John Spero and the LGBT book group at the Barnes & Noble in Fort Lauderdale, who invited me to their group for one meeting and made me so welcome I decided to stay.

My mother, Shirley Globus Plakcy, and my agent, Richard Curtis, have provided great support, as have my friends, including Lois Whitman and Eliot Hess, Steve Greenberg, Pam Reinhardt, Andrew Schulz, Sally and Bob Huxley, Zita Goldfinger, and Debbie Prince.

And, as always, my deepest appreciation to Marc, for love, support, and services rendered. You're my soul and my heart's inspiration.

Chapter 1

BACK TO WORK

I PARKED MY BATTERED PICKUP at a meter on South Beretania Street, about half a block away from Honolulu Police Headquarters, and sat there with the windows open for a few minutes. Keola Beamer was playing a slack key guitar piece on KTUH, the radio station at the University of Hawai'i, and a light breeze rustled the palm fronds. It was nice to sit there, rather than face what was waiting for me inside.

The pickup was a hand-me-down from my father, a small-time contractor who supported my mom, my brothers, and me by building everything from an addition to somebody's house to small shopping centers all over the island of O'ahu. He yelled a lot when I was a kid, and let my older brothers pick on me too much, but he and my mom instilled a sense of honor in me, a need to do what's right. That's partly why I became a police officer six years ago.

I think it was that sense of honor, too, that made my coming-out so hard. Admitting, to myself and others, that I had been lying about being gay for so long was tough, and it was even tougher because the media dragged me out of the closet, when my sexuality became an issue during a case I investigated. My family had to learn I was gay from a TV report.

They stood by me, though, while I was suspended from the force, and they rejoiced with me when the suspension was voided and I was offered a new job, in a different district, with the boss I was about to report to.

Keola finished and the station segued into Keali'i Reichel, who sang, "Every Road Leads Back to You." I figured that was a good cue to see where my road was going to lead me, so I locked the truck and headed down the sidewalk.

The sour-faced aide manning the metal detector looked like he knew exactly who I was, and he wasn't happy to see me. I took the elevator up to Lieutenant Sampson's office, and the two cops already on it stopped talking as soon as I stepped in. Neither said a word to me, and I didn't say anything to them.

I started to understand what it was going to be like to come back to work again, now that everyone on the island of O'ahu knew who I was.

Though I had met Sampson when my suspension was voided and he had offered me a transfer to his division, I didn't know much about him, just that he seemed to be a fair, no-nonsense guy. "Come on in, Kimo, have a seat," he said, standing up to greet me. "How've you been holding up?"

"It hasn't been easy," I said, keeping my back stiff as I shook his hand. I looked around as I sat. The furniture was standard-issue HPD, simple and utilitarian. Sampson's desk was loaded with paperwork and a few framed pictures. A paperweight on a shelf caught my eye; it was a scale model of what looked like a Civil War–era cannon. "Coming out is tough enough when you're just telling your family and friends. When the media gets involved and you nearly lose your job, it's even tougher. But I appreciate your willingness to bring me into your team, and I'm looking forward to getting back to work."

"Good. I'm embarrassed that this department, which I believe in, didn't treat you right, but I think we can put all that behind us." I noticed that he was mimicking my posture, staying stiff and serious. Finally, he smiled. "I'm looking forward to having you work for me. So let's get going."

I relaxed a bit in the chair, crossing my legs, and he leaned over and dropped an 8 x 10 blowup of a dead man in front of me.

I've seen a lot of bodies and I always feel an initial stab in my guts. I think when I stop feeling that I'll have to turn in my badge. This one was no different. After I blinked and swallowed, I forced myself to look closely at the photo.

I saw a Caucasian male, early twenties, obviously fit. He wore a wetsuit, which meant that he had been either a surfer or diver, and he was spread-eagled on the sand, one arm turned at an awkward angle. Someone had carefully parted his wet, dirty blond hair to show a gaping hole in the right side of his head, but otherwise he looked unharmed.

"Michael Pratt," Sampson said. "Twenty-two. Born and raised in Absecon, New Jersey. Lived on the North Shore, in Haleiwa. He'd been using it as his base off and on for the last two years, following surf competitions around the world when he could. He was surfing at Pipeline one morning about five weeks ago, and bang! somebody shot him right off his board. Dozens of people in the water and on the beach, and nobody saw the shooter or even heard the shot. Witnesses said it looked like he fell, and it wasn't until the body washed up with a bullet hole in the head that anybody thought to look around. By that time, of course, it was too late."

I took another look at the photo, trying to imagine Pratt on a board. Pipeline was one of the prime surf spots on the North Shore, a unique combination of an extremely shallow coral reef and waves that break close to a soft, sandy beach. It's the standard by which all tubular waves are measured. When Pipeline waves are six feet and under, they have enough juice to allow you to try any maneuver. But as the waves get taller, you focus simply on the thrill of flying so high and so fast—and then try not to kill yourself when the wave dumps you unceremoniously on the shore, or worse, on some outcropping of spiky coral.

I had spent countless hours surfing there as a teenager, sneaking out of my parents' house with my best friend, Harry Ho. I'd lived about a mile from it during the year I'd spent immediately after college, learning that though I was good, I would never be good enough to make a living from surfing.

"Damn good aim," I said, thinking of Pratt speeding across the face of a wave. "A moving target like that."

"An M4 carbine, based on the ballistics analysis," Sampson said. "Standard military issue since about 1994. Gives you distance and accuracy."

He dropped another photo in front of me. This victim was female, Filipina, black hair, olive-colored skin just a few shades darker than mine. She, too, had been shot, this time just above the heart. She wore a hot pink strapless mini-dress with matching stiletto heels, and she had the trim, fit physique of a jogger, an aerobics instructor—or a surfer.

"Lucie Zamora," Sampson said. "Another surfer. Same weapon. Shot about three weeks after Pratt, outside a club in Haleiwa. Again, no witnesses; she had walked out by herself, about two A.M., and there was no one else in the parking lot at the time. She was found just a few minutes later, but even though a bouncer tried CPR, she was already dead."

I studied the photo. She had obviously fallen just after she'd been shot, her right leg tucked under her, a pink clutch spilling cosmetics onto the black pavement next to her. She wore huge pink hoop earrings and nearly a dozen skinny pink bangle bracelets. "She know Pratt? Any connection to him or his murder besides the weapon?"

Sampson shook his head. "Not that we've been able to figure out." He threw another picture in front of me.

"Jesus, how many of these have you got?" I said, pulling back. This photo was the most gruesome of all. The body had been in the water for some time before being pulled out, and it was bloated and shriveled and had been nibbled on by various sea creatures.

"This is the last one. Ronald Chang. Washed up off Puaena Point about two weeks after Lucie Zamora was shot." Sampson walked back behind his desk and sat down. Around me, I saw the evidence of his investigative and managerial success—commendations, plaques, photographs. Sampson himself was a bear of a man, tall, burly, and bearded, and I was interested to note that he wore a navy polo shirt and khaki slacks, not a suit or uniform.

"Let me guess," I said. "Same weapon."

"Nope. This was a handgun, probably a Beretta. From some faint bloodstains we found in the parking lot of his apartment building, we think he might have been shot there. We don't know how or why he ended up in the water; probably just dumped."

"What makes you think they're connected, if the weapon was different?"

"He knew Lucie Zamora, and he disappeared the same day she was shot. He was a computer technician, twenty-eight years old. Originally from Maui, but he had been living in Haleiwa and telecommuting for a firm in Honolulu for the last few years. He was a surfer, too, though not a competitive one like Pratt or Zamora."

"If somebody's shooting surfers," I asked, "how come I haven't heard about this before?"

"The press haven't made the connection yet, and we haven't helped them. We don't want to cause a mass panic on the North Shore. Yes, somebody's shooting surfers, but we aren't sure if they were targeted *because* they were surfers, or because they have some other connection entirely." He looked at me. "That's where you come in."

The Honolulu Police Department covers not just the city of Honolulu, but the county of Honolulu as well, which encompasses the entire island of O'ahu. District 2 covers the North Shore of the island, including the central island communities of Mililani and Wahiawa, as well as civilian crimes on military bases such as Wheeler Army Air Field and Schofield Barracks. Some detectives work out of downtown, others out of the substation in Wahiawa, about halfway between Honolulu and the surfing beaches. "Would I work here or in Wahiawa?"

"We'll work that out." He looked at me. "Tell me what you know about surfers and cops."

I laughed. "Well, lots of cops surf. But that doesn't mean the two groups get along. Though the state owns the beach up to the high-water mark, some landowners, particularly hotels, try to restrict access, and so you can't always get the best breaks without trespassing on someone's property. The non-surfing cops tend to enforce the letter of the law, especially if the surfer in question has long hair, no visible means of support, and the faint aroma of marijuana lingering around him."

"Exactly why the original detectives have had trouble getting people to talk, and exactly why I need somebody who can go in there and talk to surfers who might shy away from speaking to a cop." Sampson leaned forward. "I need somebody who can hang out on the North Shore and dig deeper in this case than the original detectives could. I need you."

I was baffled. "But anybody on the island of O'ahu who reads a newspaper or watches TV knows that I'm a cop, thanks to all the media attention my coming-out story and my suspension got. Even though I've been surfing my whole life, nobody who's a serious surfer will trust me."

Sampson looked me straight in the eye, something I admired him for. "Actually, all they know at present is that you *were* a cop, until you were suspended. The department hasn't made a public announcement of your reinstatement, and I know you haven't either."

It took a minute for Sampson's words to sink in. "You want me to go undercover?"

Sampson nodded. "Who have you told about the deal we made with you?"

I started ticking people off on my fingers: my parents; my brothers and their families; Harry Ho, my best friend since high school; Terri Clark Gonsalves, my best female friend. I didn't know if any of them had told anyone else, but it wouldn't have surprised me. I had been in the news, and that made me fair game for anyone's gossip, even those who were near and dear to me.

Sampson's expression was grim. "Well, I can't blame you. If I were in your shoes, I'd want the world to know, too." He paused. "Unfortunately, that leaves us with a problem. In order for this to work, the world has to believe that you've left the force, and that includes your family and friends."

Sampson put his hand to his cheek and thought for a minute, while I looked up again at a photo in which he was being commended by the mayor. I had known guys in vice who were allowed to tell their friends and families that they were undercover, just not the specifics of the investigations. I wondered why I couldn't do the same. It's not that I had gone into police work for the glory, but it would be nice someday to get my name in the papers for something that would make my parents proud of me. Something that reflected my skill as an investigator, not some sleazy investigation into my personal life.

Sampson finally steepled his fingers and looked at me. "Basically, you'll have to pretend that you've decided that this job offer just isn't what you need at this time of your life. You need to think about who you are, where you're going from here, that sort of thing." He released his fingers and motioned with his right hand. "Being who you are, you'll want to do that kind of soul searching near a big wave, so you'll head up to the North Shore and plunge back into surfing. That'll be a good cover to get you up there, where you can get to know people, ask questions, and find out who's behind this."

"Tell me why I can't tell my parents," I said. I noticed my back had gone stiff again, that I was clutching the arms of the chair. "My brothers. Why do I have to lie to them?"

"Your oldest brother's the station manager at KVOL, isn't he?"

I clenched my teeth and nodded. KVOL was the scandal-mongering TV station of the islands, with the slogan "Erupting News All the Time." KVOL had broken the news of my suspension from the force, and though my brother had been able to tone down and eventually stage manage the coverage in my favor, he and his station were in large part responsible for how big the story had become.

"You may trust your brother, but I don't," Sampson said. "I know what these media types are like. And if you tell him a different story than you tell your parents or your other brother, he'll figure it out. I can't have this investigation compromised."

By the time he was finished, I was shaking my head. "I can't do it. You're asking me to lie to everyone who matters to me. I can't do that, not after what I went through just to be able to tell the truth."

The fact that he didn't trust my brother Lui stung me. Sure, I didn't have the best relationship with him and my other brother, Haoa, when we were kids. They were ten and eight years older than I was, and they picked on me mercilessly. But as adults, we'd become friends, and both my brothers had stood by me during that time—only a few days before, though it seemed like a lifetime—when I had been suspended from the force and needed their help to reinstate my good name and get my job back. Hadn't Lui shown that family mattered to him?

But then again, he had run the story about me without telling me in advance, without letting our parents know that their youngest son's life was going to be splashed across the evening news. Did that prove that he couldn't be trusted, when there was a story at stake?

"There is a greater good here, Kimo," Sampson said, leaning across the desk. "I want you to remember that. There's a murderer killing surfers on the North Shore, and you're the only one who can get in there and find out what's going on." He paused. "And you know the only way you can do that is by pretending that you've left the force."

I didn't know what else to say. He wasn't asking me to step back into the closet, as God knows I couldn't. But after all the hurt I'd caused my family and friends, I couldn't imagine tearing everyone up yet again. "But . . ." I began.

"No buts," he said. He handed me a pile of folders. "Take

these home and read them. Don't tell anyone we've had this conversation. Think about it. Then come back here tomorrow morning and we'll talk again."

"What if I say no?"

Sampson sat back in his chair and stared at me for a minute, and in that show of confidence I had an inkling of why he had received so many of those commendations. "You're a good cop, Kimo. I need you on this investigation. If you can't do it, well, we'll talk about that when we have to."

When I left Sampson's office I didn't quite know what to do or where to go. I'd prepared myself to begin work again that morning, and that clearly wasn't to be. I walked to my truck, turned the engine on, and started to drive, not really knowing where I was going.

There was a lot of traffic in Honolulu as I circled past the Aloha Tower, that old 1920s building where people used to gather to watch the cruise ships go in and out. Past the Iolani Palace, the only royal palace on American soil, across the street from the tall gold statue of King Kamehameha. Around and around, through downtown, along Ala Moana Beach Park and the Ala Wai Yacht Basin, where Gilligan and the skipper left with their boatload of tourists for a three-hour tour.

I ended up at the top of Mount Tantalus, overlooking Honolulu. It was a real tourist office day: temps in the low 70s, trade winds off the ocean, just a few puffy white clouds floating across the sky to add interest to what otherwise would have been an unbroken expanse of light blue.

From up there, you could see all the way from the extinct volcano of Diamond Head to the naval base at Pearl Harbor. It was only about a dozen miles, but it was a trip that ran from the origin of the island all the way to the latest innovations in military technology. I looked out at the city for a while, saw the line of surf where waves broke against the shore, plane-loads of tourists landing and taking off from Honolulu International, and the steady traffic of tiny cars along the ribbon of the H1, the highway the federal government requires us to call an interstate. I guess subconsciously I'd hoped that coming up there would allow me to put all my troubles into perspective, see myself as just one of those infinitesimally small people below me, going about their daily lives.

I'm not sure it worked, but I did get out of the truck, sit on a bench, and start to read the dossiers, as Sampson knew I would.

Though there was a lot of paperwork—crime scene reports, interviews with witnesses, friends, and relatives—there wasn't really much information. There appeared to be no thread that tied together all three victims other than the fact that all three were surfers. Michael Pratt was *haole*, or white, a mainlander who lived in Haleiwa when the surf was high, traveling around the globe to compete, from France to Australia and Costa Rica to South Africa. He usually finished in the money in surfing championships, and supplemented his income by teaching surfing at clinics and exhibitions.

Nineteen-year-old Lucie Zamora was a Filipina who had moved to Honolulu at age ten when her mother, a maid at a Waikīkī hotel, was finally able to send for her and her younger brother. She had been living on the North Shore for the last two years, working as a clerk and waitress while struggling to become a professional surfer. She had a couple of high finishes in local tournaments, but was nowhere near Pratt's caliber.

Ronald Chang was twenty-five, a computer technician and weekend surfer. Born in Hong Kong, he had grown up on Maui, where his parents ran a Chinese restaurant. Like me, he'd been surfing most of his life, and like me, too, he had a full-time job. But he'd never placed in the money at a surf competition.

Though Zamora and Chang knew each other, neither seemed to know Pratt. Zamora and Pratt were shot with the same gun, and Chang had disappeared earlier on the day that Zamora was shot. There had to be a connection between these three that had led to their deaths, but the detectives on the case hadn't been able to find it. Did I think I was better? No. I knew I was good, but almost every detective I'd met on the force was as smart, or as dogged, or as lucky, as I was. Sampson believed that because I was a surfer, I'd have some special entrée to the world of North Shore surfing that would provide the missing clue. But was it worth lying to people I cared about (and the general population as well) and putting my life on hold to find out if he was right?

That phrase struck me. Putting my life on hold.

Michael Pratt's life, Lucie Zamora's life, and Ronald Chang's life had been put on permanent hold. How many others would suffer the same fate if I didn't do anything?

I closed the dossiers and looked out at the landscape again. Those big puffy clouds had multiplied and were massing over the Ko'olau Mountains. O'ahu is an island of microclimates— it can be gloriously sunny in Kāhala, but rainy in Mānoa, just a few miles away; partly sunny in Pearl City, windy in Laie, cool in Haleiwa. And yet, they say if you just stay where you are, the weather will change soon.

I felt as unsettled as the weather, and equally vulnerable to being blown one way or the other. So I decided to get my father's advice.

Chapter 2

TELLING LIES

MY DAD HAS SPENT MOST OF HIS CAREER as a general contractor, building the homes, stores, and offices where the people of our island live and work. He has always impressed upon me and my brothers the honorable nature of hard work, the need to put others before yourself, and the importance of remaining true to your ideals no matter what pressure is brought to bear on you.

When I was born, he was working as a construction supervisor for Amfac, one of the "Big 5" companies in Hawai'i. At night and on weekends, he was building a small house on a piece of land his friend Chin Suk had given him. When the house was finished, he planned to sell it, and use the money to start his own construction business.

But it was tough providing for a family of five on a superintendent's salary, and he often had to wait weeks before he could afford to buy the materials he needed. One day, a man from a mainland company offered him a thousand dollars to approve a lucrative contract that would have been very costly to Amfac. That thousand dollars would have been enough to buy the rest of the materials my father needed, and get his business launched. But he turned the money down, and reported the bribe to his boss.

The house wasn't finished for another six months, but my father made up for it by working harder and working smarter, avoiding waste and watching every penny. He has always held that up to us as an example of how a man must listen to his conscience and not take the easy way out.

Now, toward the end of his career, he worked out of an office above a small shopping plaza he owned in the industrial neighborhood of Salt Lake, near Pearl Harbor, and I knew if I hurried I could make it there just in time for lunch. And indeed, I pulled into the parking lot just as he was descending the exterior stair, headed for his truck.

He has lost a little height, the osteoporosis compressing his spinal column in tiny increments, and his hair is flecked with silver. As my mother often points out, though, he is still as handsome as he is in their wedding picture, framed in our living room. She keeps him on a strict diet, but he is a big man, broad-shouldered and a little paunchy in the gut. If I age as gracefully as he has, though, I will be glad.

"Kimo!" he said, when I pulled up next to him and leaned out my window. "This is a nice surprise. How's the first day back at work? You on a case out this way?"

"Not exactly. You have lunch plans?"

"I'm having lunch with you. Come on, I buy you a plate lunch."

A plate lunch is an island tradition, developed to serve to plantation workers who needed to keep up their strength through long days. A main course, usually fish or chicken, two scoops of rice, a scoop of macaroni salad, and some shredded lettuce. As we walked past the storefronts, I noticed an odd pattern in the flooring—random tiles with unusual patterns. "Hey, Dad, what's with the floor here?" I asked. "Surfboards? Footballs? Movie cameras?"

As I walked I figured out the pattern. The tiles came in groupings of threes, scattered down the walkway as if tossed there. "Not movie cameras, TV cameras," my father said. "For my sons. I wondered which of you would be the first to see the pattern. Haoa comes here couple times a week, he never looks down. Lui even came once or twice, he never saw. This is the first time you've noticed."

"For your sons," I repeated. The TV camera for Lui, the football for Haoa, the surfboard for me. While we had been going on about our lives, leaving our parents behind, our father had been memorializing us in tile. "I hope you have the same number of each tile," I said. "You don't want us to get jealous."

"The same," my father said. "Always the same for each of my sons. No different."

We ate our plate lunches at my father's favorite restaurant, a hole in the wall at the far end of the shopping center called Papa Lo's.

I didn't know if there was a Papa Lo; if there was, I'd never met him. Instead the place was staffed by eager Vietnamese women who spoke only enough English to take orders and make change. While we sat at a linoleum-topped table and waited for our food, I said, "I met with Sampson today, and things aren't going to be as easy as I expected."

"How come?"

I squirmed uncomfortably on the hard plastic chair. "He wants me to lie about something. And I don't want to."

"Lie? About what?"

"Something in an investigation. One he wants me to work on."

"I don't like he ask you to lie," my father said, shaking his head. "Why you be a policeman if you can't tell the truth?"

"You told me once," I said, recalling a conversation we'd

had only a few weeks before, "that you and Uncle Chin, when you were younger . . ."

"Yes, yes," he said. "What?"

Uncle Chin is my uncle in all but blood. My father's best friend, he was once a powerful leader of a Honolulu tong, or Chinese gang. Now he is old and sick, but he and my father have always been, well, as thick as thieves, though I've never for a moment had reason to doubt my father's honor.

"You told me you had always acted with honor, no matter what you did. Was that true?"

The waitress brought our lunches and laid them before us, bowing her head slightly. My father began to eat, without answering my question. Finally, he said, "You know expression, 'no honor among thieves'?"

I nodded.

"You may not understand, but your Uncle Chin, always honorable man. And me, too, I try to live with honor and respect, try to teach that to you boys, too."

"I'm not sure we always paid attention."

My father made a noise in his throat that is impossible to render into an alphabet, but it is the same noise he made when any of us came in late with improbable explanations. Its meaning was something along the lines of "You expect me to believe that?"

We ate for a while in silence. Eventually, my father finished, wiped his hands on his napkin, and crumpled it into a ball. "Will you still have job if you don't agree to do this thing he wants, that will make you lie?"

I understood then that whether he knew it or not, my father was giving me the opportunity to take the job, even if it meant lying to him, to my mother, my brothers, and everyone else I knew. All I had to do was lie. I could tell my father that there would be no job for me with the HPD if I turned this opportunity down. It would give me a reason why I was leaving the force, a reason my parents, with their strong beliefs about honor, could understand. Instead of appearing weak, making it look like I could no longer handle being a cop now that I was out of the closet, I could appear to be strong, holding on to my values in a world that didn't appreciate them.

Of course, the irony was that I would be lying as I pretended to be unable to lie.

But what else could I do? Six years of work with the Honolulu PD had shown me that being a cop touched something deep inside me. It was a privilege and a responsibility, and I could not turn my back on either of those things. If I had to make a few personal sacrifices for the public good, tell a couple of small lies to my family and friends in order to catch a killer, that was nothing compared to the men and women who had given their lives in the line of duty. To pretend otherwise would demean them, and the badge I believed in.

It was time for me to make a decision, and there would be no going back on it. While my father waited for my answer, I felt that my senses were magnified. I smelled the chickens roasting in the back kitchen, and the pineapple an elderly couple were sharing next to us. The sun streaming in the front windows was almost too strong, hurting my eyes. When the door opened, I heard a siren outside, police, fire, or ambulance rushing to provide help to someone who needed it.

"Sampson said we'd talk about that," I said. "But I have a feeling I won't be reporting to work at the headquarters downtown any time soon. And if that happens, I think I might just go surfing for a while."

≈

I MET WITH SAMPSON AGAIN the next morning, ready to make a deal. "Who will I report to up on the North Shore?"

"No one on the North Shore will know you're working on this case," Sampson said. "I'll give you my personal e-mail address and my cell phone number, and that's the only way I want you to contact me."

I raised my eyebrows. "Any particular reason?"

"I have no idea who's behind these murders," he said. "But I have to be suspicious when I have two good detectives in District 2 and they can't come up with any information. I'm not saying that I think there's a cop, or cops, involved in this, but something doesn't smell right."

I didn't like the sound of that. I never liked to believe that cops could go bad, though I knew of course they did. The thought that someone on the North Shore could be sabotaging the investigation made me more than a little uncomfortable, but it was just one more problem heaped on my plate, a plate that had gotten fuller and fuller since the day my closet door opened.

We mapped out a strategy. I would tell my family and friends that I had decided not to accept the department's offer, in order to sit back and think about all that had happened to me in the last few weeks; not just my coming-out, but the man I had killed in the course of solving my last case. I was going to take my severance check and head for the North Shore, to surf while I thought about my next move.

Sampson would issue a press release to local media indicating that while my name had been cleared, I had chosen not to return to the force, and he would field all inquiries regarding me. He would work out the details to ensure that my salary would continue to be deposited into my bank account, and that my benefits, including health and life insurance, would continue.

One of my brother Lui's reporters, a Korean guy named Ralph Kim, had followed my story from the beginning. In order to further spread the word, I made plans to call Ralph and break the news of my resignation from the police force. Beyond that, all I had to do was get out of town.

I had to leave a message on Ralph's voice mail, but it wasn't more than a few minutes before he called me back at my home number, excitement and feigned outrage in his voice. "I knew this was going to happen," he said. "That department is never going to accept an openly gay cop."

"It's not about the department," I said. "It's about me. That's why I want to talk to you."

"Have you hired an attorney?" he asked. "You know that series we ran last week, about gay cops around the country? There's some big money in discrimination settlements."

I stretched out on my sofa, the phone at my ear. "I need some time off, Ralph," I said. "That's the story. It's not about discrimination or how the HPD treats its cops. If you want to talk to me, those are the ground rules."

"I want to talk to you," he said. "But that's not much of a story."

"Sure it is, if you pitch it right," I said, sitting up. I found myself waving my free arm around, even though I knew Ralph couldn't see it. "What effect does coming out have on somebody's life—career being one part of that? You could talk to that guy at the power company, and that top salesman at the big car dealership near the airport. Some other high-profile gay men and lesbians. You might even get a series out of it, following up on last week's series." I paused, giving Ralph a chance to think. "This could be a big career move for you, Ralph. But the story's got to be about me, and my decisions, not a smear campaign against the HPD."

"It's still a so-so story, but I'll pitch it to my news director and see what he says. In the meantime, let's schedule something."

I didn't want to do the interview at KVOL, because I didn't want Lui to know about it until it was over. I knew he'd waste a lot of time trying to talk me out of it, or putting obstacles in my way, out of a misplaced sense of family loyalty. Once he got over that, I was sure his newsman's instincts would take over, and he'd run the story. So Ralph and I met just after lunch at Kuhio Beach Park, with the squat, single-story Waikīkī station right behind us. I wore a pair of khakis, a dark green polo shirt, and brown leather sandals, trying to look relaxed and confident.

Ralph knew something was up, but couldn't figure out what. "You're just walking away?" he asked me. "After all your years on the force?"

"I need some time to think about my future," I said. We strolled along the beach together, the cameraman walking backward in front of us. "My life has been in turmoil for the last couple of weeks, and I need some time to process everything that has happened to me. Remember, I solved a high-profile murder case, acknowledged my sexual orientation to the world, and killed a man with his own gun. That's a lot for anybody to handle."

Ralph found a dozen ways to ask the same question, but every time I gave him a variation of the same answer. Finally he shifted tactics.

"What about that murder case?" he asked. "Will you be testifying?"

"That's up to the DA," I said. "I'll make myself available whenever the department needs me."

"And yet you don't want to be a cop anymore?"

"I don't know what I want, Ralph," I said, and something about the honesty of that remark made him finally believe me.

"So what's next?" he asked. "There are forces on the mainland where you could work, aren't there?"

"There are. But I haven't looked that far ahead. Right now I just want to step out of the limelight and think about what's right for me."

"Going to hit the waves?"

"You bet," I said. "I've got a long board and a short board, and they're both calling my name."

"I'll let you answer that call, then," he said. The cameraman moved around to get a beauty shot of the waves. Ralph said good-bye, wished me luck, and told me to keep in touch. "You have a lot of fans here in town, Kimo, and I'm sure they'll all be looking forward to your next move."

I felt a little funny walking back to my apartment after the interview was over. A little depressed, maybe. A part of me liked the spotlight, even though most of me didn't, and so I was torn between being happy that I could slip into anonymity and knowing that my visibility might be helping others.

And of course, the fact that I had lied through my teeth during most of the interview didn't help.

Chapter 3

NORTHERN EXPOSURE

MY CELL PHONE RANG late that afternoon, as I was packing my truck with everything I would need on the North Shore. "You trying to get me killed?" Lui asked, without preamble. "Because you know that's what Mom is going to do if I run this story."

Our mother still had not let Lui forget that he had broken the news of my sexuality, and my suspension from the force, without calling either me or our parents before the story ran.

"I'll take care of Mom and Dad," I said. "I'm going there for dinner. Before the story runs, I'll tell them."

"But why, Kimo?" he asked. "If you're going to leave the force, fine. But why make more of a story of it? I'll square it with Ralph, we'll forget you had the interview, and you can go up to the North Shore and surf. Nobody will even notice you're gone."

"That's the point," I said. "I want people to know I'm leaving the force, and I love the way Ralph is making the story more than just about me. I know a lot of people have been following what's happened to me, and I want them to know how it all has come out. You have to run that story, Lui. You owe me."

"You're crazy, brudda, but it's your own special kind of crazy. It's a great story and a good interview, so I'll run it, but you make sure and tell Mom that I didn't want to."

"I will."

≈

I GOT TO MY PARENTS' HOUSE LATE that afternoon. It's the house where I grew up, in St. Louis Heights, a nearly vertical suburb of Honolulu that backs up against Waahila Ridge State Park. The houses are older bungalows or split-levels stacked at a forty-five degree angle down the streets. "Your father said he had lunch with you yesterday," my mother said, as I kissed her cheek. "I wondered when you were going to come and see me."

My mother has always stood in sharp contrast to my father. Where he is casual, letting his hair get sloppy before he cuts it, or allowing half a shirttail to escape his pants, my mother is the picture of perfection. Her black hair is cut and styled and sprayed into submission, her skin smooth and wrinkle-free even in her sixties. As a teenager, she was the Pineapple Festival Queen, glittering in a rhinestone tiara and satin sash, and she has always retained that aura of poise and grace. She only comes up to my father's shoulder, but she exerts a subtle force that easily allows you to forget her height.

My parents and I sat in their elegant living room, in elaborate armchairs imported from France. It was an odd room to find in a house in Hawai'i, one dropped in from the pages of *Architectural Digest,* circa 1975. As kids, we never set foot in there, for fear we'd break something. My mother folded her hands in her lap and gave me the look that had terrified all of us, my father included, for years.

"You know I had a decision to make about work," I began. I realized my mouth was very dry, but it was too late to ask for a glass of water. "And it was a really difficult one to make, but I thought a lot about the way you brought me up, the things you taught me mattered, and I've decided that I'm not going back to being a cop. At least not right now."

"I don't like to see you quit a job. We didn't bring you up that way."

"I know." I squirmed in my chair, trying to find a comfortable position, finally giving up. And there was no way she was letting me stretch my legs out and rest them on the glass and gilt coffee table. "But you didn't bring me up to lie, either."

"What exactly do they want you to lie about?" she asked. "Being gay?"

"That cat is pretty much out of the bag," I said. "It's something else. I don't really want to go into it."

"But . . . "

"Let the boy be, Lokelani," my father said. "If this is what you need to do, then we support you. Being a cop is a bad job for a gay man, anyway. You go surf for a while, then you come back, maybe you work with me. You could go back to school, learn about decorating."

That thought horrified me. I missed that gay decorating gene; my apartment looks like the "before" picture from some TV show. It was killing me to have my parents think I was a quitter, that I couldn't do my job anymore just because I'd come out of the closet.

My mother clearly wasn't happy. Short, petite, and pretty in a china doll way, she has ruled her big, tall husband and three big, tall sons with a raised eyebrow, a tone of voice, a deep sigh. It's rare that she comes out and takes a stand so definitely, but there was nothing I could do at that point. Once I'd made my decision, chosen my wave, so to speak, all I could do was ride it until it crashed to shore, doing my best to manage the fear and exhilaration, and avoid getting crushed on the coral that always lurked just below the water's surface.

"There's more," I said.

My mother looked wary. I could only imagine what was going through her head, after all that had happened. "What?"

"There's going to be a story, on KVOL, on the evening news."

"No, Kimo," my mother said. "No more stories!" She reached for the phone. "I'm calling your brother right now."

"You can't, Mom," I said. The words rushed out, in my haste to keep her from spoiling those carefully laid plans. "It's not really about me, so much. It's about the decisions gay people have to make when they come out, about who to tell, and how to tell, and what you have to do once the secret's out."

I leaned forward. "It's not just my story. The reporter interviewed other people, too. I mean, I'm the hook, the reason for the story. But they're making it into another series, like the one on gay cops around the country. This is about gay and lesbian people in Honolulu, and how they live their lives every day."

My mother looked at my father. Some kind of unspoken message passed between them, and finally my father said, "News on soon. We don't want to miss it."

We moved out to my father's den to watch the news—there was no way my mother was letting a television set into her re-creation of Versailles. My parents were both tight-lipped during the interview.

After the interview with me, Ralph gave the audience a preview of what was to come in this new series: gay men who had lost their jobs after coming out, lesbian moms who had lost custody battles, gay ministers who had been forced to leave their churches. There were other, more positive stories coming too, about people who had found faith, given up addictions, chosen new careers, and established new families. It was going to be a good series, I thought, one that might change minds and move hearts. And it was going to do all that because I had told a lie.

The segment ended with a shot of Ralph framed against the surfers at Kuhio Beach Park. "This is Ralph Kim, in Waikīkī with former Honolulu PD detective Kimo Kanapa'aka, who has just announced his decision not to return to the force after his very public coming-out story. Stay tuned to KVOL, 'Erupting News All the Time,' for more stories about ordinary men and women and their experiences coming out of the closet."

When the news was over, my mother stood up, said, "Dinner now," and we went into the equally formal dining room and ate, talking carefully about my brothers and their wives and children. I could tell the story had moved them, though we didn't really talk about it. That didn't change the fact that I had lied, and I would have to live with the consequences of that lie, particularly when it came to light, but it did make me feel a little better.

I went up to my room shortly after dinner, just the way I had as a teenager. The room was frozen as it was when I was seventeen, leaving Hawai'i for college on the mainland. The walls were lined with surf posters, the shelves crowded with every trophy I had ever won in a surf competition. I sat on my twin bed and tried to remember that boy, or the young man he became, who returned to the islands with the idea that he could be a champion surfer. I remembered the day my parents picked me up at the airport, how I told them I was moving to the North Shore to surf even before we had left the parking garage.

In many ways I am lucky to be the youngest. By then, my oldest brother, Lui, was married, a father, and moving up in the hierarchy at KVOL. Haoa, two years younger, had just gotten married and started his own landscaping business. Their success bought me a little freedom, and eventually my parents agreed to let me take a year to surf. My father hired me on as a laborer and carpenter until the fall, letting me bank every penny I earned to fund my North Shore adventure, and I surfed every morning before work, rising in the pre-dawn darkness, and every evening. I left them in September, as the North Shore waves began to improve, and didn't return until winter had passed and I had given up that dream.

I tried to read but I couldn't concentrate. I checked my gear again, read some old high-school papers, and reorganized the books on my shelf, which I hadn't read since my teens and wasn't likely to read ever again. At eleven, I turned the lights out.

I couldn't sleep well, hepped up by the nervous energy of what the next day was to bring, but I did doze a little. I was grateful when light began seeping in my window and I heard the slap of the morning paper in the driveway. I pulled on a pair of board shorts, flip-flops, and an old T-shirt that read HUG A PINEAPPLE. Before I opened the door, I looked outside for reporters lurking in the underbrush. Fortunately there were none.

There was a breeze blowing up from Diamond Head and I could smell just the faintest hint of salt water. Down the street, I heard the soft whoosh of someone's sprinklers, a dog barking, a siren passing far below. A yellow and orange sun was just coming into view over Wilhelmina Rise, to the east, and

there were thin wisps of cirrus clouds high in the atmosphere.
I picked up the paper and went back inside.

Opening it, I saw that I had reclaimed the headlines I'd
been so glad to relinquish only a few days before.

"Gay Cop Resigns," they read. Someone, identified only as
an "unnamed police source," said that while gay men and lesbians had been successfully integrated into police forces
around the country, and there were clearly other gay officers at
HPD, some officers might not feel comfortable serving with
someone who was openly gay. Sampson himself was quoted
as saying, "Mr. Kanapa'aka has gone through a very difficult
time in his life, and the Honolulu Police Department wishes
him only the best in whatever the world brings his way."

My father was up at first light, too, and while my mother
slept in we read the paper and he made scrambled eggs and
Spam for both of us. We Hawai'ians take pride in the fact that
we eat more Spam per person than any other group in the
United States, something like five and a half cans per person
per year. Hormel has even made a special limited edition hula
girl can for us, available only in the islands.

"At least you get to surf for a while," my father said, as we
sat down to eat.

"I will," I said. "Big waves coming soon." It was October,
and the best surf of the year was on its way to the North
Shore, monster waves that attracted the best surfers from
around the world.

"You have to be careful," my father said, between forkfuls
of egg. "People will know who you are, and some of them
won't like you. You won't have your badge or your gun to protect you."

"They never really protected me while I had them," I said.
"The badge is just a way of convincing people to give you the

information they know they should. And a gun doesn't protect you; it's a means of last resort. The only protection you really have is your own common sense." I reached over and touched his shoulder. "Besides, if I get in any trouble, I still have that pistol you gave me."

When I left for the North Shore the first time, after returning home from California with a B.A. in English and no job prospects in sight, my father had given me a .9 millimeter Glock, one he'd had for years. It was more male bonding than out of any sense that I was in danger. I had grown up around guns; they were as much a part of our family life as luaus and slack key guitar music. Another father might have given his son a book, an heirloom watch, or an embroidered ball cap. Mine gave me a pistol.

He'd kept it lovingly polished and oiled, and I had tried to take as good care of it as he had. At that moment, it was locked in the glove compartment of my truck—which of course he had handed down to me, too. I'm of the general opinion that you don't draw a weapon unless you are ready to fire it, and you shouldn't be ready to fire it until you have exhausted every other opportunity. I'd never fired either the pistol or my service revolver at anything more than a paper target, though I had killed a man with his own gun only a short time before. The memory of that incident still haunted my dreams, but I had done it to save my brother Haoa's life, and I did not regret it.

"Good," he said, smiling across at me. "You know I worry about you." He took a forkful of eggs and Spam, and smiled at the taste. "Just don't tell your mother."

"Don't tell me what?" my mother asked, coming in to the kitchen in her white terry cloth robe, a gift from a spa vacation my father had treated her to the year before.

My father's eyes widened. "I wasn't supposed to tell you he had Spam for breakfast," I said. "You know how you worry about his cholesterol."

I was surprised at how quickly the lie came to my mouth. I try to believe I am an honest person, but years of harboring secret desires, lying to myself as much as others, had made the habit easier. So much for my new honesty; like the position I thought I was getting at District 1, in downtown Honolulu, it had evaporated quickly.

"You shouldn't eat like that, Al," she said, taking the half-eaten plate from him and scraping the Spam into the garbage. "You know what the doctor said."

"He said, 'no eat anything taste good'," my father grumbled to me.

Chapter 4

LET'S GO SURFING NOW

I LEFT THEM A LITTLE LATER, taking the H2 freeway and then the Kamehameha Highway up through the center of the island, past pineapple plantations and tourists in rented cars. It was a sunny day, clear skies and gentle breezes ruffling the papery blossoms of wild red and purple bougainvillea along the highway, and I rolled down my windows, turned the volume up on an early Hapa CD, and tried to relax.

It had been a rough couple of weeks, emotionally and physically, and I knew it would take me a long time to process everything that had happened. But now I had to focus on the case, and solve it quickly so I could get back to Honolulu and get on with my life.

My cell phone rang about halfway up the Kam. It was my second brother, Haoa, the one who had the hardest time with my coming-out. "Eh, brudda, howzit?"

"Heading for the big waves," I said. "How you doing?"

Both my brothers had helped me put away the case that had been the cause of my coming-out, and Haoa had nearly been shot. That experience seemed to have shaken my big, solid brother, and I was sorry I was leaving Honolulu when he might need me.

"Keeping busy," he said. "We're redoing all the planting for an office building out in Kāhala." Haoa's landscaping company had continued to grow, and he sometimes worked with our father on projects. I was a little jealous of that.

I asked about his wife, Tatiana, and their kids, and heard all their news. Then there was an awkward silence. I thought for a moment the connection had been broken, even pulling the phone away from my ear to check the display and make sure he was still there. Finally, he said, "How you sleep, brah? Going through everything you do?"

"I get nightmares," I said. "And sometimes my nerves keep going and I can only doze. But then whatever's bothering me passes, and I sleep again. For a while." I held my breath, waiting for him to say something, and when he didn't, I said, "You will, too. Give it time."

"Yeah. I hope so." He yawned. "Gotta make a living," he said. "You take care, brudda."

"You, too."

I hung up, feeling like shit yet again. Add Haoa to the list of all those I owed. I should never have involved civilians in a case, least of all my own family, but I hadn't had a choice; I had been suspended at the time and knew the only way I could get back to the force was to solve the case myself, however I could.

Thunderclouds moved overhead and began to spit then shower me. I turned on the wipers, flicked on the headlights, and kept going. I drove directly to Haleiwa, where the bodies had all been found, passing the big carved Haleiwa sign with the surfer catching a wave right in the middle. Every time I go through that arched bridge over the Anahulu River, I get excited, because it means I'm going surfing, and there's nothing better.

There are no motels anywhere in the area, so I stopped at Fujioka's Supermarket, where all the visiting surfers check out the bulletin boards for rooms in private homes, for shacks with no plumbing but great ocean views, even for just a stretch of concrete floor with room enough for a sleeping bag and a surfboard.

Though any of the above might have served when I was twenty-two and broke (and many did), I could afford to be a little pickier at thirty-two, with a credit card in my pocket and some money in the bank. I copied down information from half a dozen listings, and might have copied one more from a flyer being posted by a heavyset Filipina with too much eye shadow and lipstick like a bloody gash across her mouth. But she saw me looking, recognized me, and put the flyer in her handbag instead.

I turned down one place where the landlady eyed me like a rib roast in the refrigerated meat case, another where I would have shared a bathroom with half a dozen surfer dudes in their twenties, a third that was the size of my closet back in Waikīkī, and a fourth that was so close to the Kam Highway that I could almost reach out the door and touch the trucks heading up from Honolulu.

Fortunately, I found Hibiscus House, a wood-frame home that had been added onto like a crazy quilt. The main house faced the street, but the driveway ran up alongside it, and the owners had built a series of rooms, one after the other, each with their own entrance and bathroom. It was as close to a cheap motel room as I was going to find, so I paid $500 for a week in advance (in cash, thank you, requiring a quick trip back into Haleiwa to find an ATM), and set about getting my feet wet in the cool Pacific.

That first day I didn't get into the ocean until late afternoon, after the rain clouds had passed over, and the sinking sun welcomed me back with water temperatures in the high 70s and light trade winds. There was still a line of cars parked on Ke Nui Road, but I snagged a spot, then dragged my board off the roof rack of the truck and headed down the sand.

People were starting to pack up, pulling off their lycra tops, called rash guards, coiling up their leashes, and shouldering their boards, but I made my way down the hard-packed sand and felt the frothy water swirl around my ankles. I dropped my board into the surf, paddled outside the breakers, and rode my first wave, a mid-sized one that broke to the left. It felt good to be back on the water.

My room at Hibiscus House came equipped with a miniature refrigerator (the tiny freezer compartment was fused solid with ice that looked like it had been there since before statehood) and a working toaster, so I swung past Fujioka's on my way home and picked up bottled water, barbecue flavored Fritos, and brown sugar and cinnamon Pop-Tarts. Not exactly hitting all the food groups, but I did also get some takeout sushi and chocolate chip cookies for dessert, and then retreated to my room like an animal holing up in its burrow.

There was water damage by the window, a brown stain the color of dried blood dripping from the sill to the floor. The twin mattress was bowed in the middle and smelled like generations of men had jerked off into it. The water in the bathroom was rusty, and the bulb in the overhead light flickered like something from a bad movie. But it was home, at least until I earned the right to go back to Waikīkī.

The next morning I went back to Pipeline, but before I got into the water I visualized the scene, based on what I'd read in the case dossier. Someone had been able to bring an M4 carbine to the beach, take careful aim, and shoot a surfer off his board. An M4's not the kind of gun you can stash in the waistband of your shorts; it can be close to three feet long, and can be fitted with a dizzying array of scopes, lights, magazines, and other apparatus. How the hell could you bring something like that to a beach and set it up?

After strolling casually up and down the beach a couple of times, making occasional eye contact, smiling and saying aloha, I saw a guy pulling his board out of a bag and had one of those *Eureka!* moments. Lots of surfers actually transport their boards in bags; with a little creativity you could probably fit a rifle in there, too.

So you can bring a rifle to the beach, pretty much undetected. But how do you set it up? Looking around, I figured the only solution was to hide behind a dune, using that surfboard to shield you from curious onlookers. There were a couple of likely prospects; if you were careful you could hunker down, letting only the top of your head and the barrel of the rifle peek above the sand.

Standing at the water's edge and looking back, I could see you'd be protected. But you'd still be vulnerable from the street. It wasn't until I saw an amateur photographer begin to set up his gear that I realized how the gunman had completely avoided suspicion. Bring enough gear with you—a couple of cameras with big lenses, some umbrellas, coolers, and other paraphernalia—and everyone on the beach would simply assume you were there to shoot pictures, not surfers.

Once I figured that out, it was time to get wet. I hadn't tackled big water for a long time, and I knew it would take a few days before I looked like I knew what I was doing. I stuck to Pipeline, because Mike Pratt had been killed there, and because both he and Lucie Zamora had been contest-class surfers. At Pipeline, I'd be likely to meet up with other surfers who knew them.

Pipeline is actually a series of three reefs, meaning it can generate a variety of swells, from small to monster. You almost never get a wave to yourself there: if the surf is low, then every surfer and bodyboarder is out, fighting for those few precious feet at the top of the swell. Even when the surf is high, there are daredevils all around, dropping into your wave and pushing you out.

The potential for disaster is everywhere, and maybe that's what makes Pipeline so much fun. The drops can be so high that you get giddy with exhilaration—yet that reef is waiting for you when you fall. You may have mastered a tall wave, but watch out for that guy cutting across in front of you. With every tube you face the possibility of getting sucked under the water.

Pipeline requires the most basic skills: getting in early and placing your turn just right. Those were things I knew I could do, if I worked at them long enough. I took the small and medium waves, often sharing them with other surfers when the beach was busy, and I let the really big ones go. If you aren't prepared for those, you can end up hurting yourself on the rocky, coral bottom.

I alternated between Pipeline and Backdoor, a perfect right only about 150 feet away, and though every muscle in my body ached by the time I dragged myself back to my little room, I was starting to feel like a real surfer again. But all the time, I was thinking about the case, too, trying to come up with ways to learn about the dead surfers and who might have killed them.

Occasionally as I surfed I'd run into my cousin Ben, who was about ten years younger than I was. He was doing what I'd done at his age, trying to see if he could make it as a professional surfer. My mother is the oldest of five daughters, and his mom was my Aunt Pua, the youngest. Pua was a hippie, far from my prim and proper mother. She was an aromatherapist at a posh resort in Kāhala, and had been married and divorced three times.

Because of the age difference between us, and the attitude difference between our mothers, we didn't know each other that well, but we recognized each other and made small talk about the family and the surf. He was a Pipeline expert, making it his home break, and I learned a few tricks from talking with him.

Some people seemed to know who I was, and sometimes they wanted to talk. A *haole* guy with Rasta hair and tattered board shorts wanted to know if I knew a good attorney—I didn't. A middle-aged Japanese lady waiting with me to buy bottled water asked me if I knew where her son could get information about AIDS. I told her about an agency in Honolulu.

Nobody seemed aware that three surfers had been killed, and though I dropped names with everyone I met, I got no reactions to Mike Pratt, Lucie Zamora, or Ronald Chang. I could see why the original detectives hadn't made much progress, and started to doubt whether I could learn anything they hadn't.

That night, I called my parents, just to check in. They were full of well-meaning suggestions for my future. "You could come work with me," my father said. "I do big projects again, I have you to help me. No more *malasada* shops." The *malasada* is a kind of Portuguese donut, and of late my father had been building tiny shops to sell them around the island.

"Al, let the boy alone," my mother said. "He should go back to school, get a graduate degree, and become something—an architect, a businessman, a lawyer."

"Pah, back to school," my father said. "Why go back to school when he can learn everything he need from his father?"

"I'm not making any decisions for a while." I had already heard that my brother Lui was sure he could find me a job of some kind at KVOL, if I wanted it. My brother Haoa wanted me to join him in the landscape business. My sisters-in-law and my friends all had their own ideas.

And I had to lie to each and every one of them, telling them all I was still figuring out what I wanted, that I was enjoying just surfing every day. More lies than I had ever wanted to tell. Telling them kept getting harder and harder for me, and would only keep getting harder until I could come home with a solved case.

Chapter 5

THE NEXT WAVE

BY THE END OF MY FIRST FULL DAY of surfing, I was beat. I collapsed on the beach, catching my breath and massaging my calves, when a *haole* girl who couldn't have been more than eighteen or nineteen stuck her board in the sand, sat down next to me, and said hi. She was wearing a neon yellow bikini, and had her sandy blonde hair pulled up into a ponytail with a matching ribbon. Her skin was the deep bronze of someone who spends a lot of time on the water.

"Hi," I said back. I'd seen her surfing; she was pretty damn good.

"You're that guy who used to be a cop, aren't you?" she asked.

"Guilty as charged. Kimo." I held out my hand.

"Trish," she said, shaking it. "I saw you on the news."

"My fifteen minutes of fame."

She nodded toward the water. "Your style's pretty good for somebody who hasn't surfed for a long time."

"I've been surfing since I was a kid," I said. "The last few years, though, not too much. Mornings, before work. Weekends. The occasional odd trip up to the North Shore." I paused. "How about you?"

"I was born in Iowa, but my mom really wanted to be a movie star, so she divorced my dad when I was seven and we moved to LA so she could pursue her destiny."

"And did she find it?"

"If her destiny's waiting tables at the International House of Pancakes on La Cienega, then she found it, all right. Me, I found surfing."

I had a gut feeling that Trish had something she wanted to tell me, something more than just the story of her mother's failed attempt at movie stardom. I wasn't in a hurry; my calves still needed a rubdown before I could stand up. And I've learned that when somebody has something they really want to tell you, they will, if you give them enough time.

"How long have you been in Haleiwa?"

"Two years. I didn't actually run away; I waited until I was sixteen, and I left a note."

"A note's always good."

"And I talk to my mom every Sunday. Religiously."

"Admirable." I waited. Trish watched the surfers. Finally, I said, "You must know a lot of people around here after two years." I had a gut feeling, and I decided to go with it. "You know any of the surfers who've been killed?"

She looked up in alarm. "More than Mike?"

Pay dirt, I thought. "Two others. Did you know Mike?"

She nodded. "He was my boyfriend. I was surfing just behind him, and I was the one who pulled him out of the water."

"That's tough," I said. She looked like she was about to cry.

I was thinking about what to ask her next when a guy called "Yo, Trish!" from up the beach. "Come on, let's go!"

"I gotta run," she said, standing up. "I've got some stuff to think about, but I want to talk to you. You'll be around?"

"I'll be here."

"Good. Catch you later." She grabbed her board and started running up toward Ke Nui Road.

At least I was making progress, I thought. I had seen Trish around, and I was sure I would see her again. There are, after all, a limited number of spots for serious surfers. Plus, surfing is an individual sport, but after you've caught a monster wave, you want to tell everyone about it. You want to hang out with other surfers, compare notes on gear and breaks. Pipeline was one good place to meet people who might have known the three victims, but I needed more sources.

I left the beach with a plan. Each night, I'd choose a different bar, ordering a burger and a beer and showing my face around. I started with the club where Lucie Zamora had been shot, but the crowd there was very young and only interested in drinking and dancing, and there was no way I could strike up a casual conversation with anyone about her or her murder. A couple of times it was clear people recognized me— there was some whispering, and a guy pointedly moved away from me when I walked up next to him to order a beer.

Over the next few days I saw Trish now and again, but the time was never right for us to talk. She always made eye contact, though, and I knew I just had to give her time. On TV, when they compress an entire case into an hour-long show (with time out for commercial breaks), the witnesses and the suspects always talk on cue. In life, though, people tell you the most when they're ready to talk, and I was willing to wait.

I spent my first few days at Pipeline, getting to know the surfers and working on my cover story. A few wouldn't speak to me, though I didn't know if it was because I had been a cop, because they knew I was gay, or just because they were unfriendly. After long, hot showers and lots of sports cream rubbed on my aching calves, I went out every night, but finally

I realized that in the places I'd been choosing, the music was too loud and the patrons too drunk. I decided to rethink my strategy and find the best surf shop on the North Shore, the one where the top surfers would hang out to swap stories and salivate over new gear. Maybe someone there could give me a lead.

After cruising up and down the Kam Highway, I decided The Next Wave was the place. The collection of high-end equipment and the cappuccino bar made it a place not only where surfers would hang out, but where it was quiet enough to strike up a casual conversation.

As I moved around Haleiwa, I discovered that there weren't many people left on the North Shore who remembered me from the time I'd spent there; most guys and girls I'd surfed with had moved on with their lives, as I had, or else were chasing waves elsewhere around the world.

One person had remained, though. Of course, he was the one guy I didn't particularly want to see, and of course, he was the owner and manager of The Next Wave, meaning I was bound to see a lot of him.

Dario Fonseca and I had a complicated history. He was not the reason why I gave up pursuing a career as a professional surfer, nor was he the reason I had entered the police academy. But he certainly contributed to both those decisions. Dario was a few years older than I was, but no better a surfer. Unlike me, though, back then surfing seemed to be all he had; no education, no family, nothing but a board and a wave and the desire to put them both together.

He and I, along with many of our friends, regularly entered contests we had no hope of winning. Then I came in fifth in the Pipeline Spring Championships. That was in March, when the great winter waves on the North Shore have died down a little, and the best surfers have gone to chase waves elsewhere. So I wasn't facing top competition, but still, it was the best I'd ever done. I was riding high, thinking I was finally reaching my potential.

A bunch of the guys had taken me out drinking that night, buying me beers and shots until the bar closed and dawn streaked the dark sky. I was in no condition to drive, so Dario dragged me over to his place, a one-room cottage north of Haleiwa, to crash. I remember wanting to lie down right there on the beach, I was so wasted.

The next thing I remember is waking up in Dario's bed, naked, his mouth on my left nipple. He bit and sucked at both nipples until they were hard and sore, and then licked a trail down my stomach to my crotch, where he gave me a blow job.

I wasn't a virgin then—I gave up that title to a girl named Penny Phillips, who had transferred into our class at Punahou junior year with a voracious sexual appetite and was gone by the Christmas holidays. In the interim, she slept with at least a dozen of our male classmates, relieving one and all of that most unwanted commodity among teenaged boys. I'd had girlfriends in college, and one night a girl named Jocelyn had talked me into a three-way with another guy, which both freaked me out and turned me on intensely. For the most part, though, I had successfully repressed my attraction to other guys, convincing myself that it was something I could grow out of if I just ignored it.

I must have passed out after Dario finished, because when I woke again it was almost noon and there was a note on the refrigerator from Dario. "You're a champ, Kimo," it read. "I'm out in the water."

I felt paralyzed. My mouth was dry and my head pounded, and my body was sore in unaccustomed places. When I looked in the mirror I saw my nipples were raw and red, and I had a hickey on the side of my neck.

I didn't know if I was gay or not, back then. I knew that I liked to look at men's bodies, in magazines and catalogs, and on the beach when I thought no one would notice. But the only men I knew who were clearly gay were fairies, effeminate guys who flounced around. If that was being gay, then I didn't want any part of it, and I determined to hide any part of me that threatened to become like them.

Waking in Dario's bed, though, I knew I no longer had Jocelyn to blame for what had happened. Sex with Dario, even as drunk as I was, was amazingly more erotic and thrilling than sleeping with girls had ever been. And that recognition scared the hell out of me.

Once I'd had a taste, though, I knew that I would have to keep on fighting, harder and harder, to hold back. And the more effort I had to put into hiding that desire, into forcing it down into the deepest part of my being, the less I would have to put into surfing.

I was scared and confused, and somehow I decided that I had made the best showing I would ever make in a competition, because I knew you had to put 110 percent of yourself into surfing if you wanted to be a champion—it had to be all that mattered to you. And as long as I was hiding my sexuality, I couldn't give surfing that 110 percent.

So I left. I hitched back to the place where I was staying, packed up, and went home. I slept nearly nonstop for a few days, and awake or dreaming, I kept coming back to that night with Dario. It felt like my world had been turned on end and I didn't know how to make sense of it.

My parents couldn't figure me out. Of course I wouldn't tell them the details, just that I'd decided to give up on being a champion surfer. My mother wasn't exactly depressed—after all, she'd sent me to college for four years so I could become a professional of some kind—and not a professional surfer. My father knew something was up but I don't think he ever figured it out. He kept trying to get me to go down to Waikīkī to surf, offering to lend me his truck, to wax my board for me. But I was so caught up in my own internal struggles that I paid no attention to them.

After hanging around my parents' house for a while, I saw a notice in the *Advertiser* that the Honolulu Police Department was looking for new recruits. Intuitively, I knew it was the right thing for me, so I entered the police academy. It was, after all, the most macho thing I could think to do. I thought if anything could save me from being gay, being a cop would be it.

I wanted to be a pro surfer when I was twenty-two, and I let fear of being gay stop me from chasing that dream. Dario Fonseca had been a big part of that fear, but I was nine years older and out of the closet now, and I couldn't let fear of anything keep me from finding out who killed Pratt, Zamora, and Chang. I couldn't avoid The Next Wave, if going there would help solve the case, just to avoid Dario.

Dario had probably known I was gay within about five minutes of meeting me, if it took that long. I knew there was this thing called gaydar, a kind of gay radar that you developed the more comfortable you were with being yourself. It helped you figure out who was gay and who wasn't. Mine wasn't that well-attuned yet, but obviously, nine years ago Dario's had been in full bloom.

Back then, I didn't like the way he always found himself next to me when we were out drinking, the way he often rubbed his leg against mine—or the way my body reacted when he did. I was damned if I'd be dragged out of a closet I wasn't even sure I was in.

I hadn't seen him since that day I'd walked out of his shack on the beach, but he hadn't changed much. When I walked into The Next Wave that afternoon, he was standing next to a display of bodyboards explaining the principles of the sport to a customer. By then I'd been on the North Shore for six days and I was tired, sad, horny, and frustrated. Beyond figuring out that Mike Pratt's shooter had probably camouflaged himself as a photographer, I hadn't been able to come up with a single lead on the case that took me beyond what I had read in the dossiers.

Of course Dario had clearly followed everything that had happened to me over the last few weeks. "Well, won't you look what the cat dragged in!" he said, coming up to me as if it had been nine days since we'd seen each other last instead of nine years.

He hugged me and kissed my cheek, and I hugged him back. I'd never been comfortable with too much physical contact with other guys before, always afraid I'd do something that would reveal my secret self. Now I figured I had nothing left to reveal.

"You look good, Dario," I said. "Must be all that clean living."

He did look pretty good. He was probably thirty-five, but he'd hardly put a pound on his skinny frame, his face had no lines, and his hair, though thinning at the top, was still full enough. "Flattery will get you everywhere." He winked at me. "And I do mean everywhere," he said, in a low voice.

His voice returned to normal as he said, "Now, why don't you take a look around while I finish up with this customer, and then we'll go in back and get all caught up."

He went back to the girl he'd been showing bodyboards to, and I walked around the store. The Next Wave was located just off the Kam Highway, overlooking Waialua Bay. The buildings in the neighborhood were all one and two stories, simple wood-frame places often with fading paint and a motley collection of clunkers, Jeeps, and pickups parked outside. Most people on the North Shore were there because they loved to surf, and high-paying jobs in the area were hard to find. People spent their money on expensive gear rather than on fancy homes or tricked-out cars.

The Next Wave had taken over the store next to it, a discount shoe operation, at some time in the past, and Dario seemed to have moved up from occasional salesman, as he was when I knew him. A news clipping on the side wall described how Dario Fonseca, owner of The Next Wave, had been honored by the North Shore Chamber of Commerce. Maybe Dario was more serious than I'd given him credit for.

One thing was certain—I hadn't surfed competitively in years, but I still kept an eye out for the latest gear, and Dario had it. There was some serious money tied up in his inventory, everything from O'Neill surfboards to Rip Curl wetsuits, Oakley sunglasses to Reef sandals, Croakies to Sex Wax. As you moved around the store, you could shop for T-shirts, boogie boards, leashes, and cork coasters in the shape of aloha shirts. The Next Wave also sold surf guides, magazines, signs that read *Surfer Girl Crossing,* and beach towels featuring the Ford woody station wagon that the Beach Boys had made famous.

Clothing took up nearly half the store, with fake surfboards at the ends of the racks with face-outs of shirts and shorts. You could buy every type of souvenir gadget known to man, including miniature surfboard magnets, bottle openers that looked like shark fins, ball caps with a long flap around the back to protect your neck from the sun, roof racks for your car or truck, and plastic cups with The Next Wave logo. After I'd made a complete circuit of the store, I wasted time by trying on a couple different pair of sunglasses, modeling for myself in the tiny mirror. I thought I looked a little like Keanu Reeves as Neo in *The Matrix;* just give me a black cape and the ability to do those jumping, twirling moves in slow motion and I'd be the baddest detective in the Honolulu PD.

It was late in the afternoon and The Next Wave was busy with a mostly young crowd shopping, discussing, and buying. Dario had even installed a little cyber café in one corner, serving cappuccinos and lattes along with Wi-Fi Internet access. Each of the six computers was busy, and from the expectant looks of a number of the coffee drinkers sitting near the stations, I figured they would be for some time.

Against my expectations, Dario seemed to have turned himself into a solid citizen. I'd given up on sunglasses and moved on to hats by the time he came over to me again. "So, how does it feel to be out and proud?" he asked. "You're here, you're queer, get used to it?"

"Strange," I said. "I never wanted to be a celebrity. But now my face has been on TV and in every newspaper."

"It'll pass," Dario said. He gave me a smile that was half a leer. "I always knew you'd come out of the closet someday. I didn't know you'd do it so spectacularly."

"How *did* you know?" I blurted out. "When I didn't even know myself?"

"This calls for some liquid refreshment," he said. "Hey, Cindy, keep an eye on things," he called to a girl by the register. He took me by the arm and steered me back to his office, past a display of sunblock featuring life-sized models of scantily clad guys and gals.

His office was at the rear of the store, down a corridor that led to restrooms and a loading dock. He had a side view of the ocean through a big plate-glass window; I could see wind restlessly whipping waves against the deserted shore, a line of rock and scree too rough to surf.

The rest of the office was cluttered with sales props and advertising memorabilia. The walls were lined with posters of past surf champions, including a couple we'd both surfed with way back when. He opened a small refrigerator and pulled out a pair of Kona Longboard Lagers.

He used a bottle opener in the shape of a palm tree, with The Next Wave logo on it, to pop the tops and handed one to me. "To your new life," he said, toasting me.

"And to yours. Looks like you've come up in the world."

He shrugged. "I'm doing OK. Retail's tough, though. You've got to be on top of things every minute or you can lose your shirt."

We sat down in a couple of beat-up armchairs. "Back to your question," Dario said. "How did I know you were gay when you didn't know it yourself." He took a pull on his beer. "It's in the eyes, usually. Hunger. The way a guy will look at another, thinking no one is noticing. Straight men touch each other without thinking—they'll wrap an arm around another guy's neck, they'll hip-check or punch one another in the arm."

I shook my head. "I see gay men touch each other all the time."

"That's true. What you want to look for is the ones who are afraid to touch. They're the ones in the closet." He smiled.

"They're the ones who are the most fun to chase. They know they want it, but they're scared, and you have to get them past the fear."

"By getting them drunk," I said.

"That's one of the ways." He lifted his bottle to me, took a long drink. "By touching them. Giving them these deep, searching looks that say, 'I can see into your soul.'"

I shook my head. "Dario, you are so corny."

"Rhymes with horny," he said. He raised his eyebrow. "I'm always horny. How about you?"

That was something I wasn't expecting, and it took my breath away for a minute. "That was nine or ten years ago," I said, finally. "And I'm already out of the closet now. You can't drag me any further."

"Honey," he said, leaning toward me, "you don't know how far I can take you."

He must have seen that he'd gone too far, too fast, because he backed up then. "You'll come to me sometime." He smiled. "I'll be here." He drained the rest of his beer. "Now come on, let me show you the rest of the store."

If it hadn't been for Dario's obvious connections to the surfing community, I think I would have walked out rather than taken a tour. He was just so full of himself, I thought, and I imagined he was still taking twenty-something surfer dudes who were conflicted about their sexuality out for a few beers—and then back home with him, wherever home was. It sounded predatory to me, and the cop part of me didn't like it.

He walked me around for a few minutes, then had to go to the register to handle a customer, and I took that opportunity to leave. I knew I'd be back; it was clear that The Next Wave was one of the centers for the surfing community, and I couldn't avoid it for too long. I just had to manage to avoid Dario when I was there.

What was it about me, I wondered, as I drove back to my room, picking up some fast food on the way, that attracted these predatory males? A kind of naiveté? I wasn't some confused teenager. I was thirty-two years old, a cop. I had no trouble facing down the toughest criminals, but a guy who wanted to get in my pants still scared the crap out of me. It reminded me of a William Styron quote, from *Sophie's Choice,* something about being six feet of quivering nerve. That was how I felt, even though I knew it was dumb. Really, really dumb.

Chapter 6

DOWN MEXICO WAY

I BEGAN HANGING OUT at The Next Wave occasionally. On Friday afternoon, after my first full week of surfing the waves, I decided to surf the Internet. I sent a quick e-mail to my friend Harry about the waves, and then a check-in message to my best female friend, Terri Clark Gonsalves, who had gone to high school with Harry and me. She had just lost her husband a few weeks before, and I felt bad that I had left town when she or her young son Danny might need me.

I wrote to my parents, too, a quick note about the surf and how the North Shore had changed in the past ten years. I wrote to Lieutenant Sampson at his personal e-mail address, telling him that I had begun talking to surfers.

I sat back and thought about the case. If the only thing that connected the three victims was surfing, then maybe if I learned more about them as surfers, I'd find a clue. The dossier I'd been given didn't have much detail, but I found that by searching for all three names online, I could find out which events they had competed in and what their results were. I built a matrix, looking for any events where they might all have been entered.

Pratt was clearly the best surfer of the three. He was twenty-five, and had been surfing competitively since he was a teenager on the Jersey shore. He'd placed in the top ten in a number of contests, including Mexpipe in Puerto Escondido, on the Pacific Coast of Mexico.

Lucie Zamora had also competed at Mexpipe, though she hadn't placed anywhere near the top. And way at the bottom of the men's list I found Ronald Chang's name.

Interesting, I thought, sitting back. All three had been at Mexpipe. Was it just a coincidence, or a real connection? I couldn't know for a while if it meant anything. I jumped over to e-mail and sent a message to my brother Lui, asking if he could dig up any video footage of the Mexpipe championship. I told him I was interested in studying form, but I thought perhaps I could see one or more of the murder victims there.

I printed out a list of the top 100 finishers at Mexpipe; hopefully a couple would be around the North Shore, and I could ask them some questions. I also spent some time on the competition Web site, learning about the races and the atmosphere surrounding them.

The three dead surfers had been at very different places in the surf hierarchy. Pratt was at the top, a real competitor. Lucie Zamora was struggling to make it out of the pack. Ronald Chang was more a wannabe than anything else, a weekend surfer who would probably never have finished in the money.

Where did I fit, on that scale? I had to put myself somewhere between Lucie Zamora and Ronald Chang, though without Lucie's obvious drive and determination. I had some natural ability as a surfer, and I'd certainly been doing it nearly all my life. But to be the best at anything, you have to pour yourself into it, heart and soul. Dario Fonseca had shown me that I couldn't do that, not while I was hiding my sexuality. I guessed I ought to be grateful for that, but gratitude was a hard emotion to feel around him.

I saw him pass by a couple of times while I worked at the computer. I don't know why, but I tried to look busy each time he passed, so that he wouldn't stop and chat. I wasn't comfortable with him, and I didn't want to give him another opportunity to proposition me.

I found one interesting piece of information about Mike Pratt that I hadn't seen in his dossier. He rowed with the out-rigger team that practiced in Waimea Bay. Cross-referencing them, I discovered that they practiced every Tuesday, Thursday, and Saturday mornings, and competed in single, double, and six-man races. That worked for me; I could stop by the next day.

By then it was late and I was hungry. I stopped for dinner at a bar called the Surfrider, where I had a beer and a burger. Neither were that good. The waitress seemed to recognize me, and so did a guy who was about twenty years too old for me, wearing a Heineken T-shirt that was too tight. He came up to me as I was finishing dinner and asked me, in a low voice, if I wanted to go home with him. I politely declined.

The next morning, I awoke to the NOAA's surf report in my drab, dingy room at Hibiscus House, confused at first as to where I was and what I was doing. Then as my body's aches and pains began to catalog themselves, I remembered.

I dragged myself out of bed and into the bathroom, consid-ering what had brought me there, and all the unfinished busi-ness I had left behind in Honolulu. For a minute, I wanted to chuck the whole North Shore business and go back to Lieu-tenant Sampson's office, tell him to get someone else to solve this case, give me back my gun and my shield, and put me to work in District 1.

But I didn't. Instead, I looked at the case files again and again, memorizing every detail of the three dead surfers. Then

I headed down to Haleiwa Beach Park, to where the North Shore Canoe Club practiced, across the street from Jameson's by the Sea. There were already a few people there by the time I arrived, and while we waited I helped bring out the canoes.

The light was bright and harsh, glinting in shards off the placid water. Almost everyone knew everyone else. I introduced myself as Kimo and we began stretching exercises as the sun moved up over the hills behind us. A fit, blonde woman named Melody introduced herself to me and asked if I'd ever paddled before.

"Yup," I said. "In Honolulu. For a while when I was a kid, we belonged to this native Hawai'ian club after school, where we practiced speaking the language. We made leis out of *kukui* nuts, we surfed, we learned to paddle. A little hula, too, but don't ask me to dance for you."

She laughed. "I won't." She sized me up. "You want to try the back of the canoe?"

"Sure." I knew that's where they put the biggest and strongest guys. I joined a team of six in pushing an outrigger into the water, and then we all jumped in and started paddling out to sea.

I sat in the fifth seat, behind a slim Hawai'ian guy with incredible biceps and triceps, and in front of a stocky *haole* guy. I noticed that his right leg, from the knee down, was prosthetic, but he was able to move around easily on it, and use his awesome upper body strength in the outrigger. Whenever I lost the rhythm of the oars, I felt one of his jabbing me in the back. I never heard him whoop or yell as the others did when we crested the wave. He approached his rowing as if he were on work-release from prison, with a grim determination that sapped some of my fun.

We got a good workout, paddling out beyond the surf, then

turning around, picking a wave, and paddling like hell to catch it. We did some quick races up the Anahulu River as well, and then returned to the beach. The Hawai'ian guy introduced himself to me as we dragged the canoe back up on the sand. "I'm Tepano. You rowed before?"

"When I was a kid. How about you, you been doing this for a long time?"

"Couple of years. It's a great workout." The rest of the team streamed off around us, leaving me walking up toward the parking lot with Tepano. "Everybody's pretty friendly, too."

"That guy behind me didn't seem so friendly," I said, referring to the *haole* with the prosthetic leg.

"Rich? He's OK. He just doesn't like surfers."

The sun was fully up, and there was a nice breeze coming in off the ocean. It was going to be a beautiful day. "Some awful surfboard incident in his childhood?"

Tepano laughed. "Not exactly." His face got serious then. "He was actually a pretty good surfer, once. Then the army sent him to Bosnia and his leg got blown off. That prosthetic is state of the art, but he can't feel a board under him, so he could never surf again. Made him a little bitter."

"I guess." I could only imagine how I'd feel if I couldn't surf anymore.

"Plus he has this job, security guard for this crazy old guy who doesn't want anyone crossing his land to get to the water. He's always chasing surfers away."

"I'll keep my distance."

"Probably a good idea." He gave me a *shaka,* the Hawai'ian two-fingered salute, and said, "Hope to see you here again some time."

"You probably will." As I was walking the last bit to my truck, Melody was walking past with another woman, Mary, who was, like Melody, in her late twenties or early thirties, and very fit. Mary's skin was tanned dark, and her glossy black hair was pulled into a long ponytail.

Melody, obviously the group's organizer, asked me, "You going to be around for a while? We could use some strength on our B team."

"A few weeks," I said. "I can't really commit to anything, but I'd like to drop by practice again some time, if that's OK."

"Sure."

Mary said, "Gotta go, Mel. See you later," and kissed Melody on the mouth. It seemed like a pretty intimate gesture to me, and I noticed that Mary wore a yellow gold wedding band. I wondered if they were lesbian partners, but Melody did not wear a band at all.

As Mary walked away, Melody turned back to me. "What brought you out today?"

I shrugged. "I've been surfing the last couple of weeks, saw your poster." I decided to take a gamble. "I remembered that a surfer I knew recommended you. New Jersey guy named Mike Pratt?"

Melody's face fell. "I guess you didn't hear," she said. "Mike died about a month or two ago."

"No!" I said. "Surfing?"

"You could say that. He was on his board at Pipeline, and somebody shot him. Dead by the time he washed up on the shore."

Tears began forming at the corners of Melody's eyes. "Gosh, I'm sorry," I said. "Was he a friend of yours?"

"Yeah, I guess," she said. "He was on our A team for a while. Really strong guy. You probably saw, we're like a family here. Mike's death hit us all pretty hard."

"They catch the guy who did it?"

She shook her head. "Not a clue. The police came around, but they didn't know anything."

"I'm surprised anybody would even talk to them," I said. "Surfers and cops don't always get along."

"If they'd known the right questions to ask, we might have talked," Melody said. She looked at me strangely. "Hey, do I recognize you?"

"Kimo Kanapa'aka," I said. "Formerly of the Honolulu PD."

"Oh, my God, I read about you. That is so totally unfair, what they did to you." I could see the wheels turning behind her eyes. "Say, maybe you could look into what happened to Mike. I could make some introductions here for you."

"I don't know," I said. "The police aren't exactly eager to hear from me—or my lawyer—these days."

"But you could show them," she said. "Find out what happened to Mike, prove you should be a detective again." I knew the friends and family of victims were eager to see murderers caught and punished, but I'd never seen this side before, this view that the police were clueless and needed the help of someone outside the force to solve crimes.

"You think people here know something the police don't?"

"I'm sure of it," Melody said. "You got time for a cup of coffee?"

Chapter 7

CONVERSATIONS

MELODY AND I MET a few minutes later at the Kope Bean, a little coffee shop in a strip center on the Kam Highway. A lot of surfers were getting a caffeine fix before hitting the waves, and a bunch of clearly Honolulu-bound business types were doing the same before hitting the H2 down toward the city.

The place was decorated in a style I can only describe as island Starbucks; the walls were painted with murals of coffee beans, called *kope* in Hawai'ian, growing on bushes on the slopes of what looked like Mauna Loa and Mauna Kea. There were two groups of overstuffed armchairs, and a number of blond wood tables and chairs for the laptop set.

Melody ordered a tall vanilla soy latte and I got a tall raspberry mocha, and we were able to snag a pair of the comfortable chairs. She was dressed for work by then, a light yellow linen dress and sandals, a lei of shiny brown *kukui* nuts and a sports watch her only jewelry. With her tanned skin and her sun-bleached blonde hair, she could have been an advertisement for healthy summer living.

Mana'o Company was playing low in the background, encouraging us to "Spread a Little Aloha" around the world, and in one corner of the room a bust of King Kamehameha surveyed us, an electric blue plastic lei around his neck.

"So how long did you know Mike?" I asked, when we were settled.

"About three years," she said. "He came to the *halau* right after he got to the North Shore, as part of his strength training."

Halau means long house for canoes, as well as a place where you can learn to hula. "How well did you know him?"

Melody sipped her latte and considered. "Better than an acquaintance, not as well as a friend," she said finally. "We talked a lot, and I heard all about his background, but I didn't see him socially. Of course, you can't help running into people up here; it really is a pretty small world."

"I've heard he was a pretty hard-core surfer."

"Fierce. It was what he lived to do. Everything else revolved around surfing. How he trained, who he hung out with, how he supported himself."

"How did he support himself?"

She slipped one sandal off and twisted around so that her leg was under her, smoothing the edges of the yellow linen dress. "Part of the reason why he came up here was because he met a shaper at some contest who offered him a job," Melody said. A shaper's a guy who customizes surfboards by sanding, polishing, and shaping standard boards. "Mike did the scut work, he called it, for this guy, Palani Anderson. Dragging boards around, cleaning up the mess, that kind of thing. He did that for about year, I guess, and then he started having breathing problems from the Fiberglas fumes so he had to stop."

"Bummer."

She nodded. "By then, though, Mike was good enough that he was able to start teaching. He worked out of the marina for a while, giving lessons, and then he finally started landing in the money at tournaments. His career was just taking off when he died."

"When was the last time you saw him?"

Melody had to think about that one. The foot that was still wearing a sandal tapped lightly on the floor. "It was just a couple of days before he was shot," she said finally. "I remember he went down to Mexico for a tournament, and so I didn't see him for a couple of weeks, but then he was back at the *halau*. I remember he got into a fight with Rich over something and it really disrupted practice."

"Rich is the guy who hates surfers?"

Melody nodded. "He's really not a bad guy, you know, but he and Mike used to argue about property rights—whether everyone should have free access to every beach, you know, that sort of thing." She waved her hand a little for emphasis, and I saw she had a small tattoo of a sun on the inside of her right wrist.

"I heard Rich used to be a surfer himself. I'm surprised that his attitude changed so much."

"Well, he's a security guard for this guy who owns a piece of beach, and he's always chasing surfers away. I think some friend of Mike's—maybe his girlfriend—was surfing there and Rich really frightened her. So they got into an argument and we finally had to cancel the practice."

"And that was the last time Mike came to the *halau?*"

She sipped her latte, thinking. "Yes, because I didn't hear he'd been killed for a week, and I worried that he'd stopped coming to practice because of the argument."

She drained the last of her latte and patted her mouth with a napkin, then stood up and slipped her sandal back on. "I've gotta get to work. If you come back to the *halau* on Thursday for practice, I can introduce you to some of the other people who knew Mike."

"Deal." I stood up with her, cracking my back. "I'm going to get some surfing in, but I'll see you Thursday."

I left Melody and headed back to Hibiscus House, where I showered and ate my Pop-Tarts, thinking about my day. I decided I had to learn more about Mexpipe, which meant I had to find someone who had surfed there. I pulled out the printout I'd made the day before at The Next Wave of the top finishers, and scanned the names, looking for any I recognized.

Pay dirt. My cousin Ben's name was there. I made a point of keeping an eye out for him that morning at Pipeline, and when I saw him taking a break I went over to where he was hanging out on the beach with a couple of friends.

He's pretty good-looking, in a scrawny, surfer way. There isn't an ounce of fat on his six-foot-something body, and he wears his black hair loose, down to his shoulders. His father was a haole Aunt Pua married in a quickie ceremony in Vegas, who left her life, and our family circle, shortly after Ben was born. So, like me, Ben has just a slight epicanthic fold around his eyes, and his skin takes a tan well.

"Yo, cuz, how's it going?" he said as I came up. "You guys know my cousin Kimo?" he said to his friends.

We nodded all around. "You got a minute?" I asked. "I wanted to talk to you about something."

"Sure." He and I walked down the beach a little to a refreshment shack, where we both got bottles of water. "Your folks still upset about what happened to you?" Ben asked, as we sat down on benches overlooking the water.

"Pretty much," I said. "I talk to them every week and you know my mother, she's full of ideas for me."

He laughed. "Boy, I know that. You should hear my mother talk."

"I never imagine Aunt Pua as the type to tell anybody how to run his life."

"That's because you're not her son. That laid-back act is for the rest of the world. Not for me. She keeps telling me I could be teaching surfing at a resort and making good money."

"My mother keeps telling me things like when the next LSAT test is. 'You can still go to law school,' she says. 'Lots of people go back to school in their thirties.'"

"Man, those two will never change," Ben said, shaking his head. "So what's on your mind, dude?"

"You went to Mexpipe, didn't you?" I asked.

"Sure. Did better than I expected, not as good as I hoped."

"What's it like?"

He took a swig from his water bottle. "Zicatela's the beach that everybody surfs. Six to fifteen foot ground swells; lots of tubes. Wipeouts can be really bad. There's this break called the Point, and you can get some really long, fast, challenging rides."

"How's Mexpipe itself?"

"Lots of good surfers show up, and the waves can be really awesome." He shifted around on his bench. "Big party scene, too."

"Yeah?"

"Toga party, bikini contest—I mean, they really try to make it fun."

"Lot of drugs down there?"

He nodded. "I don't do anything more than pot, and never when I'm in a contest, but you could get anything you wanted there. Just had to walk around the town for a few minutes and somebody would try to sell you something."

"I'm trying to track down some people who were there—maybe you knew them. Mike Pratt, Lucie Zamora, Ronnie Chang."

Ben narrowed his eyes at me. It was obvious that he recognized the names and had an idea of why I was interested in them. "I thought you were done being a cop," he said.

I shrugged. "Old habits die hard."

Ben considered that. "I knew Mike Pratt pretty well," he said finally. "Interesting guy. Really good surfer—I think he was just about to really make a name for himself. He got in with this weird crowd, though."

"Weird how?"

"This Christian surfing ministry—they run a café at the main surfing beach, and they have Bible study sessions at this place called El Refugio. Now, I'm not against any religion—I figure, you want to believe, man, more power to you."

He stopped to take another swig from the water bottle. "But Mike, man, he really took it to heart. Then when we got back, he started bitching about his board not being right. You ask me, it's his head that wasn't right."

"You ever see him hang out with Lucie or Ronnie?"

"A couple times, I saw him with Lucie. But you know, she didn't really belong there—she wasn't good enough. I think she was just there for the party. The other guy—Ronnie—I just met him once or twice because he was with other people from the North Shore. He was a total wannabe."

He drained the last of his water. "I gotta get back. You gonna be around for a while?"

"For a while."

"Cool. See you around, then." He gave me a *shaka* and walked back toward his friends.

Ben had seen Mike and Lucie talking to each other at a party. It didn't mean that they were best friends, or involved together in some way, but it was a start.

Chapter 8

COACH TEX

I SURFED ALL DAY SATURDAY, hoping to see Trish. Though I talked to a bunch of surfers I didn't learn anything new, and I was starting to get discouraged. Once I actually heard the word "faggot" muttered under someone's breath—but I couldn't tell who had said it. I was discovering information, but very slowly, and that was frustrating. By late afternoon, I was beat. Though I had surfed regularly in Waikīkī, that was nothing compared to the punishment I was putting my body through. I couldn't even keep my promise to get out for meals—I stopped at Fujioka's and bought some takeout sushi, and nearly fell asleep eating it.

Sunday morning, I put on my rashguard and walked out into the pre-dawn darkness, dragging my board with me. I couldn't help thinking about the murders as I surfed. Usually the water is the place where I can put everything else aside, but knowing that all three victims had been surfers somehow connected the act of surfing with their deaths, making it impossible for me to forget them.

I surfed most of the day, resting between waves, scanning the sand for Trish, and talking to whoever passed by. I had some big, plump shrimp for lunch, bought from a bright yellow lunch wagon at the beach. By around three o'clock, I gave up, and after a quick shower back at Hibiscus House I drove over to The Next Wave, hoping that Dario had the day off.

Either he did, or he was holed up in his office the whole time. I was grateful, and it allowed me to focus on doing more computer searching. I already knew a lot about Mike Pratt, so I decided to spend some time on the other two. I knew it would be hard to zero in on someone with as common a name as Chang, but I wanted to give it a shot.

After a number of fruitless searches, I found a site from La-hainaluna High School in Lahaina which listed winners of a science fair. One Ronald Chang had won second prize for a case study of how one could hack into the school's computer system and change student grades. Chang's photo, which was close enough for my purposes to the one I'd seen in his dossier, clinched the deal for me.

There was a little note on the Web page thanking Mr. Chang for his insight, which resulted in a total revamp of the school's computer grading system. If Ronnie could do that at sixteen, I thought, what was he capable of at twenty-five?

I went back to the dossiers on the dead surfers. Ronnie Chang was a computer technician for a firm in Honolulu, and the investigating detectives had spoken to his coworkers, but as far as I could tell, no one had spoken to his family or friends back in Maui. I wondered about that, and sent a quick e-mail to Lieutenant Sampson asking if there had been a reason why not.

There was almost nothing online about Lucie Zamora, other than her name on the roster of a couple of surfing tour-naments. The original detectives had run all three surfers through the police system, checking for arrests, warrants, and other malfeasance, and all three had come up clean.

Sampson must have been online himself that afternoon,

because I got an e-mail back almost immediately, authorizing me to fly to Maui to talk to people about Ronnie Chang. It wasn't a big deal; an inter-island flight takes about half an hour, and the round trip, with a rental car, would be under $200. I was able to get a reservation for the next morning, which meant I needed to be at the airport in Honolulu early. I decided to drive down that night and sleep in my own bed— but I didn't tell my family or friends, because I didn't want to have to come up with yet another lie.

It was strange pulling into my own parking lot, climbing the stairs to my own little studio apartment. I had only been away for two weeks, but I had immersed myself so much in my new life on the North Shore that I almost felt like I didn't belong back in Honolulu. Or maybe it was that I knew I didn't really belong back there until I had solved the murders.

I had been waking before sunrise every day, so the next morning I was able to make it to the airport in plenty of time for my flight. The Island Air agent recognized my name at the gate and winked at me, but that was the extent of my notoriety. I figured I had finally slid out of the newspapers, and I was able to settle back into a bit of anonymity.

I got into Kapalua-West Maui Airport on the Valley Isle a little after ten. I had a list of things to check out—Ronald Chang's high school, and his parents' restaurant, for starters. I was also going to cruise a couple of surf shops, looking for anyone who might have known him.

I took the Honoapiilani Highway, which circles around West Maui, down to Lahaina, where I was looking for Victor Texeira, the computer science teacher at Lahainaluna High. I was somewhat surprised to discover, when I asked at the office for him, that I was directed to the gym, rather than to a computer lab.

There was only one teacher in the gym when I stuck my head in there, a very fit guy in very tight clothes, with a whistle around his neck. When one of the kids called him "Coach Tex" I was even more confused.

"Can I help you?" he asked, coming over to me. "You guys do two laps, then hit the showers," he called to the kids, who promptly took off around the perimeter of the gym.

I gave him my name, and he said, "I'm Victor Texeira." He smiled. "The kids call me Coach Tex, as you heard."

I had worked out a story in advance. I explained that I was a former homicide detective and that I'd been asked to look into a series of murders that had occurred on the North Shore. All that was true. I have discovered, in years of listening to lies and pulling them apart, that those lies which are most closely rooted in truth are the easiest ones to maintain.

One of the victims had been Ronnie Chang, his former student, I continued. "I'm a little confused, though," I said. "I thought from what I read online that you taught computer science."

"I do, one class. Mostly I'm the gym teacher, though." He motioned to a room at one corner of the gym with glass windows looking out on the floor. "Come on into my office and I'll explain."

I followed him, noting privately how his little gym shorts hugged his ass, the way his pecs and biceps bulged out of the skintight polo shirt he wore. I was pretty sure he was straight; he wore a wedding band and one of those little Jesus fish pins at his collar. Even so, I rarely saw a straight man dress so provocatively. I could even tell he was wearing a jockstrap under his shorts—that's how tight they were.

"I want you to know, I'm not normally the type of guy to speak ill of the dead," he said, opening the door to the office and motioning me inside. "But in this case, I'll make an exception."

"Tell me how you knew Ronald Chang," I said, sitting across from his desk. The room was lined with trophies, certificates, and commendations, including pictures of Coach Tex with the governor and two U.S. senators.

"It was my first year here," he said, sitting. "I was hired as a coach, but the state had just installed this e-mail system for us, and they needed somebody to administer it. I had just graduated from UH, and I'd lived in a computer-equipped dorm, so that made me the most qualified."

"Ronald Chang was a student then? How old was he?"

"He was a junior," Texeira said. "Ringleader of a bunch of kids who didn't take gym seriously. Every day they'd come in with obviously faked excuses—recovering from a cold, can't get overheated, that kind of thing. Then on the weekend I'd see them all at Breakwall or Shark Pit, surfing like there was nothing wrong with them."

I knew Breakwall and Shark Pit, both decent surfing spots in Lahaina. "That must have pissed you off," I said.

"It did. So one day I decided I'd get even. I came up with a bunch of exercises designed specifically for surfing. Nothing elaborate—your standard strength conditioning, flexibility, and so on, but I packaged it right. I waited to collect everybody's excuses, then I announced this special program all week. But anybody who was sick that day couldn't start, and would have to miss the whole week."

He shrugged. "What can I say? I was twenty-two and cocky. I thought I'd really put one over on them."

"Something happened, I'm sure."

He nodded. "The next day, somebody hacked into the school's computer system and sent a bunch of x-rated e-mails from my address to a bunch of the female teachers. I nearly got fired—it was clear that I didn't send the e-mails, but I wasn't doing a very good job of keeping the network secure either." He shrugged. "Like I said, I didn't know all that much about computers. Ronnie hacking into the system showed our weak points."

"You knew it was him?"

"We couldn't prove it, but I just had to see his nasty smirk to know he did it. I had one more trick up my sleeve, though."

"What was that?"

"I created a computer club, and made him the president. The computer club was charged with helping the school maintain its system. So he had to find every hole and plug it up."

"Isn't that dangerous—putting the fox in the henhouse?"

"It was a risk. But I thought if everyone knew he had all access, and then something happened, suspicion would fall directly on him. So he had to keep things clean to protect himself."

"He must have been a pretty sharp kid."

"He was. But he had a sneaky side, and I never trusted him. To tell you the truth, I wasn't surprised at all when I heard he'd been killed." Suddenly a thought occurred to him, and he got serious. "You won't tell his parents any of this, will you? I wouldn't want to trespass on their grief. I'm just telling you this because, you know . . ."

"I appreciate everything you've said, and I'll keep it in confidence." I stood up and Victor Texeira stood with me. "Thanks for your help. I appreciate your candor." I paused before walking out the door, though. "Is there anyone here in Maui who might know more about Ronnie as an adult?"

Texeira thought for a moment. "There's a guy named Will

Wong who was a classmate of Ronnie's. He works in a surf shop in Lahaina Town called Totally Tubular."

"Great. Thanks." We shook hands, and maybe it was my imagination, but I thought he held my hand a little longer than he should have, and looked a little too directly into my eyes.

Man, I thought as I left, I've got to get my gaydar working.

Chapter 9

LAHAINA HARBOR

I DROVE SLOWLY down into the center of Lahaina, thinking about what Victor Texeira had said. I pulled into a parking space in the quaint downtown area, and before I got out of the car I looked back at Ronnie Chang's dossier. He had gone to work for a computer company in Honolulu, after attending UH for two years and leaving without a degree. Even though the original detectives had been there, I figured it would be worth a stop, deciding that I'd sleep in my own bed again that night, visit them the next morning, and then head back to Haleiwa.

Which left me outside a restaurant called Wok 'n Roll, owned by Lan and Yee Chang, Ronnie's parents. It was just lunch time and the place was crowded, so instead of going in I went for a walk through Lahaina. By the time I'd strolled through the harbor, I'd built up an appetite and I returned to the restaurant.

Yee Chang was working the register, Lan behind the stove cooking. Though I'd never met them, their pictures had been included in my dossier. Yee had lost weight since the picture was taken; grief will do that to you. I waited until there was a break in the crowd, and walked up to introduce myself, with the same story I'd given Victor Texeira.

She looked like she might cry. She reached out and took my hand. "We are so happy you investigate who kill our son," she said.

"I'm doing my best."

"Eat first, then talk," she said. "What you like? Honey chicken very good today. My husband make everything fresh. Lan! Make honey chicken special for detective. Give extra rice!"

She wouldn't take money from me. I took the plastic cup she handed me, filled it with ice and lemonade, and waited for Lan to serve up my chicken, reminding myself all the while why I didn't like to interview the parents of the deceased. They almost never had anything bad to say about their child, and though occasionally they could point you in the direction of a bad influence, the dead child was almost always blameless, an innocent victim. Even when the deceased had a laundry list of warrants, arrests, and convictions, his parents always believed the best of him.

I had almost finished my chicken when Yee had a young girl replace her at the register so she could come sit with me. The dining room was bright and airy, spotlessly clean, looking out on Front Street and the harbor. It had to be expensive real estate, I thought, which meant that the Changs were doing well.

My father's best friend, Uncle Chin, is Chinese, so I was very familiar with Chinese culture. I began by telling Mrs. Chang how sorry I was about her son's death and how I knew it was impolite of me to ask questions about him, but that I believed it was important to bring whoever killed him to justice.

She nodded eagerly. "His spirit very restless," she said. "Must have peace. You can bring my son peace?"

"I can try." I paused for a minute, then began asking simple questions. She did not know much about his life on O'ahu,

but she knew that he loved to surf. He did not have any ene-
mies that she knew of, no one who held a grudge or had any
reason to dislike him.

"How about his friends," I said. "Did you ever meet any of
them?"

The few names she gave me were already in his dossier.
"And his fiancée, of course," she said.

"Fiancée?"

"We never meet her, you know, engagement too soon before he died. And not Chinese girl either." For a moment a
frown crossed her face. "But she make Ronnie happy."

"What was her name?"

"Filipina girl. Lucie . . ."

"Zamora?"

"That's it!" she said. "She must be so sad, to lose Ronnie."

"I'm afraid she was killed, too, Mrs. Chang. Around the
same time Ronnie was."

Her mouth opened into a wide O, and her hand flew up to
cover it. Her surprise mirrored my own. I was sure that there
was no formal engagement between Ronnie Chang and Lucie
Zamora; if there was anything between them at all beyond
friendship I thought it was either a figment of Ronnie's imagination, or Lucie was playing him for something.

Mr. Chang came out from behind the stove and his wife
quickly told him, in Mandarin I only partially understood,
that Ronnie's fiancée had been killed, too. His surprise was
less visible than hers, but it was clear he hadn't known.

I thanked both Changs again for the delicious lunch and
walked out onto Front Street, which was busy with tourists in
matching aloha shirts, flip-flops, and uneven tans. I strolled
down Front Street, looking for Totally Tubular and Will
Wong. The surf shop was a little hole in the wall near the har-

bor, with nowhere near the selection you could find at The Next Wave. But they were doing a good business, and I had to wait a few minutes before the exceptionally tall Chinese guy I assumed was Will Wong could talk to me.

He must have been six-four or six-five, at least, and he was skinny as a rail. I was surprised he wasn't playing basketball for some mainland team. That is, until he stumbled over a boogie board on his way to talk to me and knocked over a rotating display of sunglasses.

After I introduced myself, we sat outside in the sunshine to talk about Ronnie Chang. "We were tight in high school, man," he said. "Ronnie was like, awesome with computers. Crappy surfer, but man, he could figure out a way into any system."

"He was still a crappy surfer when he died?" I asked. "I know he went to a tournament in Mexico."

"That was a joke, man," Will said. "He only went because he was chasing some girl, and she said she'd party with him down there."

"And did she?"

"He was pretty cagey when he got back," Will said, sitting back on a bench and stretching his long legs out across the sidewalk. "I never really knew for sure. But somehow he came back with a whole lot more money than he started with, and I know he didn't win it."

"What do you mean?"

A noisy bunch of Japanese tourists passed us, on their way to a whale-watching excursion, or at least that's where I guessed they were going, from all the whale paraphernalia they were either wearing or carrying; a half dozen of them wore paper crowns that looked like whale's tails. When they passed, Will said, "He really wanted this top of the line board, but he didn't have the dough, especially with buying presents for this chick and paying for the trip to Mexico—for both of them, by the way."

"You know this chick's name?"

"Sure. Lucie. He used to make a joke about it, you know, I Love Lucie."

"And when he came back, he had the money for the board?"

"Right on. He ordered it through me, and I had it shipped to him in Haleiwa. He only had it like a week before he got killed."

"Bummer."

Will nodded. We talked for a couple more minutes, and then he said that his break was over and he had to get back to work. That was fine with me, because I had to catch my flight to O'ahu. I drove to the airport, thinking about what I'd heard. Lucie Zamora and Mexpipe connected Mike Pratt and Ronnie Chang, and something had happened in Mexico that upset Mike and brought Ronnie cash.

Could Ronnie have rigged the results at Mexpipe by hacking into a computer? Maybe he had moved Mike up in the ratings for a share of the cash prize. Then Mike had joined up with the Christian surfers at El Refugio, making him regret what he'd done. Or perhaps Ronnie had rigged Mike's board with some kind of computer sensors that gave him an edge—that would explain why Mike had been bitching about his board after he returned.

I fell asleep almost the moment my butt hit the airplane seat, and didn't wake up until we were just about to land. I was so tired I could barely drive back to my apartment, and after scarfing down a quick dinner I went directly to bed.

The next morning, Tuesday, I slept late. Sure, I could have

gotten up at dawn and surfed Kuhio Beach Park, but I was getting spoiled by those big North Shore waves. And since the park was right next to the police station where I had worked for six years, there was a good chance I'd run into an old colleague or two, people I didn't want to have to explain myself to at present.

By ten o'clock I was on my way to Aloha Security, the company where Ronnie had worked. I had called and found out that the man I needed to speak to was Ronnie's boss, a *haole* named Pierre Lewin.

Lewin was a reformed hippie with a French accent and brown hair in a ponytail halfway down his back. His office was filled with posters, half of them from rock concerts and the other half advertising computer software.

I gave him the same story, that I'd been asked to look into Ronnie's death, and he didn't question me. "Ronnie was a gifted hacker," Lewin said. "You know what that is?"

"Somebody who breaks into computer systems?"

Lewin nodded. "And what we do here is consult with folks who don't want anyone to break into their systems. Ronnie's job was to do his best to exploit all the weaknesses in customer systems. Then we'd come up with ways to block those holes, and he'd test again. We have a lot of very big clients— none of whom I can mention because of security issues."

"That's fine. So Ronnie could probably break into any system he wanted to?" Even the one tabulating the scores at a surfing competition, I wanted to add.

"Anyone other than one of our established clients," he said, leaning forward.

"That's a pretty dangerous skill, isn't it?"

He laughed. "We're not talking about Tom Cruise in *Mission Impossible,* dangling from a wire into somebody's computer bank. Ronnie mostly worked from his apartment in Haleiwa."

"You ever have the idea that he was breaking into other systems—ones you weren't paying him to test?"

"Our employees have to undergo rigorous background checks," he said. "They're bonded, and they know there are dire consequences for anybody who circumvents the law."

Yeah, right, I was thinking. We talked some more about computer security and hacking, and then I left. I wondered how seriously Ronnie had taken those dire consequences. Clearly, he hadn't recognized how dire they might be.

I decided I'd swing past the Prince Kuhio, a hotel on Waikīkī where I knew Lucie's mother worked, and see if I could talk to her. I knew the Kuhio well; it was only a couple of blocks from my apartment, so I stopped back at my place for a few minutes, to read through the file on Lucie one more time.

The investigating detectives had talked to Mrs. Zamora, and to her son, Freddie. Neither of them had any idea why someone would want to kill Lucie—she was such a sweet, kind girl. She went to church every Sunday, her mother said.

Knowing what Ronnie Chang had told his parents about Lucie—that she was his fiancée—I wanted to know if she had told her mother about the engagement. She hadn't, I discovered. Mrs. Zamora, a petite, trim woman in a gray and white uniform, was able to meet me on her break, in a garden just off the hotel's lobby.

She'd never even heard Ronnie's name. The investigating detectives hadn't mentioned him or his murder, and Lucie had certainly never told her mother they were engaged. "You're sure my Lucie knew him?" she asked.

I nodded. "They had friends in common," I said. "And he had spoken of her to his parents."

"He was a good boy, this Ronnie?"

"I think so," I said. "He had a good job. Their friends say he took Lucie out, and bought her gifts."

"She no tell me anything after she move to Haleiwa," Mrs. Zamora said sadly. "She only say what she know I want to hear. 'Yes, Mama, I go to church. Yes, Mama, I marry nice Filipino boy. Yes, Mama, I make you proud of me.'" Tears welled up in the corners of her eyes and she dabbed at them with a tissue. "She give me money so her brother can go to college. Every week, she send me an envelope with a hundred dollars, cash money. I tell her no send cash through the mail, but my Lucie, she so honest. She say no one steal the money. She say she make lots of money soon, she buy me a house, let me stop work."

I told Mrs. Zamora that I would do my best to find out who killed her daughter, and she smiled sadly. "My Lucie with the angels now," she said. "She sit at Jesus's right hand."

Chapter 10

FRANK TALK

I HEADED BACK NORTH after that, driving straight to The Next Wave. I ordered an extra large raspberry mocha and started going through my notes. I had spoken to a lot of people in a short time, and I needed to make some connections between them. Reviewing my conversations with Victor Texeira, the Changs, Will Wong, Pierre Lewin, and Mrs. Zamora, I began to get a clearer picture of the three surfers.

Lucie Zamora was the connection between Mike Pratt and Ronnie Chang. All three needed money; Mike and Lucie for surfing, Ronnie for dating Lucie. Somehow, Mexico, the Mexpipe competition, and Ronnie's hacking skills had to be connected.

I had to learn more about Lucie. But how? I turned to the Internet and began sifting through hundreds of Zamoras. I had just about given up, though I still had Lucie's name on the screen when a skinny twenty-something guy with a goofy little patch of goatee on his chin flopped down next to me. "Hey, dude, you knew Lucie?" he asked.

My sensors went on alert. I shrugged nonchalantly. "A little. You?"

"Used to date her," he said. "Man, I am wiped." He took a long drink of his cappuccino. "Need a caffeine fix something mad."

"I hear you," I said, holding up my own cup.

He took a deep sip, and then sighed. "You look really familiar. Were you at Mexpipe?"

I shook my head. "Never been." I stuck out my hand. "Kimo."

"Frank." He looked at me again. "Pipeline?"

I nodded. "Just came up here two weeks ago, but I've been there pretty much every day."

"Cool."

"How was Mexpipe?" I asked, wondering if he had been there with Lucie.

"Pretty radical," he said. "I got some awesome waves. Didn't finish in the money but I met Lucie. Man, she was a great chick." I noticed his hangdog expression. "We were really grooving together, then we got back here and she got shot."

The electricity was going full blast by then. I figured I might learn something if I played dumb. "Shot?" I asked. "How bad?"

"Like dead, man."

"Where did this happen?" I asked. "Up here in Haleiwa?"

He nodded. "Right outside Club Zinc, about a month ago. She was wearing this pink dress that she loved, and it made her look so hot that all the guys were hitting on her. So I got mad and walked out. And somebody shot her as she was leaving, alone. Probably to come look for me."

I stared but he kept on going. "I keep thinking like, maybe if I had been with her, it wouldn't have happened, you know? Like somehow it was my fault. But she had her secrets, you know?" He sighed and started tearing his coffee cup into small pieces. "I guess we all do."

He lapsed into silence, just as I was hoping to hear what kind of secrets Lucie Zamora had. But I've interrogated a lot of people, and I had a feeling that if I waited, Frank would have more to say. "It's tough," I said. "I mean, you just start to get to know somebody, and then she's gone. Makes you think."

"Totally. I mean, I had a feeling she was into something funny." He stopped tearing and leaned toward me. "For a chick who supposedly came from nothing, and who wasn't earning anything on the circuit, she lived pretty large."

"Surfing's an expensive hobby."

"Tell me about it. But this chick, she had all these designer dresses and expensive jewelry and all. I mean, she was fine. And when we got back from Mexpipe, the first place she went was this store, Butterfly, to buy some more stuff."

So like Mike and Ronnie, Lucie had come back from Mexico with money. Frank lapsed back into silence, so I said, "Where did you think she got the money?"

He shrugged. "She didn't like to give out information. I just figured she had some kind of scam going. But I didn't want to know what it was. I just want to surf, man. I'm not some kind of detective or anything. She wanted the bling bling, that's OK by me. I'm just bummed it got her killed."

"You think that's what it was?" I asked. "A dangerous taste for the high life?"

"And doing the things you gotta do to keep that taste satisfied." Frank crumpled the last shreds of his coffee cup. "Gotta go," he said. "I tend bar over at the Drainpipe. Come by sometime, dude."

"Sure." I knew that I would, too, once I'd learned a little more about Lucie Zamora and had more pointed questions to ask. The dossier on her hadn't mentioned a taste for designer labels, though that, combined with limited legal income, is often an indicator that there's something fishy going on.

I went back to the computer, and read my e-mail. There was a long message from my friend Harry complaining about the crappy surf conditions at Kaisers, our usual surf spot at Ala Moana Beach Park.

Lui still felt bad about running the stories on me, even though both the series on gay cops around the country, which ran while I was suspended, and the series on coming out, which ran during my first week on the North Shore, got great ratings and great viewer feedback. He suggested that a big family luau at Waimea Bay Beach Park might make me feel better, and I'd replied by saying I'd only agree if I could challenge him and Haoa to a surf contest. Of course, I copied the entire family on the message, leading to a flurry of responses that indicated all my nieces and nephews were eager to see their dads on surfboards.

My older brothers had been great surfers in their day. Neither had pushed it as far as I had, but both were good, and both still kept their boards in their garages, though I doubted either had been on the water for years. My father even promised that he would join us for a wave or two if we would all go out together. I could just imagine what my mother thought of that idea, but as my father got older, he never missed a chance to hang out with his boys.

I waded through all the luau-related e-mail—who would bring the chicken long rice, the *lomi lomi* salmon, the *haupia* (a coconut-milk pudding.) Haoa had an *imu,* a Hawai'ian style barbecue pit, in his backyard, so he would bring the *kalua* pig, a detail which could not help but annoy Lui. The two of them were only two years apart and had been battling for supremacy since infancy.

When I finished, I sent an e-mail to Sampson requesting any info that might indicate Lucie had expensive tastes—labels in her clothes or handbag, for starters. I looked up the store Frank had mentioned. Butterfly was a boutique in the North Shore Marketplace that sold designer-label clothing and accessories. I wasn't sure how to approach it, though, without a badge.

I didn't want to try the same tactic I'd used on Maui. There was too much chance that the news I was investigating could get back to the wrong ears—either the killer, or the police. I didn't want either to know what I was doing.

It was nearly nine o'clock. I picked up some Mexican food and took it back to Hibiscus House. I was falling asleep as I ate. By the next morning, though, I had a plan. I'd surf for a while at Pipeline, then head up to Butterfly to see what I could learn about Lucie Zamora.

Chapter 11

BUTTERFLY

AS SOON AS I ARRIVED at the store, I realized I was in trouble. The dresses in the window were by Armani, Valentino, and Versace. A tiny purse studded with rhinestones had a price tag of $2,400. The only recognizable label on my clothing was the Teva on my sandals; I wore a pair of board shorts whose pocket I had torn a few days before, and a T-shirt from Town and Country Surf Shop. Oh, and I'd forgotten to shave that morning in my hurry to get out on the water. In short, I looked like a *moke,* a native Hawai'ian criminal more likely to smash the front window in and steal something than to walk in and shop for merchandise.

I didn't know what I'd hoped to achieve by going to Butterfly, and I was kicking myself for rushing in without thinking through a plan, when the door popped open and a guy in a black T-shirt and black slacks stuck his head out. "I know you!" he said, smiling. "You're the gay cop!"

"Busted." I smiled and stuck my hand out. "Kimo Kanapa'aka."

"You are such a hero!" he said. He shook my hand. "I'm Brad. Jacobson. It is so awesome to meet you!"

"You work here?" I asked.

He shrugged. "It's not much, but it's a living. Were you looking for something?"

I decided to jump in. "Someone, more like," I said. "This girl I met at a surfing tournament. She told me she bought all her clothes here. I just moved up here, and she's the only person I know in town. I thought—oh, it's pretty dumb."

"No, what?"

"I guess I figured I might run into her around here."

"Come on inside," Brad said. Brad was in his late twenties, I figured, as I followed him into the store, which had the kind of elegant hush that comes from recessed lighting, thick pile carpeting, and price tags in the stratosphere. He wasn't what you'd call classically handsome; his nose was crooked and his blonde hair thinning, but he put himself together well. "What's her name?"

"Lucie," I said. "Lucie Zamora."

"Oh, my God," Brad said. He clutched his heart. "You don't know? Well, of course, you've been busy with your own troubles."

I tried to put surprise in my voice. "What?"

"You'd better sit down." He motioned me to an armchair that would have looked quite at home in my mother's living room. I sat, and he pulled a similar chair up next to me. "She was killed!" Brad said. "Shot down like a dog on the street." He looked like he was ready to cry. "Oh, it was just awful."

I looked away from Brad, the way I'd observed the families of victims do when they heard the bad news, then when I looked back at him I rubbed my eyes and nose, body language that I knew conveyed disbelief. I let my voice get a little higher, and rushed the words out. "When did this happen?"

"About a month ago. She was coming out of Club Zinc late

at night, and somebody shot her." He shook his head. "The police, of course, are clueless." He smiled at me and touched my hand. "I'll bet if they had you on the case, you'd already have the creep behind bars."

I took a deep breath, then put my hand up over my mouth, taking a moment to compose myself. I didn't like faking emotions in front of someone as nice as Brad, but I had a role to play, and I knew that the better I played it the more chance I would have of finding out information that could lead me to Lucie Zamora's killer.

"I'm sure the local guys did their best," I said, finally. "They probably just haven't released any results yet." I put my hand to my cheek, a thinking gesture. "They must have talked to you, didn't they?"

He shook his head again. "Nope. And I mean, I wouldn't say I was her closest friend, but, well, she was in here almost every week buying something. I knew her tastes almost as well as my own."

"She liked her labels," I said, putting on what I hoped was a weary smile.

"Absolutely. Armani was like her god. Manolo for shoes. Coach for purses and belts. I mean, I could go on and on." He waved his arm around the store, encompassing all the expensive labels around us. Each designer had a niche, I noted, with just a few examples of each style. Soft lighting highlighted the three-way mirrors in the corners.

"I'm surprised. I never saw her name in the money at tournaments," I said. "I didn't realize she had the money for such expensive clothes. She have a sugar daddy somewhere?"

Brad shook his head. "I don't think so," he said. "Most of our customers—the ones with the rich husbands or daddies—use plastic. But our Lucie was strictly a cash basis customer, even though sometimes she'd spend a thousand dollars on a dress. She said she'd gotten in trouble with credit cards once, so she didn't buy anything she didn't have the cash for." He smiled. "But there wasn't much she didn't have the cash for, I'll tell you."

"It must have been strange to you, taking in so much cash at once."

Brad leaned back against his chair, looked around at the empty shop, and then back at me. "Well, between you and me and the lamppost, at first I thought she was somebody's mistress. You know, she had a body that wouldn't quit, and she liked to show it off. But she wasn't much into sexy lingerie."

I let my voice catch. "I just can't believe she's gone."

He pushed out of the chair, squatted down next to me, and took my hand. "You poor thing, you must be devastated," he said. "I mean, to find out your only friend in town was murdered!"

"It's a shock." I caught my breath, and then sighed.

Brad nodded. "All her friends felt that way."

A bell started ringing in my head. "You knew her other friends?"

"Well, more like she knew my friends," Brad said. He stood up and walked over to the cash wrap. It looked like he was getting ready to close up. "I know this group of guys, and they all got to know her and like her." He looked up at me sadly. "I guess that's almost the same as having friends."

"Do you think I could, maybe, meet some of your friends?" I asked. Using this guy who had been so nice to me was making me feel more and more like crap, but I needed some insight into this case, and if his friends could help me get to know Lucie better, then I would do what I had to do.

"I'm just going to meet them once I close up," Brad said.

Though I really wanted nothing more than to crawl into bed and rest after a day's hard surfing, I said, "Do you think I could kind of tag along? Like I said, I really don't know anyone else up here."

Brad looked me up and down, hands on hips. "I hope you don't mind my saying, but you could use a little cleaning up before you go out in polite society."

"I've got a room at the Hibiscus House. I could swing past there, clean up, and meet you wherever you want." Finally, an emotion I didn't have to feign; the eagerness I was showing was how I really felt.

"I'll follow you there." He locked the door and shooed me toward my truck. "You need serious help, mister, and looking at you, I know you're not going to find it in your room at the Hibiscus House."

Brad drove a gold Toyota Camry with rainbow bumper stickers and a broken antenna, and he followed me as promised. I was embarrassed to let him into my room, which was a mess. There was no housekeeping staff, the furniture looked like it had come from the Salvation Army store, and I needed to do laundry, which was evident from various items of clothing strewn around on the floor.

"Are you sure you're gay?" Brad said, standing behind me in the doorway. "My God, I've seen straight men who clean up better than this."

"Well, if I'm not, then I've just knocked a big fat hole in my life for no reason," I said. "I guess I should jump in the shower."

"Not here." Brad walked into the room and pulled open the half of the sliding closet door that actually worked. There were still a couple of clean shirts and pants hanging there.

"OK, this, and this," he said, pulling out a pair of Ralph Lauren chinos my mother had bought me and a black T-shirt that was almost a clone of his own.

He looked at me. "Boxers, right?" Without waiting for my assent, he walked over to the flimsy bureau and opened the top drawer. "Bad," he said, holding up a pair with tropical fish on them. "Horrible," were a pair spattered with ice cream cones, and "Awful" were a pair decorated with Santas and Christmas trees. "Jesus, you don't get laid much, do you?" he asked. "Who would want to sleep with a man who wears these?" I didn't want to admit to him that I liked those goofy boxers, and frankly, the few times I'd had sex with other guys, they'd come off so quickly they'd never been an issue. He finally found a striped pair that met with his approval.

I watched his whole performance with a kind of baffled amusement. He reminded me of Gunter, a gay man in Honolulu I knew, except that Gunter mixed his attitude with an athletic physicality that was as sexy as it was intimidating. Brad was simply a guy with no tolerance for bad fashion. He found a pair of loafers and a leather belt on the floor, and then said, "All right. You come with me now."

I was eager to get to the bar to meet these other people who had known Lucie Zamora, but I had to humor Brad. He drove me to his apartment, a one-bedroom a couple of blocks off the Kam Highway, and led me without ceremony to his bathroom. "Strip, soldier," he said. "Get in the shower, and don't forget to moisturize."

Brad's shower was big enough for two, and I thought for the first few minutes that he might be joining me, which was a prospect I thought would be interesting—if I wasn't in such a hurry to get to the bar and meet his friends. Instead, though, I was left alone with a shelf of grooming products. Lavender-scented bath soap, lemon moisturizer, shampoo, conditioner, shave gel, and a host of other products whose function I did not understand.

I used a disposable razor and a fog-free mirror in the shower to shave, and when I finally stepped out Brad was there with an oversized bath sheet. "Feel better?"

"Almost human." I wrapped the towel around my waist and faced the mirror.

"Give me your hand."

Brad squeezed a dollop of lotion into my palm. "Massage that into your hair, from the back forward." When I finished, he handed me a comb. "You have good material. But if you don't take care of it, it'll never last. How old are you?" He turned me to face him. "Thirty?"

"Thirty-two."

He looked me up and down. "You'll do. Your clothes are on the bed."

By then, even though I knew I had to get to that bar and meet Brad's friends, I was starting to be a little disappointed. I mean, I didn't expect every gay man I met to want to drag me into bed, but Brad obviously liked me, or he wouldn't have gone to all this trouble. Yet . . . nothing was happening.

I shrugged and got dressed. Ever since I finally admitted to myself that I was gay—which had been what, six weeks before—I had been horny as hell. I felt like a kid in a candy store who'd just been given his allowance, and permission to buy whatever he wanted. But it was getting really difficult to balance those personal desires with my need to investigate this case. If I kept on thinking about having sex with every guy I met, I'd never make any progress.

I took a deep breath before I walked back to Brad's living room, willing myself to remember the three dead surfers, to focus on what I had to do. "Now you look presentable," Brad said, eyeing me up and down. "Every caterpillar has a butterfly inside." He looked at his watch. "Good. We've still got thirty minutes left of happy hour."

Chapter 12

A LITTLE SUGAR

AS BRAD DROVE US down the Kam Highway a bit, I asked him what had brought him to the North Shore. "You a surfer on your off hours?"

"Not at all," he said, shaking his head violently. "The closest I get to surfing is looking for gay porn on the Internet."

"Then what are you doing up here?"

"It's a very ordinary sort of story," he said, sighing. "I fell in love with a surfer boy and followed him up here. Of course it didn't work out, and he moved on, but by the time he did I had started to work at Butterfly. The woman who owns the store lives in LA and only comes up here once a year, so I'm the de facto manager and I can do as I please."

"Great gig."

"She's a friend of my parents," he said. "I grew up outside LA, and no, I do not have any family members in the movie business." He looked over at me. "That seems to be what every gay man asks me when he hears I'm from LA. Like if my father was some big movie producer I'd be selling ladies' *shmattes* in a strip mall."

"The question would never have occurred to me."

"I can see that," Brad said dryly. "Just from seeing your underwear selection. Anyway, after Francisco dumped me, I looked up, saw that I was making decent money and I had a bunch of friends, so I figured I'd hang around and see what happened next." He smiled. "And then you came up to my window."

He pulled in to the parking lot of a nondescript bar called "Sugar's: The Sweetest Spot in Town" in a strip shopping center just before the Kam split off to head inland. From the outside, it wasn't very appealing: the building needed paint, and it was shaded by a single half-dead palm tree. A police cruiser sat at the edge of the parking lot—tracking homos or anticipating bar fights. The wind was picking up, moving dark clouds across the sky and tossing trash around the lot. "Here we are, hon," Brad said. He took my hand. "Now I know you're upset about Lucie, but we all have to move on. I'm sure once you get a colorful cocktail in front of you, you'll cheer right up."

Brad was obviously a regular there, judging by the chorus of hellos that greeted us as we walked in the door. He steered us to a big round table at the back of the bar, in front of sliding glass doors. Outside, I could see a deck overlooking what looked like a small pineapple plantation, endless neat rows of spiky bromeliads, many already with a tiny pineapple nesting in their centers.

Five guys sat around the table, and I tried to connect their names to their characteristics as they were introduced to me. Jeremy was chubby, Rik was skinny, Larry was cute, and George was butch. The last guy, older than everyone else by at least ten years, was Ari. Every one was gay, though; I figured that out. As was pretty much everybody else in the place. But there wasn't the desperate, sex-based atmosphere I'd seen in gay bars in Honolulu; this was more like a place that friends got together for a couple of drinks. How it might change as the evening wore on, though, I couldn't say.

I felt a wave of excitement building in me, almost as good as being out on the water, as each of the guys was presented. It was just as I had hoped when I convinced Brad to bring me—this network of men could be just the entrée I needed, and I could begin mining each of them for information about the murders.

"Guys, this is Kimo," Brad said. "For those of you who are totally unaware of current events, he used to be a cop in Honolulu until they figured out he was gay. Now he's like, totally a surfer dude."

"You know we shun people who use that kind of language," I said, only half joking. Most of the real surfers I knew could speak just as well as any college professor, though there are always a few really dumb ones who perpetuate the stereotype.

"Why, Brad's a genius," Jeremy said. "We all find ourselves, from time to time, though we know it's fruitless . . ."

"Literally speaking," his skinny friend Rik interrupted.

"Though we know it's pointless," Jeremy rephrased, "pining after straight surfer boys. But you're the antidote to all that—a gay surfer boy!"

"Hardly a boy," I said.

"Metaphorically speaking," he said. "So as long as Brad is willing to share, we can pass you around amongst ourselves, whenever we feel that surfer-boy urge."

"Jeremy Leddinger, I am not your pimp," Brad said. "I am not anybody's pimp. And I'll have you know, Kimo is my friend. Not my boyfriend."

"Then what's with the Brad Jacobson makeover?" Jeremy

asked. He leaned over to me. "Tell me you didn't start out to-day looking like that."

"I didn't," I said. I felt the way I thought a ping-pong ball must, in the middle of a tournament. Funnily, though, I didn't mind. It was kind of flattering.

"He needed a makeover," Brad said. "I complied. End of story."

"Gee, I hope it isn't the end," I said. I batted my eyelashes at him. It seemed like the right thing to do.

The table roared and Brad blushed. I felt a stiffening in my still-pressed chinos, and wondered if Brad was feeling the same thing.

"So do you make over every guy you meet?" I asked, when I finally had a chance to talk to Brad again.

"Just the ones who need it," he said. He looked at me and lowered his shoulders. "OK, they all seem to need it. But you more than most."

He looked around, and then leaned in close to me. "You actually never met Lucie, did you?"

"What makes you think that?"

"Because I've been watching you, and you're asking questions about things you would know if you really had known Lucie."

I looked at him in amazement. "Geez, you ever thought of becoming a detective, Brad? 'Cause you know there are departments on the mainland that take in gay cops."

"I figured as much. I'll bet you think that if you can figure out who killed Lucie, those cops might take you back."

Give Brad points for seeing through me, though his take on the situation wasn't quite correct. "I need to show them I'm still a good detective," I said, thinking fast. Although it wasn't far from the truth.

"We can help you," Brad said. "Larry is a shopaholic like Lucie was; they used to compare notes all the time. Ari owns an apartment building where Jeremy lives, and where Lucie used to. George swings both ways, and he slept with Lucie at least once that I know of, because I walked in on them. And Rik was really friendly with Lucie, always wanting to know where she was. I'm sure he spent a lot of time with her."

I was amazed yet again. It was just the kind of network that Sampson had hoped I'd tap into as a surfer. Behold the power of the homosexual.

"Let me get things moving," he said. He sat back, and when there was a lull in the conversation he said, "I was kind of teary this afternoon. We got some new Armani in and the first person I thought of was Lucie."

"Have they found who killed her yet?" Rik asked.

Brad shook his head. "But I have a little news flash for you." He motioned for everyone to lean in close to the center of the table. "We now have our very own cop. If we all tell him what we know, maybe he can find out what really happened to her and Lucie can rest easier in her grave."

"Our own Hawai'i Five-O!" Jeremy said. "I still think Jack Lord is so masculine and handsome." He sighed.

"We could be your—what do they call them on TV—your confidential informants," Rik said.

"You mean snitches," George said, laughing.

"If there's anything you know, that you want to tell me," I said, "I can guarantee that it will get into the right hands. I know for a fact the investigating detectives weren't able to find out much about Lucie or the others who were killed."

"There were others!" Jeremy shrieked. "No one told us anything!"

I immediately regretted that slip of the tongue. But Brad saved me. "See, Kimo already knows a lot about the case. I mean, none of us even knew that anyone else had been killed. So we have to help him."

"Who were the others?" Ari asked.

"A championship surfer named Mike Pratt," I said. No response from the crowd. "And a Chinese computer guy named Ronald Chang."

"Lucie had a friend named Ronnie," Rik said. "He was a computer guy."

"Yeah, I met him once," Brad said. "Is that him?"

"I think so," I said. "But I don't know much about him either, so anything you guys know would be helpful."

They all seemed eager, and very quickly my date book filled up. Breakfast the next morning with Ari, the landlord. I could surf until about three, when chubby Jeremy, who was a fourth grade teacher at Sunset Beach Elementary, could see me after school. Then cocktails with butch George Olsen and cute Larry Brickman followed by dinner with skinny Rik. "What about me?" Brad pouted.

"Ahh, you and I have tonight," I said, taking his hand.

Brad blushed and the table cheered. The party broke up a little later, the rest of the guys going off wherever, leaving me and Brad at the big table at Sugar's. I felt that I had made a lot of progress that evening, and I deserved a chance to put aside the homicide detective for a few hours and just be who I was—a lonely, horny gay man who had only recently admitted his sexuality, and who had no idea how to manage the feelings that kept welling up inside. "I didn't mean to embarrass you earlier," I said to Brad. "I really appreciate everything you've done, and if you're not into me, I totally understand."

Brad nearly spit out the last of his strawberry daiquiri. "Not into you!" he sputtered. "You have the face of an angel and the body of death."

I laughed. "Yeah, the guys are just lining up to date me." I stood up. We'd already settled the check. "I just need a ride back to my truck, if you don't mind."

"Oh, honey," Brad said, standing up too. "I'm giving you a ride, don't you worry about that."

And ride me he did, once we got back to his apartment, where he massaged my back and certain other body parts. I don't know why I pursued him as I did; he seemed grateful enough for the chance to be nice to me, to be able to present me to his friends. Maybe that's why I did it, because I thought he ought to know that wasn't enough. That he deserved somebody to be nice to him for a change.

Not that he was any kind of charity case. Under the designer pants and form-fitting black T-shirt was a body any Waikīkī boy would be pleased to call his own, or to use for an evening of passion. While his abs might not have been rock solid or his biceps bulging, he had a mouth, a penis, and an ass, and he knew how to use all three.

"Mmm, you know what's the best part about this," Brad said, snuggling his backside up against my groin, where my penis was too tired to even consider responding.

"What's that," I said, leaning over and kissing his shoulder.

"I can spoon up against you and fall asleep, and though I know you won't be here in the morning, at least I know my wallet and my stereo will be."

On that terribly sad note, I let Brad fall asleep, and then, as he expected, crept out the door and back to Hibiscus House.

Chapter 13

BREAKFAST

I WAS AT PIPELINE AT SIX, about half an hour before sunrise. It was kind of creepy moving across the beach in the pre-dawn darkness, but nothing I wasn't accustomed to. I caught a couple of five-foot waves, getting barreled on both, but by seven the swells were getting bigger and it was time for me to pull out.

I met Ari at seven-thirty at Rosie's Cantina, a little Mexican place known for its surfer breakfasts, and when I sat down opposite him I suddenly felt a week's worth of hard surfing, the night before with Brad, and my lack of sleep swell up inside me. I yawned when I shook his hand and took the card he handed me, which read *Aristotle Papageorgiou, President, North Shore Real Estate Investments.* "You see why people call me Ari," he said.

"It's not you," I said. "I really need to get more sleep."

Ari simply raised his eyebrows and smiled. Coffee revived me a bit and we ordered breakfast. "So what kind of real estate investments?" I asked, fingering the card. "Brad said you owned the apartment building where Lucie lived?"

Ari nodded. "I went to college in Minnesota," he said, "and while I was there I got interested in real estate. I saw people buying houses near the college, living in them while they were in school, then reselling them after graduation. I convinced my dad to front me the money for a down payment, in lieu of paying for a dorm room, and while I lived there I rented out rooms to other students. By the time I graduated I was able to pay my dad back and make a nice profit."

"A mogul in training," I said.

"Not quite Donald Trump, but it was a start. I wanted to get the hell out of Minnesota, though, so I came to Hawai'i and started looking for property to fix up and resell. I found a niche up here on the North Shore."

"That's what you do—buy up houses and then fix them up?"

"Among other things." The waitress brought our breakfast and we dug in. "I bought a run-down apartment building a couple years ago. The place was full of drunks, drug addicts, and surfers, and I can't tell you which were the worst tenants."

He took a forkful of eggs. I figured him for about forty, and it looked like he'd been at least moderately successful—Ralph Lauren shirt with the little polo player over the left breast, thick gold chain around his neck, gold coin pinky ring. His hair was immaculately groomed, his fingernails clearly manicured. In contrast, I was still in full surfer mode, in board shorts, flip-flops, and a Banzai Pipeline T-shirt with an incongruous bird of paradise superimposed over a picture of a monster wave.

"Lucie moved in as I was trying to upgrade the quality of tenants," he said. "Pretty girl, you know, very athletic, great sense of style."

"She have a job that you know of?"

"Yeah, she was working at the time at The Next Wave—you know it?"

I nodded.

"Guy who runs it, Dario Fonseca, he's a business partner of mine. He recommended her."

Interesting, I thought. Of course I'd never mentioned my interest in Lucie, or any of the dead surfers, to Dario. We'd had too much old ground to cover. "Dario invests with you?"

"I've got this project in the works," Ari said, pushing aside his empty plate. "Up on a ridge overlooking Kawailoa Beach. Quirk in zoning lets me build a multi-family property up there."

"Condo?"

He nodded. "Nothing too tall, you understand. Even so, I'm fighting against a community organization." He shook his head. "Idiots don't want any development. 'I've got mine, the rest of you get the hell out.' You know the attitude." I saw him tensing up. "They cloak themselves in this false environmental shit. 'Preserve the open space, keep the old Hawai'i.' Well, I got news for them. Time moves on. That's my land, and I'm going to build on it."

"Dario must be doing pretty well if he's a partner with you on that."

"He's one, among others. Right now, the property's tied up in litigation, but as soon as I get rid of these Save Our Scenery jerks I'm breaking ground."

"Lucie involved in any of that sort of thing?" I asked casually. "Protest groups, anything like that?"

He laughed. "Not Lucie," he said. "Lucie had her eye out for Lucie only. She wanted to surf, and she wanted nice things."

"You can't make much money working in a surf shop," I said.

"She quit The Next Wave a few months after she moved in. I never did find out what she was doing for money, but her rent always came in on time."

"Cash?" I asked, as the waitress approached to refill our coffee.

Ari smiled at her, and she smiled back. "How'd you know?" he asked, when she'd left.

"Just a hunch."

"You think she was doing something illegal?" he asked. "I swear, I didn't know anything about it. Only reason I really knew her at all was first, because of Dario, then I knew she dated George for a while."

"George is bi?"

He laughed again. "George is a little bit conflicted," he said. "He can pass for straight, six days out of seven, so every now and then he tries a little pussy just to remind himself what he's missing. Lucie had a trim little body, turn the lights off and stay away from the front, you could almost imagine she's a boy. My personal belief, that's the only way George could do her. But what do I know? Forty years old and I've never been with a woman. Never wanted to." He eyed me. "You?"

"I was more than a little bit conflicted," I said. "For a long time."

He leaned in close. "And you could—get it up?"

"I could." I shrugged. "And I did, more times than I can count. But I always knew something was wrong. Just took me a long time to figure out what."

We both sipped our coffee for a minute or so. Finally, I asked, "What happened to Lucie's stuff?"

"Her mom and her younger brother came up from Honolulu to pick it all up," he said. "They were both pretty broken up. You could tell they had no idea she was into anything illicit. Kept talking about her being such a good girl, going to church on Sundays, how she had promised her mom that after she got surfing out of her blood she was going to marry a nice Filipino boy and settle down."

"Our parents never really know us," I said.

"You're right about that." He drained the last of his coffee and signaled for the waitress. "The apartment's still vacant, if you want to take a look at it," he said. He wrote the address down on a Post-it Note he took from a little leather case. "I've got a lock box on it so brokers can show it. I wrote down the code for you. She covered the walls in surfing posters and I didn't take them down—I thought maybe they might help rent the place."

"I'll check it out."

He took the check from the waitress and wouldn't even let me leave the tip. "This one's on me," he said. "Hell, I can't say I knew Lucie all that well, but consider this my way of saying thanks for looking out for her." He frowned, and in that moment he looked all of forty, and more.

The wind was still up, throwing a chill into me as I left the restaurant, and I knew that meant Pipeline and Banzai Beach would be almost unsurfable for anyone but the best, so I ended up at Chun's Reef, a much easier break. A guy picked up his stuff and moved away when I dropped my towel near him, and a couple of girls giggled and pointed at me. One asshole even said, "Out of my way, faggot," as he cut across me on a wave, but overall the atmosphere wasn't any worse than Pipeline on a bad day. I surfed for few hours, and then a little before three I made my way to Sunset Beach Elementary.

Jeremy Leddinger had obviously been the class clown growing up, from the sarcastic tone I'd heard him use the night before. A chubby gay kid who defended himself with a rapier wit, who depended on being able to make his tormentors laugh to save his hide.

I found him in a classroom decorated with posters of the solar system, grading homework assignments at a wooden table at the front of the room. I wasn't sure what he could tell me; I knew that he had once lived in that same apartment complex where Lucie lived.

"So, Brad's newest project," he said, when I walked in the door. "I have to admit, you clean up well."

"Brad's the kind of guy who picks up strays?"

He laughed. "Unfortunately, it's a problem I share with him, so I can't criticize too much."

"You lived in the same building as Lucie," I said. "Sounds like a rough kind of place. What were you doing there?"

"I was in the first wave of Ari's gentrification effort," he said. "But I have an unfortunate taste for bad boys. The kind who lie to you, steal from you, and give you unpleasant diseases. So putting me in there was like giving crack to a junkie."

If Jeremy lost about fifty pounds, I thought, he'd be pretty cute. But the weight was probably tied up with his self-image, with the little boy inside looking for attention and probably only accustomed to getting it packaged around abuse. "How'd you get to know Lucie?"

"I was in lust with a little Filipino with a big ice habit," Jeremy said. "He and Lucie used to get together and jabber away in Tagalog. Eventually he stole too much from somebody who wasn't interested in his dick or his ass, and he got sent away to do some time. I still used to see Lucie, so I'd say hello."

"You think your boyfriend got his ice from Lucie?"

Jeremy nodded. "I don't know where she got it, though. But I'm pretty sure that's how she was able to afford the designer clothes and the trips to surf contests."

"She wasn't the kind of girl who'd use sex to get what she wanted?"

Jeremy shrugged. "She wasn't trying to sell it to me, that's for sure. But that guy you mentioned—what was his name—her friend, the computer guy. Ronnie. She certainly led him around by his dick."

"He was her boyfriend?"

Jeremy laughed. "What a quaint expression to use regarding Lucie. She didn't 'do' the whole boyfriend thing. Even that bartender she was sleeping with when she died—Frank—she was just using him. An excuse for her to hang out at the Drainpipe, so her customers would know where to find her."

He neatened the corners of some papers on his desk and then looked back up at me. "But what do I know? I didn't even know Georgie boy was doing her until it was all over."

Something in Jeremy's eyes told me the thought of anyone else having sex with George made him very unhappy. "Well, thanks for your time," I said. "I hope you find someone who treats you the way you deserve."

"Oh, I've found him a bunch of times."

I looked him right in the eye. "No, you haven't."

"I don't suppose there are any more at home like you."

I shook my head. "I've got two brothers, but they're both straight."

"Brad's a lucky guy."

I held my hands up. "Brad and I had a little fun, that's all. Maybe we'll have some more fun, maybe we won't. I don't know how much longer I'll be up here, anyway."

Jeremy smirked, and I left him to his grading. The wind was still up, so I decided to head over to the apartment building where Lucie had lived. Though Ari said he had cleaned it out, if felt like a loose end I should check out.

On my way, I stopped at Fujioka's and bought some rubber gloves and plastic zip-lock bags. In case I found anything there, I didn't want my prints getting in the way. The building was just off the Kam Highway, on the south side of Haleiwa, a two-story U with parking around the edges of a grassy square.

I drove past slowly. A row of fantail palms separated the property from the street, and a hibiscus hedge was struggling to take root alongside the parking area. A pair of young guys were camped out on a tie-dyed blanket in the center of the grass and music blared out of an open door. It was obvious Ari hadn't completed his gentrification project, though the lawn was neatly trimmed and the building had been freshly painted.

I circled back and pulled into a parking space.

The two guys on the lawn regarded me with interest. "Hey," I said, walking up to them. "I'm looking for a girl I think lives here. Lucie? Surfer chick, brown hair, drives a Volkswagen Bug?"

The guys had the glassy eyes of habitual drug users. "She's gone, man," the first guy said.

"You know when she'll be back?"

They both laughed. The first one had a hiccupy laugh, as if he was trying to get enough air to keep on breathing. "No, she's gone-gone," he said. "Gone to heaven, gone."

He made wiggly motions with his hands, simulating, I suppose, the progress of Lucie's soul rising to heaven. This set his friend into paroxysms of laughter again, and he quickly joined in, hiccupping all the way.

I left them laughing and made my way to the apartment, pulling on the rubber gloves as I went. Looking over my shoulder, I saw that they were now lying on their backs, comparing clouds. They'd forgotten all about me.

I punched the code into the lock box on the door and it swung open. The place was an efficiency, one room with a galley kitchen along one side and a closet and the door to a bathroom opposite. A window next to the door looked out at the parking lot.

The appliances in the kitchen were pretty new, and the carpet was in good shape. The rest of the room was empty, though, as Ari had said; the walls were covered in surf posters, just like my bedroom when I was a teenager. My surfers had been all male, of course; Lucie's were female. I recognized a couple, including Melanie Bartels and longboarder Belen Connelly, and there was a promotional poster for the MTV series *Surf Girls:* fourteen girls following big waves around the Pacific and competing to be number one. It was a show that was tailor-made for Lucie Zamora and her goals.

All around me, strong, confident women dropped down wave faces, zoomed through tubes, or charged really big waves. I stared at them, trying to get into Lucie's head, and then I remembered something from my days in Vice. Drug dealers often keep a private stash, one that is carefully hidden. I knew from reading the dossiers that the investigating officers hadn't known that Lucie dealt, so they would have had no reason to search.

I started in the galley kitchen, pulling the appliances away from the walls. Nothing there except dust bunnies. The cabinets were empty, and there was nothing in the toilet tank except water and hardware. I tested the tape holding each poster to the wall—it was all strong, and all of roughly the same vintage. The indoor-outdoor carpeting was firmly fixed to the floor.

I had worked on enough construction sites with my father to know how buildings like this were constructed—a framework of studs covered with drywall. There had to be a way to get into the hollow spaces between the studs, and it had to be easy enough to give Lucie access as she needed it.

I walked around the room once more, trying to see the room as Lucie might have. I ended up in the bathroom, staring into the mirrored medicine cabinet. And then it hit me. Looking in there, I saw the cabinet was held to the wall by a set of screws, and when I jiggled it, the cabinet was slightly loose.

Back at my truck, I had a tool kit. Once I had the right screwdriver in my hands, the cabinet came off in minutes. There were a half a dozen small baggies in the hollow space behind where the cabinet sat. I opened one and sniffed.

Without a chemical analysis, I couldn't be sure, but I thought what Lucie had stashed there was crystal meth, which was often processed in the islands into its smokeable form, called either "ice" or "*batu.*" I didn't know why Lucie had left so much crystal meth there, and I had no idea how much it was worth.

Tucked into the back of the compartment was a piece of paper, folded and then folded again. It looked like a computer printout from a police database, an arrest record for someone named Harold Pincus, who had been charged with wire fraud, mail fraud, securities fraud, and first-degree fraud in connection with his alleged operation of a Ponzi scheme. I had no idea who Pincus was, what a Ponzi scheme was, or why Lucie had kept this paper with her stash, but I copied down all the information before I replaced the paper in the niche.

I called Sampson's cell number and a recorded voice told me that he was either out of range or his phone was off. I left him a message, telling him that the investigating detectives ought to check out the hollow place behind the medicine cabinet in Lucie's apartment. I even left the access code for the lock box. Then I put the cabinet back in place and left.

I had been hoping I'd get some kind of vibe from the place, maybe a message Lucie Zamora had encoded in the building's DNA, but instead I got a sad feeling that this was the best she'd been able to do before her life was snuffed out.

On the way back to Hibiscus House, I tried to recap what I had learned. I knew from both Brad and Ari that Lucie paid for everything in cash. That's a typical profile for someone with illicit income who doesn't want a paper trail. Jeremy thought his Filipino boyfriend had bought ice from her. And I'd found her private stash of crystal meth behind her medicine cabinet.

There were still a lot of questions, and I missed my partner in Waikīkī, Akoni, a big, beefy Hawai'ian guy I'd gone through the academy with. I wanted to go over everything with him, get his opinion, but I couldn't, because I was flying solo. I wanted to know if Lucie had brought the crystal meth in her apartment back from Mexico, and if she'd recruited Mike Pratt and Ronnie Chang to help her. Why was there still so much left, though? Had she held some back as part of a private deal? And if someone killed her because of her drug connections, why hadn't they torn apart her room to find the drugs I had? I pulled my pad and pen back out and started making notes.

I had some time to kill before meeting George and Larry for cocktails, and I was pretty surfed out, so I decided to go back to Hibiscus House and take a nap. I thought I'd earned one.

Chapter 14

THE PLAINS OF AFRICA

LARRY AND GEORGE HAD SUGGESTED I meet them at Kahuna's, a surfer bar on the Kam Highway just outside Haleiwa. I remembered the place all too well; it was where my buddies had taken me that fateful night after my fifth-place finish. How many more messages from my past were waiting for me, I wondered, as I parked my truck in the lot and walked up to the ramshackle thatched-roof bar, which was pulsing with the sound of the Beach Boys, who were singing about the joys of California surfing.

I went to college in Santa Cruz, and I surfed up and down the California coast during the four years my parents thought I was studying the great works of literature, perhaps as a prelude to law school. I'd take surfing on the North Shore any day.

Neither Larry nor George were at the bar when I arrived, so I went up and got myself a Corona. At the bar, I saw Melody, from the outrigger club, with the blonde who had been introduced to me as Mary. They looked very intimate, clasping each other's hands. As I was getting ready to go over and say hello, I saw Mary kiss Melody, and decided they probably wanted to be alone.

I staked out a high-topped table with a view of the front door. Around me I saw a couple of guys I recognized from Pipeline, but for the most part the crowd seemed to be a tourist one. Nobody moved away from me or muttered insults, and for that I was grateful.

George arrived first. Since my gaydar still wasn't very well developed, I never would have thought George was gay. He wore a sleeveless T-shirt that showed off his well-muscled biceps, a pair of khaki board shorts, white socks, and work boots. He seemed to be a popular figure, high-fiving and laughing as he worked his way over to my table. Like me, he seemed comfortable moving in a straight world.

"So how did you know Lucie?" I asked, when he'd finally got himself a Heineken and came over to sit across from me.

"Met her at the gym," he said. "I'm a personal trainer and I work with a lot of surfers on conditioning. Another client referred Lucie to me."

"Tell me about her."

"Really tough," he said. "She could take whatever I dished out for her. Super motivated, didn't understand a lot of the physics involved in surfing, so she didn't know which muscle groups she had to work on, but she wanted to win and she was willing to do what it took to get there."

"What can you tell me about Lucie that nobody else knows?"

George thought for a minute. "She was nosey," he said finally. "Always snooping around. At the gym, I caught her going through a guy's locker once. She swore she wasn't looking for cash, and I believed her. Whenever she was over at my place, she was always looking through my mail, my bills. I know she did the same thing to Larry and to Ari."

"She ever find anything she wasn't supposed to?"

"Not that I know of." He drained his beer. "Gotta piss. I'll be back."

While George was in the restroom, Larry came in. Wheat blond hair, with a slim, but muscular physique, he was the kind of guy who attracted attention wherever he went. It seemed like every girl in the place swiveled her head toward the door when he walked in.

He saw me and came directly over to the table, where he leaned over and hugged me. "It's great to see you again," he said. There seemed to be a genuine warmth there that wasn't manufactured, and it surprised me. Of all the guys, I expected Larry to be the most standoffish, just because he was handsome. Wrong again, detective.

"I think it's really cool that you care enough to look into what happened to Lucie," he said. "Too often nobody cares about people on the edges of society."

"Was Lucie on the edge?"

"She came from a poor family," he said. "She didn't actually finish high school. She didn't want anybody to know that, and sometimes she told people that her family back in the Philippines was rich, that they were bankrolling her surfing career."

"Did she lie a lot?"

Larry shrugged. "Sometimes. Occasionally she shoplifted, and I know once or twice she picked up tourists, had sex back at their hotel rooms, and stole their wallets. I wouldn't say she had a lot of morals. And even though she was pretty, and smart, and talented, she wasn't successful yet, and she didn't have rich or influential friends to make sure that the police investigated her murder."

"They investigated," I said. "A friend of mine showed me

the report. They just couldn't find anyone who would be honest with them about her."

"It's hard," Larry said.

George reappeared, with Heinekens for all three of us. "You talking about sex already?" he asked Larry.

"Get over yourself, George," Larry said. "I'm talking about Lucie. According to Kimo, nobody would talk to the police about her."

"Nobody asked me," George said. "Not that I had that much to say. Or that I'd trust the cops too much anyway."

"George has had a couple of run-ins with the police," Larry said. "He's a little too fond of having sex outdoors. With strangers."

"Up yours."

"You've been there." Larry turned to me. "Always with a condom, though. You don't know where that thing has been."

"How'd you know Lucie?" I asked.

"We used to go shopping together. I was at Butterfly one day, hanging out with Brad, when she came in. We totally hit it off. She had great taste in clothes. We'd go down to the outlet mall in Waikele together and look for bargains."

"She didn't strike me as the bargain hunter type," I said. "Butterfly certainly isn't a discount operation."

"Lucie loved labels," Larry said. "More than she loved a bargain. Me, all I can do most places is browse, but I can actually buy at Waikele. Lucie'd go with me, help me pick out what worked best for my coloring, my build."

He was dressed beautifully, I had to admit. His linen slacks caressed his body, and the Dolce & Gabbana logo T-shirt he wore seemed almost to have been custom-made. He wore suede shoes that looked like they were fresh from the box.

The conversation turned to more general topics, and I was

just enjoying their company when Larry turned to George and said, "Did you ask him yet?"

"I was just about to when you showed up."

"Ask me what?"

"If you were interested. In us."

I must have looked as confused as I felt. "In a three-way," George clarified. "You, me, and Larry."

I was nonplussed. "Wow, I'm flattered."

"Good," George said. "Let us flatter you some more, over at Larry's place."

"I've never actually done it with more than one guy," I said. "And I can't say I've met two better looking guys up here, guys that I'd be more interested in experimenting with."

"Then let's go," George said.

I felt like I was flailing around wildly for an excuse. My dick had already decided for me, and its vote was clear: get naked with Larry and George. But I was trying to learn to think with the big head, too, when it came to sex. And the big head was telling me I had a case to investigate, and I had one more guy to meet with that night. "I'm supposed to have dinner with Rik," I said. "I don't have any way to get in touch with him to cancel."

"Fuck him," George said. "Tomorrow night, if you want. That is, if you like ribs."

"That's George's charming nickname for him," Larry said. "Rik is so skinny you can see his ribs when he strips off his shirt."

"The truth is that Brad wore me out last night," I said. I saw George and Larry raise eyebrows at each other. "Swear to God." I thought for a moment, searching my fried brain cells for a detail that would convince them. "He said something like, 'Oh, Jesus, open up those pearly gates because I'm coming!'"

Larry laughed. "OK, you proved you've actually had sex with him. That's Brad's trademark line. But that doesn't get you off the hook permanently."

"I don't mind being hooked," I said.

"Larry's a bottom and I'm a top," George said. "So we can take good care of you."

I was starting to feel like one of those zebras on the plains of Africa that's been cut away from the herd, the predators circling. There was no reason why I shouldn't have sex with two guys at the same time, if I wanted to. And there was no reason why the prospect should scare me. But somehow it did, which meant I would have to follow through with it—eventually. It's the only way I know to overcome the things that scare me—to face up to them. For now, I could use the excuse of meeting Rik for dinner to get the hell out of that bar.

Chapter 15

TRISH DISHES

RIK AND I HAD SWAPPED e-mail addresses and he was supposed to send me a message confirming time and place for dinner, so I had to swing back past The Next Wave to get the information. Disappointingly, though, he had cancelled on me—he said he had to work late.

I sat back in my chair. It was almost seven, too late for me to head back to the water. Was I disappointed that I'd given up on George and Larry's offer? Well, my dick thought so. But then it's an unreliable monitor of what's right and wrong, and besides, it had gotten an amazing workout the night before, courtesy of Brad. Like the rest of me, it could use a little R & R.

I decided to use the time productively, making copious notes on all the day's conversations. Then I switched over to e-mail. I responded to a bunch of messages from friends, worried about how I was doing. I had a stock message I wrote back, about how I was taking some time to think about my next step, and that I appreciated their support. It sucked to have to lie to people.

I was excited by the case, eager to solve it, and frustrated that I couldn't talk about it with anyone. I had to put on a façade for my family and friends, telling them I was still getting my head together, and listen to their well-meaning advice. With every day that passed, I knew it would get harder to tell them the truth. Just one more reason why I had to settle this case quickly.

When I finished my e-mails, I tried to track down Harold Pincus, but there were just too many men with that name, and I didn't know the jurisdiction where he had been arrested. Shelving that idea, I did some computer searches on ice, cross referenced to Hawai'i and the North Shore. The problem seemed to be worsening, in all the islands. Drug treatment programs reported more patients with methamphetamine problems, and for the first time more people entering pro- grams reported problems with ice than with alcohol.

Child Protective Services estimated that 85 percent of their cases involved meth, and the number of methamphetamine- related deaths was climbing on O'ahu. I found a study which showed a jump in use by high school students as well.

On the mainland, users are more likely to inject metham- phetamine, or speed, into their veins, but in Hawai'i we tend to prefer the smokable form, called ice. The pleasurable and addictive effects are immediate, and can last up to twelve hours. Most of the powdered drug was smuggled in from Mexico; processors used solvents to create the powerful, nearly pure crystalline version, which could be smoked.

Because meth is so powerful, it can be profitable even in small chunks, and smugglers often brought it in from the mainland on their bodies, in luggage, and even in hand-held coolers. I wondered if somehow all three of the surfers who'd attended Mexpipe had been recruited to bring some of the drug back to Hawai'i, for processing into ice. That would ex- plain the crystal meth that I found behind the medicine cabinet at Lucie's apartment; she could have brought it back from Mexico. That would also explain how all three had lots of extra cash upon their return.

Now I just had to find the person or persons who connected the three dead surfers to the ice business. Easy peasy.

With that revelation, I left The Next Wave. I knew the logical, rational thing to do would be to go back to Hibiscus House, take a long, hot shower, and crawl into bed. Alone. But I was tired, and lonely, and my body hurt in a dozen places. I wanted someone to be nice to me.

My truck seemed to know that, too, and very shortly I was in front of Brad Jacobson's apartment building. From there, it was only a few steps up to his door, and a single press of the doorbell. He opened it, and the momentary look of confusion on his face was replaced by one of pure joy.

≈

THE NEXT MORNING, Friday, I tried to get surfers to talk to me about drugs, but no one was willing to say anything. Finally, I pulled my board up on the sand and sat there, staring out at the water, trying to think of what to do next. I'd only been there for a few minutes when Trish came up and sat beside me. "Hey," she said.

"Haven't seen you for a while."

"I had to take extra shifts at the place where I work because one of the other waitresses has been sick."

She sat back on the sand, and we watched the surfers together for a few minutes. I wondered how long it would take Trish to get around to what she wanted to tell me—and if we'd be interrupted again before she could say it. Even so, I knew I couldn't rush her. We watched one guy really carve on a monster wave, and I said, "He's not bad."

"He's got a lot of talent but no discipline," she said. "See how he gave up there? He could have gotten another turn out of that if he'd tried. But he's getting better—six months ago he wouldn't have gotten in as many turns as he did."

"You must know all the regulars," I said. "Didn't you tell me you were Mike Pratt's girlfriend?"

"I loved him, OK?" she said fiercely, and I saw that she had started to cry. "And it just really pisses me off that he's dead."

I put my arm around her and she leaned into my chest, crying. An older couple on folding chairs a few feet away looked at us. They were wearing matching aloha shirts, and looked settled and comfortable—the kind of people who never set foot in the water. She had a pair of heavy duty binoculars on a string around her neck, and he was holding a camera with a big lens. I smiled at them and patted Trish's shoulder, and they went back to watching the surfers.

"It's tough losing somebody you care about," I said, when Trish had recovered enough to sit up. "How long had you known Mike?"

She wiped her eyes with the back of her hand and got a smudge of sand on her right cheek. "About two years. But he had this girlfriend back in New Jersey, and he didn't break up with her until last year. Then it was another couple of months before we actually hooked up."

"Did you go to Mexpipe with Mike?"

She shook her head. "I couldn't. I had to work. But I know something happened down there."

"What do you think?"

"I couldn't say exactly, but I knew him, and I knew something was wrong. He kept complaining about his board, about how his rhythm was off. Whenever I'd press him, he'd say I didn't want to know about it."

"But he never told you what was wrong?"

She shook her head. "When they came to take him away, I talked to the cops. I told them I thought there was something funny about his board, and that they should take it into their office and look it over. But this fat cop just laughed."

"I've heard Mike was having problems with his board. What happened to the board after that?"

"I took it to my house, and I left it outside, along the wall, with my boards and my housemates' boards. But then the next day when I was at work, somebody walked off with it. That's when I knew there was really something funny. I mean, whoever it was didn't steal any other boards—just Mike's."

"Did you report the theft to the cops?"

"I wasn't talking to those jerks again," she said. "They care more about donut shops than about what happens out here." She turned to me. "Look how they treated you. Assholes."

"Some cops are better than others," I said. "I worked with a lot of good ones. A few bad ones, too, but you get that anywhere. Even surfing."

"Yeah, I guess."

Trish lapsed into silence, hugging her knees close to her and staring out at the waves. This was about the time when my partner on Waikīkī, Akoni, would start to get frustrated, thinking that Trish didn't really know anything specific. But me, I was just getting started. I had all day to hang out under the sunshine and the blue skies, watching the surfers and the waves, and waiting for Trish to talk. "You have any theories about what was going on with Mike?" I asked.

"You won't believe me either."

"I know you don't really think that. Or you wouldn't have been trying to tell me this for the last couple of days."

She was still wavering, so I stood up. "Come on, let's see what the waves are like from the other side of the breakers."

Reluctantly, she followed me. We duck-dived through the breakers and then sat on our boards near each other, waiting for waves. I caught one first, and then she did, and we surfed like that for almost an hour before she dragged her board back up to the sand where we'd been sitting. I followed her.

"Have you decided that I'll listen to you?" I asked, sitting next to her.

Most of the people out at Pipeline were in the water, so we had the beach almost all to ourselves. The photographer couple had packed up and left. There were some kids up by Ke Nui Road, and a grizzled old guy asleep on the beach a few hundred yards away from us, but that was about it. The sun was high in the sky and it felt good to dry off in the hot sun. Overhead, a few cumulus clouds floated lazily past, and the shrieks of seagulls, terns, and other seabirds mixed with the roar of the waves pounding against the beach and the occasional cries of a surfer who'd either caught or lost a good wave.

"I think he was smuggling drugs from Mexico in his surfboard," Trish said finally. "I know, it sounds like something out of a bad movie."

"Actually, it sounds pretty close to what I think was happening," I said. I turned to her. "There have been three surfers shot so far, and all three of them were at Mexpipe. They were all shot within a few weeks after they got back. So it's likely that the trip to Mexico was somehow related. I heard Mike was having problems with his board, and I know the girl who was killed sold drugs, but I never thought of smuggling drugs in a surfboard. What made you think of that?"

"I just put it together," she said. "I never asked him about it. He was dead by the time I figured it out." She ran her hand through her wet hair, pushing loose blonde strands back off her face. "He had, like zero money. Everything he made went for paying his basic bills and for travel to surfing competitions. Then he got back from Mexico, where he didn't win very much, but he suddenly had enough to pay entry fees and airfare to this tournament in Tahiti."

"And you thought he'd made that extra money from smuggling?"

"Not at first. But then he told me something was wrong with his board. That it had gotten a hole drilled in it."

"So you assumed the hole was for smuggling drugs."

She squared her shoulders and turned away from me. "You're talking like one of them."

"Like a cop? But isn't that why you came to me in the first place? Because you knew I used to be a cop? People don't change, Trish. At least not so fast." I watched her back for a minute, and thought I saw the pressure on her shoulders lessen just a bit. "Another thing that hasn't changed about me is that I care about catching criminals. I want to do what I can to make sure that the person who killed Mike gets put away for it. But I have to ask questions in order to do that."

She turned back. "I know I sound paranoid. But something's just not right."

"It's not that I doubt you, Trish. I believe you. I just have to learn everything I can." I paused. "The girl who was killed after Mike appears to have been an ice dealer. He didn't use drugs, did he?"

"Nope."

"Do you know if he knew a girl named Lucie Zamora?"

"Sure. Most of the pretty decent surfers know each other. Is she the one who roped him into smuggling?"

"I don't know. There may be somebody above Lucie, who put it all together."

She fingered a gold surfboard on a thin gold chain around her neck. "What are you going to do now?"

"Keep asking questions," I said. The sun passed behind a cloud bank that was rolling in off the Pacific, and it suddenly got chilly on the beach. I stood up. "I'm going back in the water. You coming?"

She shook her head. "I gotta work in an hour," she said. "But I'm out here most mornings. If you hear anything else, will you tell me?"

"Sure."

I walked her back up to Ke Nui Road and watched her drive off toward Haleiwa. I remembered that Mike Pratt had worked for a board shaper when he first came to the North Shore, and put that together with the fact that something had gone wrong with his board after coming back from Mexico. It made sense to me that before throwing the board away, he'd try to salvage it. And who better to go to than his old boss? The shaper was an old hippie named Palani Anderson; I'd read about him but had never met him. Maybe it was time I did.

Chapter 16

THE OLD HIPPIE

I FOUND PALANI'S WORKSHOP in Mokuleia, just off Puuiki Beach. The first thing that struck me was the aroma of polyester resin, which I could smell from a block away. When I approached the open garage I heard the noise of an orbital sander, and I saw Palani standing in front of a shaping rack, working on what looked like a nine-foot board. His white hair was pulled back into a ponytail, and he wore goggles and a dust mask.

The room behind him was painted black, with lights mounted on the walls just above the shaping rack to highlight any bumps in the white foam. Scattered around him, on the floor and on shelves along the wall, were the tools of his trade: a dozen different types of planes; a spokeshave, used for shaping curved work; a Japanese curved planer; several different kinds of surforms (used to shape noses, tails, and rails); and piles of different grades of sandpaper.

I also saw stacks of foam blanks in sizes from six feet up to ten feet longboards, and cans of resin. When Palani looked up and saw me approaching he turned the sander off, pulled down the mask, and flipped up the goggles.

I introduced myself. "I remember you," he said. "You used to be a pretty decent surfer. You still surf?"

It was amazing how good it felt to be remembered for something other than coming out of the closet. "Try to."

"You looking for a board?"

I shook my head. "Information. About Mike Pratt."

"Poor son of a bitch," Palani said. "I wasn't surprised to hear he died. Still a shame, though."

He put the goggles and the mask down on a table and we walked behind the garage. The air was fresher there, a nice breeze coming up off the ocean. He pulled a pack of Marlboros from his pocket and offered me one, which I declined.

"Why weren't you surprised?" I asked, as he lit his cigarette.

"He got himself in with the wrong crowd," Palani said. He took a deep drag on his cigarette. "I'm not opposed to recreational drugs. Hell, I smoked enough dope in my life to save a ward full of cancer patients. But the drugs these kids do today, they're bad news. Crack cocaine and ecstasy and crystal meth."

"Nothing like the heroin of the good old days," I said.

Palani laughed. "You got me there." Then his face saddened. "But Mike got himself on the business end of the deal somehow. He was a good kid, you know, a real talented surfer. Had a feel for the waves you can't train into somebody."

"So I've heard. What made him go bad, then?"

"Money. Makes us all do things we shouldn't sometimes. He was determined to be a real competitor, and to do that you need backing. Entry fees, travel, training time. Somebody offered him the money he needed, and he took it."

"He ever tell you who that was?"

Palani shook his head, and his ponytail swung from one side to the other. "I didn't want to know. But I knew he was in trouble."

"Did he ever come up here with something wrong with his board?"

Palani looked at me. "You know a lot about him, don't you?"

"I've been learning. Somebody asked him to smuggle drugs in his board, didn't they?"

"Yup. Really pissed him off, because he loved that board. He customized it himself, right here in this shop."

"The board wasn't fixable?"

Palani laughed. "Not with the center of it cored out," he said. "You can fix a broken plug, a stringer. Something simple. No way to fix something like that."

"What I still don't understand is how that could get him killed."

"It was him complaining about it. He bitched to anybody who'd listen. I told him to shut his mouth, it was going to get him in trouble, but he kept on. I guess whoever it was got worried he'd complain to somebody who would listen."

We made small talk for a few minutes, and then Palani showed me around his garage. I'd done a little shaping when I was in high school, mostly trying to customize my own boards, and it was cool to see a master at work. But eventually I had to tear myself away—I had the information I'd come for.

Leaving Palani's place, I finally felt like I was getting somewhere. At long last, a real motive for Mike Pratt's death. He was pissed off that his board had gotten ruined, and he couldn't keep his mouth shut about it.

I dragged myself back to Hibiscus House. I thought I might take a nap and then think about going over to see Brad, but my nap stretched all night, until I woke up Saturday morning as fingers of light were beginning to crawl through the window that looked out over the driveway.

The next morning, as I waited for waves, I couldn't help trying to organize what I had been discovering. There were certain pieces of evidence. All three of the murder victims had been to Mexpipe, though that was the only thing, beyond surfing and murder, that seemed to link them. Therefore it was probably an important fact.

Mike Pratt knew Lucie Zamora. After a trip to Mexico, a trip Lucie had also made, Mike returned with the money for travel and entrance fees. Trish believed he'd gotten that money by bringing crystal meth back from Mexico, and that he'd used his board to hold it. Palani confirmed that a hole had been cored in Mike's board. Shortly after he returned, after he'd complained about the condition of his board to anyone who'd listen, he was dead.

According to Jeremy Leddinger, who had a drug addict ex-boyfriend, Lucie Zamora sold ice, the powdered form of crystal meth. I had found a stash behind her medicine cabinet, and I doubted it had been left there by a previous tenant. Further evidence was provided by the cash she had to spend on designer clothing at Brad Jacobson's boutique, Butterfly, and on shopping trips with Brad's friend Larry Brickman.

Larry and George had also verified that Lucie knew Ronnie Chang, the computer-nerd-slash-weekend-surfer, who had also gone to Puerto Escondido for Mexpipe. He seemed like a straight arrow, but a sexy woman has been known to draw even the straightest guy into troublesome waters, and Jeremy had said Lucie led Ronnie around by his dick.

A huge wave washed over me and knocked me into the cool Pacific, reminding me that I was in troublesome waters as well. I kept on surfing, all day long, though I couldn't stop turning over the questions I had about the three dead surfers.

Whenever I was on the beach I tried to talk to other surfers, looking for anyone who had known Mike, Lucie, or Ronnie, or anyone else who had gone to Mexpipe. I didn't have any luck.

That night, I thought about calling Brad, but I decided first to head to the Drainpipe, the Haleiwa bar where Lucie's one-time boyfriend Frank worked. I was hoping he could shed some more light on where Lucie got her drugs from, and how her dealing might tie in with her trip to Mexpipe. I wasn't sure how much he could tell me, particularly if the bar was busy, but it was Saturday night and I was thirsty, and the Drainpipe seemed as good a bar as any.

Jeremy had said that dating Frank was just a cover so that Lucie could hang around the Drainpipe and meet up with customers. Perhaps someone there had bought from her—or someone had moved into her territory.

Frank wasn't on duty, which was disappointing, but I got myself a beer and relaxed. I got roped into a dart game, talked to a couple of guys and girls, and remembered what my Saturday nights had been like before I came out of the closet.

It was funny, but I found myself having a pretty good time, partly because there was absolutely no sexual agenda going on—at least not on my part. I wasn't sizing up the *wahines*— or the guys, for that matter—and trying to figure out my chances of scoring. While there might have been a girl or two checking me out, none were blatant, so I didn't have to do anything to discourage anyone. I played darts, I drank my beer, and I laughed. A lot.

It was obvious to me, though no one said anything directly, that people knew who I was, so I couldn't be too blatant about asking for drugs, or asking if anyone knew Lucie, Mike, or

Ronnie. Around ten o'clock I was surprised to see Brad's friend Jeremy, the elementary school teacher, but we did nothing more than shout hellos before he appeared to have left the bar. I figured there were probably few gay places he could go, and if he was bored at Sugar's it was worth checking out the straight bars to see what kind of action was going on.

About a half hour later, George and Larry, the macho guy and the cute guy, came in together, and my radar went into overdrive. Sure enough, as soon as they both had beers, they were heading my way.

I was a little drunk by then. Still able to function, still able to drive, but my defenses were dangerously low. They clinked their bottles up against mine and made their greetings, and I followed them to a dark corner of the bar.

"How's it going?" George asked. "You finding anything out about Lucie?"

"Still picking up information," I said. "Haven't really processed it all yet."

"If there's anything we can do to help," Larry said.

"Anything at all," George said. His leg brushed against mine, so casually that it might have been nothing, but my adrenaline level soared. I decided I could put my homicide investigation on hold for one Saturday night and enjoy myself.

I knew I could play coy with them, ignore the subtext, come up with another excuse to leave. But what was stopping me from heading out with them, enjoying what they had to offer? Some outdated code of ethics that said sex should be only a two-person sport? Or some deeper programming, which indicated that sex had to be involved with romance, which had to lead to me and Mr. Right living together behind a white picket fence?

I didn't think either of those should control me, and frankly, I was horny, so I said, "That offer you made the other night. That still stand?"

"You bet," George said.

"Didn't think you'd be so easy," Larry said.

I licked my lips. Might as well go for the gusto, I thought. "I'm not easy," I said. "I'm hard."

Both George and Larry laughed out loud. "Well, that's a good state to be in," George said. "You're staying at that sleazy old Hibiscus House, aren't you?"

"Yup."

"Well, let's get over there and make it a little sleazier."

They'd come in George's pickup, in response to a phone call from Jeremy, as I thought, so Larry came with me and George followed. His truck was a lot like mine, banged up and yet still serviceable.

Larry sat next to me, playing first with a curl of my black hair, then stroking one finger down my thigh as I drove. "You'd better not do too much of that, if you want us to get there in one piece," I said. I could feel my erection straining against my jeans and thought if he touched it, I'd probably explode right there.

"We'll get there," he said. "Don't worry."

Fortunately, Hibiscus House wasn't too far away, and very shortly the three of us were standing in my slightly messy room. I'd learned from Brad's visit that I had to keep it neater, so the only thing I had to do was move some dirty clothes off the chair and the place was fit for company.

George and Larry didn't wait for hospitality, though. George was behind me and Larry in front of me, one stroking my back and the other kissing me. In short order, and almost without my noticing it, I'd shed my clothes and stood there, nude, between them.

"If you guys don't strip down, we aren't going to have much fun," I said, in between my tongue's dueling with Larry's.

"Oh, we'll have some fun," George said.

There was something quite erotic, on the edge of dangerous, about my being naked with the two of them fully clothed. I'd exposed myself to them completely, while they had exposed nothing at all to me. I'd relinquished all the power, and that was a powerful aphrodisiac itself.

I felt Larry's stiff dick rubbing against mine through his pants fabric, and George's finger, magically lubricated, exploring my ass, and gave myself up to the pleasure. Soon enough, both of them were naked, too, and Larry had turned his ass to me. George handed me a rubber and squeezed some lube onto my hand, and I practiced doing to Larry what George was doing to me.

In short order, we were making a Kimo sandwich. Larry's hole was loose and slippery and I slid right in. Mine was more difficult for George to penetrate, but he seemed to have a lot of experience. I felt the rubbery head of his condom-enclosed dick knocking up against my back door, and then in one strong push that sent waves of pain through my body, he was inside me.

He led the rhythm; as he pushed into me, I pushed into Larry. Soon my ass got used to the intrusion and the pain somehow melted away. I had my hands on Larry's prominent hipbones, more for balance than for anything sexual, while George was balanced enough to let his hands roam around my body, tweaking my nipples, cupping my hips, running down the outer edges of my thighs.

I shut off all thinking, opening myself to pleasure, and pleasure was provided. I felt incredibly connected to both of them, as if an electrical current that began in George pulsed through me and into Larry.

I couldn't control the noises I made, and it seemed George couldn't control his, either. They worked together until, with one massive push into me, he filled his condom's reservoir and I did the same with mine. We held the position for a moment or two, and then with a squishy plop George had pulled out of me, and I pulled out of Larry.

Larry turned to face me and we began to kiss again. Then I felt George move between us down at crotch level and realized he was blowing Larry, my limp dick nested in his hair. Larry came quickly, and then the three of us fell onto my bed, where we spooned up together. "Man, that was awesome," I finally said.

"That *was* pretty good," George said.

"You guys do this kind of thing . . . often?"

"When we find somebody we both like," Larry said. "Not so often as all that, but occasionally."

"Are you—together?"

George laughed. "Tonight's about as together as we get," he said. "I like a little pussy now and then, and Larry mostly likes to get fucked—as often as he can."

I didn't pretend to understand. I loved what we did—while we were doing it—but I didn't think I'd make a habit of it. After a while, Larry and George both kissed me good night, and slipped out the door.

I looked at the clock. It was just midnight. I could get some sleep and then the next morning . . . I suddenly realized: the next morning was Sunday, and my family was coming to the

North Shore for a big luau. My room was littered with condom wrappers and lube bottles, my ass felt like it had been reamed by a beer bottle, and my nipples felt like raw meat. Jesus.

I hoped it would all be better in the morning, and went to sleep.

Chapter 17

LUAU

MY CELL PHONE WOKE ME AT EIGHT. "We're passing Helemano Plantation," my brother Lui said. "We'll be in Waimea soon. You got the picnic area reserved?"

"Shit."

"You still in bed, sleepy head? I figured you'd be surfing already, trying fruitlessly to improve your surfing skills before your big brothers show up and blow you out of the water."

"Rough night. I'm getting up. I'll be there in a few minutes."

"Get lots of tables. We have a whole caravan here."

"Caravan?"

"Mom, Liliha, and Tatiana are each driving a car full of food. The three of them have been cooking for days—it's like those three witches from *Macbeth*." His voice turned away from the phone for a second. "Jeffrey, you tell your mother, your auntie, or your *Tutu* I called them witches and you get no Xbox for a month." His voice returned to normal. "Dad's got every surfboard this family owns packed into his truck. I've got a car full of kids and toys and so does Haoa. Harry's back there somewhere, and so's your friend Terri with her son."

"Jesus."

"He's probably trailing along behind," Lui said. "Get your skinny butt moving. I can almost see Matsumoto's."

I stumbled out of bed, into the shower, and into board shorts and a T-shirt. I could just imagine the wrath of my entire family if they showed up at Waimea Bay Beach Park and I wasn't there with a batch of picnic tables.

Fortunately, the near-perfect surf conditions meant that everyone who'd considered heading up to the North Shore had gone directly into the water, and I was able to secure the perimeter of an area I thought was big enough for all of us. Only moments after I arrived I saw my father's pickup, loaded with surfboards, enter the parking lot.

There was indeed a caravan behind him. Lui had recently surrendered his pickup for a dark gray Mercedes sedan, which was in second place, filled with Jeffrey, his brother Keoni, and their sister Malia. Right behind was Lui's wife Liliha in her gold Mercedes, which was filled with food and picnic supplies.

My mother drives a Lexus, and she and her load were sandwiched between Liliha and my brother Haoa's panel truck, in which he had the *kalua* pig, fresh from the *imu* pit in his backyard, along with barbecue supplies.

His kids, Ashley, Alec, Ailina, and the newest baby, Apikela, rode with their mother, Tatiana, a big-boned daughter of Russian immigrants to Alaska who had floated up on our shores and fallen in love with Haoa. She drove a Chrysler PT Cruiser which was perennially loaded with kids, toys, and various levels of debris.

At the rear were Harry, his girlfriend Arleen next to him, her son Brandon strapped into a car seat, Harry's longboard strapped to the roof of his BMW, and Terri Clark Gonsalves, my high school friend, in her Land Rover, with her small son Danny. It struck me that we probably had every variety of luxury car on the islands represented, along with my father's beat-up old truck, the previous beat-up old truck which he'd passed down to me, and Haoa's landscaping van.

The parking, hugging, kissing, and unloading seemed to take forever, especially with the kids all clamoring to get out on the water. Harry and Terri finally volunteered to chaperon the lot of them, and while the rest of the adults unloaded, they trooped down to the Pacific to check out the surf conditions. The littlest kids had boogie boards, but Ashley and Jeffrey, who were already teenagers, both had graduated to real surfboards.

I helped Haoa lift the pig out of his van, and noticed him wincing. "How you doing, brah?" I asked. He'd gotten banged up pretty badly over the last month, between getting himself into a variety of fights, and then redeeming himself, at least in my eyes, by rushing to save me when a bad guy was about to shoot me.

"I'm getting old, Kimo," he said. "Forty. Jesus."

"Cool," I said. "So I can beat your ass when we go surf."

"You never do dat," he said.

"I'll beat both of you," Lui said, coming up to join us. "When we go surf?"

"Soon as we get rid of this stuff," I said. Lui helped Haoa and me carry the pig over to where the women were putting the food together, and then the three of us dropped our shirts, grabbed boards, and raced each other to the water's edge, then out into the surf.

"Go, Daddy!" Ashley cried.

"My dad's the best surfer," Jeffrey said.

"Uncle Kimo's the best," Keoni said defiantly. "You watch."

"You don't know anything," Jeffrey said, cuffing his brother.

"Loser buys everybody shave ice," I called, launching myself into the waves.

My brothers were always so much older than I was, Lui by ten years, Haoa eight, that I never really got to hang out with them as equals. Even once I returned to the islands from college, both of them were so busy with their families and their careers that sometimes they seemed more like uncles than brothers, though I felt a visceral closeness to them whenever we were together.

That day, for the first time, I really felt like we were three brothers. I hadn't seen Lui shirtless, in board shorts, since he was a teenager; my oldest brother is rarely seen without a suit, or at least a sports jacket.

Haoa's more relaxed; in his landscaping business he usually wears polo shirts embroidered with the name of the business, khakis or chinos, and deck shoes or sandals. But I hadn't been on the water with him in years, either. The three of us raced through the breakers, laughing and talking stink, as the rest of the family gathered on the beach to cheer and watch.

I knew I was the best surfer in the family, at least in part because I was the only one who'd kept on surfing, year after year, and because I secretly thought I was the one with the most talent, too. But my brothers gave me a run for my money. I remembered being a little kid, watching Haoa and Lui surf and being amazed at their prowess. Those feelings came back to me as I watched them both jump on their boards, catch waves, even do a little carving. They were both rusty, sure; and the waves at Waimea Bay, though nothing like Pipeline, were still pretty strong. But my brothers, like me, were Hawai'ian to their core, and for us, surfing is like riding a bicycle; you never forget how to do it.

The kids on shore exploded into laughter any time one of us fell, and cheered wildly as we bobbed, turned, and rode the waves in. We must have surfed almost an hour like that before we called a truce. "So who wins?" I asked, as the three of us trudged up the shoreline, dragging our boards.

The kids had obviously been practicing together, because with one voice, they shouted, "Uncle Kimo!"

I gave an exaggerated bow, and one of my brothers kicked my behind, knocking me head first into the sand. Immediately, all six of my nieces and nephews, along with Danny Gonsalves, were on top of me. Ashley and Jeffrey wanted a private surfing lesson, and then I had to fool around with the other kids and their boogie boards. It was almost noon by the time I finally dragged them all up the shore to the picnic area so we could start the luau.

I found myself in line next to Terri Clark Gonsalves. She was wearing a navy polo shirt and black shorts, and when she pulled off her dark glasses for a moment I saw dark circles under her eyes. Her husband Evan had died just a month before, and the grief was still wearing on her. "How are you holding up?" I asked.

She shrugged. "I get through the days. Tatiana's been great. She's always inviting Danny over to play. He and Ailina go to kindergarten together. They're like little sweethearts."

"Good for them." I smiled. "I'm glad you guys could come up here today."

"I wasn't going to, but Tatiana insisted. I didn't want to intrude on a family thing."

"You know you've always been part of our family." Terri and I had gone to Punahou, a Honolulu prep school where both my brothers had preceded me, and even though her family was one of the wealthiest in the islands, we'd always been great friends.

"I know, and I appreciate it, now more than ever." She paused. "I know that you're working undercover," she said in a low voice. "Harry told me. I know he wasn't supposed to, but I was feeling so miserable about what happened to you that he thought he had to tell me."

"I'm not sure I know what you're talking about," I said, loading my plate with *lomi lomi* salmon, *kalua* pork, long rice, and vegetables. I saw Harry coming toward us. He looked as skinny as ever, though his mop of black hair seemed to have been cut at a fancy salon, instead of with a bowl and a pair of scissors. "I left the force. I'm just up here surfing, trying to figure out what to do with the rest of my life."

"Harry," Terri said darkly, as he arrived in line behind us. Back in Honolulu, I had counseled him to start working out, to bulk up some of the muscles he would need to improve as a surfer. After not seeing him for a couple of weeks, I noticed the workouts were starting to have an effect; his arms seemed at least a little more muscular under his short-sleeved aloha shirt.

He looked from my face to Terri's. "Shit," he said. "Were we not supposed to know?"

"Get some food, Harry. We'll talk."

Terri and I walked over to a picnic table under a stand of palm trees, and sat down. Harry joined us a few minutes later. Across the way, I could see Arleen, a sweet Japanese girl Harry had met through me, holding Brandon, all the moms swarming over the new baby in our midst. "What makes you think I'm working undercover?" I asked.

Harry looked sheepish. "As long as you're not a cop anymore I can tell you," he said. "I hacked in to your bank account."

"You did what?" Terri and I both said, almost simultaneously.

"I was worried you'd run out of cash," he said. "You know with all those patents in my name, I'm running a big surplus. So I was going to transfer some money to your account. I figured if you didn't know where it came from, you couldn't complain."

"That's a really—nice—sentiment," I said. "Strange, but nice."

"Once I got in—and by the way, your bank's site really isn't very safe from hackers, any teenager could break through—I saw that your paycheck was still being deposited. But some of the codes on the deposit changed two weeks ago, and just for my own amusement, and to see if I could do it, I decoded them. You were switched from District 1 to District 2, on temporary assignment undercover."

I shook my head. "Jesus, Harry. How many crimes do you think you committed just doing all that?"

"Well, if you're not really a cop anymore then you aren't obliged to report me, are you?"

I sighed. "Lieutenant Sampson—he's my new boss. He was worried that if Lui got wind of my assignment, he'd find some way to get it on TV. So I had to promise to tell everyone that I had given up the job and was coming up here just to surf."

"I don't know that I'd trust Lui either," Terri said, wiping her fingers on a napkin. "Sorry, I know he's your brother, but look what he did to you, Kimo. If he ran that story about you being gay without telling you—or your parents—I don't think he really has any ethics at all."

"I wouldn't go that far," I said. "But I guess I agreed with Sampson, because I said I'd do it his way."

"So your parents don't know you're still working?" Harry asked. "Your mother must be having a cow."

"A herd," I said. "New cows popping out daily."

The three of us ate in silence for a few minutes. "Are you making any progress?" Terri finally asked.

"I've been learning a lot, but without a partner to bounce it off I'm feeling swamped."

"We can help," Harry said. "I provide the logic, Terri provides the heart. Together we're a full person."

"Arleen thinks you have a heart," Terri said.

"You know what I mean. You've always been better at the touchy-feely stuff, I've always been better at the logic. Kimo's always been the one who just bulls through and gets things done. We've been like this since high school and we're not likely to change."

When we were at Punahou, Harry and I were mad to surf, sneaking off every available moment to drag our boards into the water, ignoring homework. He was the only reason I'd made passing grades, though somehow he'd scored straight A's and gone off to MIT for undergraduate and graduate degrees in computer science. He'd come back to the islands just a few months before, teaching a little at UH, fiddling with some inventions, and managing the money he'd made on the mainland.

Terri had been the good girl, president of the honor society, homecoming queen, a straight-A student herself. She had made sure we knew when our tests were and dragged us to extracurricular activities. It was good to be together with them both again.

I outlined the facts. "That poor girl," Terri said, shaking her head.

"Hey, there's two dead guys, too," Harry said.

"I know, but I keep thinking that this Lucie is at the center of things," Terri said. "I'm getting a really clear picture of her from the details. She sounds determined to succeed, but it's not just a lack of money that's standing in her way, it's her attitude toward money."

"What do you mean?" I asked, sitting forward on the picnic bench.

"You said she loved labels—name brand clothes. Usually people wear those clothes because they want to fit in, to be like people they see as better, and they want everyone to see that they're worthwhile, too."

Harry and I must have both been looking skeptical, because she continued. "It's like that saying, 'dress for the job you want, not the job you have.'" That was a saying I'd heard. "Lucie was dressing like the person she wanted to be—successful and rich—the person she wanted people to think she was. Combine that with her drive to succeed as a surfer and you have somebody who's willing to do almost anything to achieve her goals."

"OK, I get it," I said. "So then what do you think got her killed? Somebody who perceived her drive as a threat?"

"It's possible. But you also said she was Filipina, right?"
I nodded.

"And the Philippines is almost completely Catholic."
"Your point?"

"My point is that she probably had a strong moral upbringing, but her desires overwhelmed her morals. Then maybe something happened that changed the balance again."

I was starting to see where she was going. "Mike Pratt was killed," I said. "You think maybe either she knew who killed Mike, or suspected, and her morals were resurfacing, maybe making her a threat to the killer."

"I think it's a possibility," Terri said. "Plus you said that Mike had gotten involved with a Christian surfing group in Mexico, didn't you?"

"Yeah."

"And you think maybe he was involved in smuggling some drugs back from there. It's possible those Christian surfers got him thinking that what he was doing was wrong, and he tried to back out, go to the authorities."

"This is very interesting," I said. "So let me see if I can construct a scenario. Lucie's this very determined girl who needs a lot of money to feed her habits—surfing and shopping foremost. She overcomes her Catholic upbringing to become a low-level drug dealer. She plans to go to Mexpipe, and makes arrangements to bring some crystal meth back—some of which I found in her apartment."

"Makes sense so far," Harry said.

"She knows Mike Pratt and knows he needs money, so she recruits him to help her. They come up with a scheme to smuggle the crystal back to the U.S. in their surfboards."

I stood up and started walking around. "But while they're in Mexico, Mike hooks up with the Christian surfers, who make him see that what he's doing is wrong. By the time he gets back to the States, he's really upset—both on moral grounds and because the board he loved is ruined."

"Where does the Chinese guy fit in?" Harry asked. "Don't forget the Chinese guy."

"Ronnie was Lucie's friend, right?" Terri asked. "Maybe she recruited him, too."

"OK, the three of them bring the crystal back from Mexico and turn at least some of it over to Lucie's supplier. I found the rest behind her medicine cabinet."

"Then there ought to be a money trail," Harry said. "These guys weren't sophisticated enough to cover their tracks. Maybe the supplier, but not Lucie, Mike, or Ronnie. You could subpoena their bank records."

I shook my head. "Not without some probable cause. Judges don't sign subpoenas based on speculation."

"I could check it out for you," Harry said. "I already know how to get into your bank."

"I'm still a cop, Harry, as you have already figured out. I can't ask you to do that—and I can't use anything you find in court."

"E-mail me their names, addresses, anything you have," Harry said. "That's all you need to know. But you still haven't established why the Chinese guy got killed. Just the *haole* and the Filipina."

"Ronnie disappeared the same day Lucie was shot," Terri said. "Maybe she confided in him. He was a smart computer guy, right? Maybe she was trying to atone for her sins by finding out who killed Mike, and she recruited Ronnie to help."

"That's as good a scenario as I can get for now," I said. "Though there isn't much I can do to prove any of it."

"You need to find the supplier," Harry said. "That's the guy who has the motive. But I hope you're not going to tell me you plan to buy some ice yourself. Because you're not officially a cop up here and you could get yourself into a whole heap of trouble."

"The idea did cross my mind," I admitted. "But I met a guy who bought from Lucie. He must be buying somewhere else now that she's dead."

"That's the guy who was supposed to meet you for dinner but cancelled?" Terri asked.

"Yeah. His name is Rik. He's hard to get hold of because he works at Waimea Falls Park and he's always having to cover for other guys' shifts."

"Or he's dodging you," Harry said. "Is he working today?"

I nodded. "I see a plan forming," I said. "You think we could take the kids over there this afternoon?"

"It's a good diversion," Terri said. "That way you kind of stumble on him. We can keep the kids busy while you talk to him."

We agreed to head to the park after lunch, just as we were inundated by a flood of my nieces and nephews.

Chapter 18

A WALK IN THE PARK

IT WAS ALMOST TWO before we could break away a group of kids to head to Waimea Falls Park. Ashley and Jeffrey wanted to keep surfing, and Alec and Keoni wanted to stay in the water on their boogie boards. We left my parents, Lui and Liliha, and Haoa and Tatiana in a pleasant after-lunch stupor to look after them.

Terri's Land Rover was the biggest vehicle, so we piled in for the brief drive inland. Terri drove and I navigated, with Lui's youngest daughter Malia on my lap. Arleen and Harry shared the back seat with Arleen's son Brandon. Terri's son Danny and Haoa's daughter Ailina, the baby sweethearts, sat together in the back cargo area.

I checked with the elderly Chinese woman who took our money and found that Rik, one of the nature guides, was somewhere in the gardens; unfortunately, she couldn't be more specific. We all took the electric tram up to the falls, but instead of swimming we elected to walk around through the gardens. The four of us concentrated on showing the kids the flowers and exotic birds, stopping at the country store to buy candy for the kids.

It was as we were coming out of the store that we ran into Rik. It couldn't have appeared more innocent, yet Rik was immediately suspicious. Fortunately, just as I said hello, Malia tugged on my pant leg and announced, "Uncle Kimo, I have to go bathroom."

"Why don't we all take a bathroom break," Terri announced. She picked up Malia and took Ailina's hand, while Arleen scooped up Brandon.

Harry, carrying Danny, said, "I saw the bathrooms over there. Kimo, you can wait here, we'll all be right back."

"So you had to miss dinner Friday night," I said to Rik, as the entourage began its trek to the bathrooms.

"Yeah, we had a big party here, and a couple of us had to stay late to close up." He looked around nervously. "I really should get back to work."

"Why don't I walk with you, and it'll look like you're showing me the park." I put my hand on his shoulder and gently steered him toward one of the paths. He was painfully skinny, and I felt like there was almost no flesh between my hand and the bones of his shoulder.

"Look," I said when we were out of earshot of the country store. "I know you used to buy your drugs from Lucie, and I'm not looking to jam you up. I just want to find out who killed her."

Rik relaxed noticeably. "I want to help you."

"Do you know where she got her supply?"

He shook his head. "I think she was afraid if I knew, I'd go direct."

"Did she ever say anything to you about Mexico, about going to the Mexpipe competition, about maybe some of the crystal meth coming back with her?"

"I know she went," he said. "And the drugs were really good down there. She told me I should go with her next year, that she could really make it worth my while."

"Was she having any supply problems that you know of? Anybody want her territory, anything like that?"

He shook his head. "We used to talk all the time," he said. "If she was having problems like that, she would have told me. As a matter of fact, things were going really well for her. She was on the verge of making a big deal, she said, and everything was going to be really sweet after that."

"A big drug deal?"

"I don't think so. I think it was about real estate."

That was a stumper to me. "Real estate?"

"She had her license, you know. I think it might have had something to do with that big project of Ari's."

I remembered talking about real estate with Ari at breakfast. "He said something about zoning problems on some big property," I said. "You think that was it?"

He shrugged. "I just remember worrying that if she went legit I wouldn't be able to score from her," he said. "That's what I was concerned about. You should talk to Ari about her."

I stopped and took hold of his arm. "Look, I told you before that I'm not interested in jamming you up, and I'm not, but I've got to know one thing. Who took over Lucie's customers?"

Rik's body went rigid. His arm was so skinny I could feel the bone. He looked like he was ready to cry. I didn't say anything more, though; I waited for him to speak. Finally, he said, "I cop in Honolulu, all right? Through my cousin. After Lucie died I didn't know anybody else up here to buy from and I didn't want to risk getting caught. I swear, that's all I know."

I believed him, and let go of his arm. We started walking again, neither of us saying anything. He had steered us in a big circle and we came back to the country store just as the rest of the party was exiting the restrooms. "Great to see you," he said, when my attention was distracted. "Gotta go. Bye!" And then he was off, down another of the winding paths.

"Hear anything interesting?" Terri asked as she approached me. The kids surrounded Harry and Arleen, who looked like they were practicing for having a large family of their own.

"He wouldn't say anything about drugs, but he did say she was mixed up in some big real estate deal, that she thought it was going to make her some real money."

"There's a lot of money to be made in real estate," Terri said. We started to stroll slowly down toward the car, Harry and Arleen following us with all the kids. "Especially up here, where there are so many restrictions on building. That jacks the price up a lot."

"Since when did you become a real estate mogul?"

"My family has some property up here," she said. We stepped into the shade and she pushed her sunglasses up on her head. She was a very pretty woman, in an all-American kind of way: dark brown hair in a bob just above her shoulders, fine features, smooth skin. I saw those bags under her eyes again, though, and remembered all she had been through since her husband had been killed.

"You doing OK?" I asked, taking her hand.

"Today's a good day," she said, smiling. "I'm having fun, and I'm glad to see Danny enjoying himself too. I haven't been up to the North Shore in ages, though I know I'm going to have to come up again soon, for this real estate thing."

As one of the wealthiest in the islands, there isn't much Terri's family isn't involved with. Her father sits on the boards of many of the island's biggest corporations, and her family trust is one of the biggest donors to island charities. All the money comes from the Clark's chain of department stores, a rival of the old Liberty House for the home grown market. "Clark's planning to put a store up here?"

She shook her head. "Not commercial land. Just some property that's been passed down in the family, by Kawailoa Beach. My grandparents used to have a summer house up there, and my uncle Bishop lives there now."

I remembered someone else saying something about Kawailoa Beach, but couldn't place the connection. My attention wandered, trying to think, and by the time I came back to the conversation Terri had moved on. "Uncle Bishop was supposed to take over the stores, but he wasn't interested in working, so my dad had to step up. Now Uncle Bishop has run through his inheritance and all he's got is this property he lives on, just north of here." I'd met Terri's uncle, and knew his relations with the rest of the family were strained, at best. "He wants to sell the property to developers and cash out. That's why I've been learning about all the development restrictions."

We stopped at a lookout point where we could look down on the gardens. "Surely they can't restrict you from building on property your family has owned for generations."

"Surely they can," she said. She waved her hand around. "Most of the North Shore is reserved for agriculture and open space. They're only letting new housing go up in what they call the infill areas, around existing neighborhoods. And even if they do let you build, you have to reserve a certain number of spaces for what they call 'affordable' housing."

"Wow. I had no idea. This place was always so sleepy."

"When they put the highway through, it made commuting down to Honolulu a lot easier, and more people decided either to move up here or keep weekend houses. Even the most run-down old shack is selling for six figures now. The rental market is getting tighter all the time—if you can rent your house out for two hundred bucks a night during surf season, you can afford to leave it empty the rest of the year, and you don't have to worry about poor tenants tearing the place up."

Danny came running up and she picked him up. "Of course, that doesn't help the surfers who are making ends meet by working at minimum-wage jobs. Lucie was probably talking about some new gated community with million-dollar homes."

"Probably the one Ari is planning to build. But how could she make money from something like that?"

She kissed Danny's head and took his hand in hers. "Commissions. Suppose Ari offered her the chance to work in his sales office. She could make a lot of money, legally, and still have some flexible time to surf."

I couldn't put it together so I kept thinking out loud, as we started to walk again. "But how could that lead to her getting killed?"

Terri shook her head. "It doesn't make sense to me. But you're the detective."

"So they say," I said. Malia and Ailina came running up then and we had to shelve all talk of murder for the drive back to the beach, and then the rest of the afternoon.

My family began to pack up around five. I was just helping Haoa load the barbecue equipment back into his panel van when I noticed a familiar car pull up—Brad's gold Toyota Camry with its rainbow bumper stickers and a broken antenna.

"Uh-oh," I said, as Brad screeched to a halt next to the van. "I'm not getting a good feeling about this."

"You know him?" Haoa asked.

"In the biblical sense," I said. "You know, not Adam and Eve, but Adam and Steve."

"Let me guess," Haoa said, as Brad jumped out of his car and slammed the door behind him. "You cheated on him."

"Well, not cheated, really," I said. "I mean, it's not like we were married."

"Yeah, that excuse works," Haoa said.

"Boy, you sure get around," Brad said, stalking up to us. "Where'd you meet this one?"

"At the hospital, when I was born," I said dryly. "Brad Jacobson, my brother, Haoa Kanapa'aka."

He looked from me to my big brother. Although Haoa is my height, 6' 1", he's broader in the shoulders and the waist, and he looks more like the Hawai'ian side of our family, with less of the *haole* than seems to have landed in me. Still, if you look closely, you can see the resemblance. Brad saw it.

"You still slept with George and Larry, didn't you, though? Those guys are my friends, Kimo. You didn't think that was a little cheap and sleazy?"

"I don't think I want to hear the rest of this conversation," Haoa said, backing away. Although he's come around, he was the member of my family who had the most problems with my homosexuality, and I could see we were stretching the limits of his tolerance.

Lui came up then, his newsman's knack for following the story guiding him. "Who's this?" Brad demanded.

"My oldest brother, Lui," I said. "Brad and I had some fun earlier last week, and I didn't realize I would be hurting his feelings to um . . ."

"Sleep with anything with a penis?" Brad finished for me.

"You could say that," I said, frowning. "I certainly didn't mean to upset you."

"Yeah, tell me another one."

I saw my father approaching, trailed by a couple of his grandchildren. "Brad, this isn't really the time," I said. I took his arm and steered him toward his car. "Why don't I come over later and we can talk about it, OK?"

"Why don't you stick your dick up your ass and fuck yourself to death," Brad said, shaking off my arm and stalking back to his car.

"I don't think that's anatomically possible," I said, as my brothers snickered behind me.

Brad sprayed gravel making a fishtail turn, then sped out of the parking lot.

"Oh, to be single again," Lui said. "Not."

"Yeah, I take back what I said about envying you the studly life," Haoa said. "I'm remembering what a pain in the ass it was." Suddenly he held up his hands toward me. "Don't take that literally," he said. "And don't give me any details."

There was a lot of kissing and hugging as everyone got ready to leave, and my mother even got a little teary. "You can come home any time you want," she said, hugging me.

"I know, Mom," I said. I leaned down and kissed her cheek. "Really, I'm fine. I'm relaxing, I'm surfing, I'm meeting people. I'm going to come home sometime, but there's stuff I have to work out up here first."

I felt a little choked up, watching the cars all back out and head down toward Honolulu, wanting so badly to be able to get in my truck and follow them, to reclaim the life I had left behind. But like I told my mother, there was stuff I had to do on the North Shore first.

There was still a little daylight left, so I went back to my truck and pulled out my notes on the case. I wrote up my discussion with Rik, along with a reminder to talk to Ari again. He might know more than he had let on at our first meeting.

I wrote up Terri's observations about Lucie's character, wondering if her Catholic upbringing really had caught up with her. And I made a note to e-mail Harry the names and addresses of all three victims. I didn't want to think too hard about what kind of computer mischief he'd get up to, but I knew I needed all the information I could find.

By the time I was finished it was dark and I started to feel bad about Brad, thinking of him brooding in his apartment. I had hurt him, and I needed to apologize. I drove over there, but his car wasn't in the parking lot.

I didn't want to go back to Hibiscus House, but then again, I didn't want Brad to think I'd turned into some kind of stalker, that I was chasing him around Haleiwa. So I decided to go back to the Drainpipe, where I'd been looking for Frank, the bartender, the night before. I still had a couple of questions for him about Lucie. And if I drowned my sorrows in a beer or two, well, that wouldn't be all that bad either.

Chapter 19

BACK TO THE DRAINPIPE

THE DRAINPIPE was not nearly as busy on Sunday evening as it had been on Saturday night, and I saw Frank behind the bar as I came in. I picked a stool, and when he came over I ordered a Kona Pacific Golden Ale. Even though it's brewed on the mainland, it's about as local a beer as you can get these days.

It took a little while before Frank had a free moment to come over and chat with me, and I busied myself with enjoying my beer and checking out the rest of the patrons: a few surfers, a few tourists, a few locals. George and Larry were nowhere in sight, which I guess I found a relief. I'd had enough wild sex to last me for at least a few days, though I wasn't sure I'd be able to resist temptation, if it was placed before me.

"How's it going, dude?" Frank said, coming over to stand in front of me. He wore a San Francisco 49ers ball cap and a Budweiser T-shirt, and still had that annoying little goatee.

"Just chilling," I said. "If you've got a minute, though, I wanted to ask you more about Lucie."

"I'm taking a break in about ten," he said, looking at the clock.

"Cool." The time passed quickly and he came out from behind the bar, bringing me a fresh beer, and led me to a table at the far side of the room where it was quieter.

"You're the guy that used to be the cop, aren't you?" he asked.

"Word gets around."

"You gonna find out what happened to Lucie?"

"I'm going to try. That's why I had some questions for you."

"Fire away."

"I know she was dealing ice," I said. "I've talked to somebody who used to buy from her. And I know she used to hang out here to meet up with customers. I'm not trying to jam you or anybody else up over that. What I'm trying to trace back is where she got the stuff from."

"She was always real cagey about that," Frank said. He pulled a packet of sugar out of the dispenser and swung it back and forth between his fingers. "But I think she had a contact at the place she used to work, The Next Wave. Even after she quit working there, she'd be stopping by, at weird hours like after closing or first thing in the morning."

"She ever mention any names? Even a first name or a nickname?"

He shook his head. "Like I said, she was pretty secretive about it. It was like she was a little embarrassed, you know? Her mom was this real sweet lady, hard-working, totally honest. A maid at this hotel in Waikīkī. Lucie'd tell me stories all the time about stuff her mom found, that she'd turn in to the hotel, because it was the right thing to do. Her mom'd have died to know Lucie was selling drugs."

He looked at the clock. "Gotta get back behind the bar. You think of anything else, just ask me."

"OK."

He stood up and walked back behind the bar. Based on what Rik had told me, I needed to talk to Ari. I looked at my watch. It was just nine o'clock; I could probably make a stop by Sugar's and not seem like I was stalking Brad.

I drained my beer, waved at Frank, and drove the mile or two to Sugar's. Like the Drainpipe, it was pretty quiet, but I was lucky to see Ari sitting alone at a table by the window, sipping something that looked like a Cosmopolitan and making notes on a Palm Pilot.

He looked up as I got close to his table, and said, "If you're looking for Brad, he's already gone."

"I was kind of looking for him," I said. "But for you, too. Got a minute?"

"Sure."

"Let me just get a beer." I got another Kona ale, and sat across from Ari.

"So Brad found out about your little dalliance?" Ari asked, tilting his head toward me.

"Yup. I guess I didn't realize it would bother him. I mean, I hardly know him. He was really nice to me, getting me cleaned up, and we had sex a couple of times. But it's not like we had any kind of relationship."

"He's a little sensitive," Ari said. "And this isn't the first time this has happened."

"So why'd he come yell at me? Why not go after Larry and George?"

Ari crossed his legs and leaned back in his chair. "Because we all live here, and we see each other all the time."

"OK. Doesn't make much sense to me, but I can see it."

He closed his Palm Pilot and put it away in the briefcase by his side. "So what did you want from me?" he asked, as he looked back up.

"I wanted to ask you about Lucie. I've been hearing that she was trying to get away from selling drugs, go legit. She got a real estate license."

"Yup. I told her that if my project went through, I'd hire her to work for me, selling units. And she'd have been good at it, too. She was hungry, and hungry people make the best salespeople."

"By hungry you mean . . ."

"She had a big appetite for life," Ari said, waving his right hand around. "She liked designer labels and expensive meals and traveling to surf competitions around the world. She had been brought up poor and didn't want to be poor anymore. Somebody with that kind of motivation will do what it takes to close a deal."

I took a drink of my beer. It was just as good as the first two had been. "You think she would have given up dealing drugs if she came to work for you?"

He shrugged. "I hoped so. I had a feeling she was heading for trouble. I guess she didn't get ahead of it fast enough."

"Is there any possibility that whoever she worked for might have resented her wanting to get out, or that she knew more than she should have?"

"Always possible," Ari said. "It wasn't like we sat around and talked about her dealer or anything. I deliberately didn't talk about any of that stuff with her, because I didn't want to know."

I nodded. I didn't really have anything else to ask, but I was happy enough to sit there with Ari drinking my beer. By the time I'd finished it, though, he'd finished his Cosmopolitan, and we both stood up at the same time. "Give Brad a day or two to simmer down," Ari said. "That is, if you're still interested."

"He's a nice guy. I don't want to hurt him."

"I'm glad." We walked out to the parking lot together, and he hugged me before we parted. "Take care of yourself."

"You too." I got into my truck, and felt the accumulation of all my surfing and my late nights. I drove back to Hibiscus House and fell promptly and soundly asleep, not waking until six the next morning.

I woke feeling refreshed, yet somehow very sad. Seeing my family the day before had made me realize how much I missed my old life in Honolulu, my friends, my job. But the only way to get back there was to solve the three murders, and I had to keep on surfing, and pretending to be a disgraced former detective who had nothing better to do than hit the waves.

It was enough to make you crazy. And when I get crazy, I surf—that's how I let go of what's bothering me and clear my head so I can get back to work. I knew I needed to think about Brad and what had happened on Saturday night and then on Sunday, and I hoped that I could work it all out in between waves. Which led me to Pipeline, just a little while before the bodies were found.

Chapter 20

BODIES IN THE SAND

IT WAS ABOUT HALF AN HOUR before sunrise when I slipped into the water, and the sky above Haleiwa was already lightening from black to gray. Around me, inky silhouettes of surfers in wetsuits paddled their boards out beyond the breakers, the slap of their hands in the cold water an intermittent counterpoint to the crashing waves. I lay flat on my board and tried to feel the water.

I saw a wave coming, knew intuitively that it was my wave, and started paddling, fast, as the motion of the water thrust me forward. As soon as I could, I stood up, and then I wasn't thinking anymore, I was part of the wave, holding on to it, following it, running with it, first toward the shore, then parallel, surfing the curl, sliding along the crest as the wave and I made our way toward the moment when it threw itself onto the shore in its final dance with death.

I cheated the shore's embrace just in time, sliding away and dunking myself in the cold surf again. For about three minutes I had forgotten everything about my life, what was right and what was wrong, and just lived in the moment. That was why I loved to surf, why for four years as a patrolman and then two as a detective, surfing most mornings had been the way I made it from day to day with some piece of myself still intact.

The sun finally peeked over the Leilehua Plateau, and the dark shapes around me began to become recognizable. I kept on surfing, pushing myself as much as I could. If I couldn't be a cop for a while and had to be a surfer again, then at least I was going to be the best damn surfer I could be.

I had just mounted a mid-sized wave when I heard the scream. It was far away and the surf was roaring, but something about the pitch or the urgency in her voice penetrated my consciousness. From my peak, I could see her—a young girl, late teens at most, dragging a wide board down the sandy strip from Ke Nui Road. Something had stopped her in her tracks, kept her screaming, hiccupping, and finally crying by the time I'd surfed in and run up the beach to her.

I saw what the morning light had revealed to her, in a hollow of sand: two naked men, in the act of embracing, both of them quite clearly dead from bullet wounds to the head. The blood had run downhill and what had not yet sunk into the sand was pooled around their feet. Though one body was unfamiliar to me, I was able to recognize the other immediately, and I felt my heart rate accelerate and sweat begin to accumulate on my forehead and under my arms.

There was already a small crowd standing around, staring at the bodies. "Anybody got a cell phone?" I asked.

A blond *haole* guy in surfer shorts that revealed a cast on his right leg held one up. "Call 911," I said. "Everybody get back. Try not to disturb anything."

"You're that cop, aren't you?" a dark-haired girl said. "The gay one."

"Still gay, but not a cop anymore," I said, as I tried to get everyone to back away. I shrugged. "I guess old habits die hard, though."

I couldn't see either of their faces, but the naked man I did not recognize was lithe and trim, a true surfer's physique. The man I knew was a little older, a little out of shape, but still handsome. I resisted the impulse to kneel down and touch Brad Jacobson because I knew I would only be contaminating the crime scene.

I calmed the screaming girl down, and a girlfriend of hers volunteered to keep an eye on her. Everybody else was eager to get back to the waves, and I had no right to keep them around. While I waited for the cops, I practiced bringing my breathing and my pulse rate back to normal. I had seen a lot of dead bodies, and I tried to remind myself that whatever essence had lived in both of them was now gone, leaving behind only an empty shell.

To keep from staring obsessively, I forced myself to take a look around, as if I was the investigating detective and this was just another crime scene. I found a pile of clothes just behind the rise that sheltered the bodies. I noticed that the men were lying on a faded, oversized towel, the kind you keep in the back of the trunk for picnics. Or midnight cuddles on the beach.

Seeing Brad and that other man there, I finally understood that it was my responsibility to find out who was killing surfers, and why. That I had to solve the case to make all my sacrifices have meaning. That whether I could flash a badge or not, I cared about righting the wrongs of the world, about speaking for the dead and making sure that their killers did not go unpunished.

A black and white was there a few minutes later, parking up on Ke Nui Road, leaving the flashers going. Two cops from the 268 beat began balancing their way over the sand, belts weighing them down with nightsticks, flashlights, radios, handcuffs, and more. I had stripped off my rashguard and stood there in only a pair of board shorts, feeling less like a detective than I had at any point in my career.

I stepped up as the two cops, a *haole* and a Chinese, approached, and laid the story out for them. "The girl over there was the first one to see the bodies," I said. "Just after sunrise. I was surfing, heard her scream, came running up."

The *haole* cop, Luna, looked at me but couldn't figure out where he knew me from. "I ever pick you up?" he asked.

I had to laugh. "I'm sure I'd remember you," I said. I stuck my hand out and introduced myself. "I used to be on the force."

Luna's face turned bright red. He wouldn't shake my hand but his partner, whose name was Chan, did. "Good to meet you," he said. "I admire you, standing up for yourself."

"Thanks." I stepped off to the side as Luna and Chan took over the site, calling in for a detective, blocking off the area. They didn't seem to need me, so I went down to the water's edge, pacing around and talking to other surfers, returning only when Chan waved me back.

He introduced me to the detectives, Ruiz and Kawamoto. "Detective . . . er . . . Mr. Kanapa'aka secured the area," he said.

Kawamoto was probably in his mid-fifties, and maybe fifty pounds overweight, including a belly that rolled over his belt. He reminded me of that caricature you see of Southern sheriffs, only Japanese. He was missing the ten-gallon hat, but I wouldn't be surprised to find out he chewed tobacco.

Ruiz was *haole* and younger, maybe mid-forties, dark hair thinning on top. He wore a UH class ring in addition to his wedding band.

I repeated what I'd seen, being careful not to reveal that I knew anything about the other three murders. I gave them an

ID on Brad, but didn't reveal our relationship and told them I didn't know his companion. "Might have been a lovers' quarrel," Ruiz said, pulling on a pair of plastic gloves.

"Might have been," Kawamoto said. Something about his face, though, told me he was already making the connection I wasn't mentioning.

I hung around for a while, memorizing the scene, trying, unobtrusively, to take a look at any evidence they found, but there wasn't much. There were too many footprints between the hollow and the road, even that early in the morning, and it was clear, at least to me, that both had been shot at close range, because of the stippling and powder burns I saw around the wounds. Finally, Ruiz and Kawamoto turned the bodies, so I could get a good look at both faces.

The guy with the surfer physique was young, in his late teens or early twenties, and he didn't have much of a tan, which probably meant he hadn't been on the North Shore for very long.

I think maybe up to that point, some part of me had been denying that the other dead body belonged to Brad. But seeing his face, I couldn't believe that anymore. My heart rate zoomed up, and if I'd been connected to an EKG at that point I'm sure it would have gone off the scale.

I realized, too, that I had to tell Ruiz and Kawamoto everything I knew about Brad, including the fact that we had slept together, because they were going to find out quickly enough from Brad's friends and I didn't want them to think I was hiding anything from them. "I'd better tell you more about Brad Jacobson," I said to Ruiz.

He stepped away from the bodies, motioning me with him. He pulled out a pad and a pen. "He worked at Butterfly, a ladies' clothing store at the North Shore Marketplace." I gave him Brad's address.

"How well did you know the deceased?"

"We met up at the shopping center," I said, being as vague as possible about why I'd be at an exclusive ladies' boutique. "We got friendly quickly, and he took me to a bar called Sugar's to meet a couple of his friends. After that we went back to his place."

Ruiz made a bunch of notes. "You had an intimate relationship?"

I nodded. I turned a bit, facing toward the water, because I couldn't keep Brad's body in my peripheral vision. I knew soon enough that the coroner would arrive, and I knew only too well what would follow that. Looking at his body kept reminding me that at least in a small way I was responsible for his death, all that had happened, and all that would.

"That was Wednesday night," I said, "and then I went back to his place again on Thursday night as well. I didn't see him again until yesterday afternoon." I took a deep breath. I was sweating and my heart was still racing. "A couple of the friends Brad introduced me to were interested in me, and I ended up spending Saturday night with them. Intimately," I added. Might as well get all the dirty laundry out there in the air.

"Somehow Brad found out, and he wasn't happy about that. His impression of our—relationship—was somehow deeper than mine was."

"Mmm hmm." Ruiz made more notes.

"My family came up from Honolulu yesterday for a big luau at Waimea Bay Beach Park. Brad found out I was there."

Ruiz raised his eyebrows.

"I think you'll find Brad's friends form a pretty effective gossip network," I said. "Word spreads around quickly." I felt another emptiness at the bottom of my stomach. Brad's friends would miss him. And they'd probably blame his death on me. I didn't like that idea.

"So he came to your family luau yesterday and what—confronted you?"

"That's a good word for it. He let me know that he was angry, and that he wasn't interested in seeing me again. He left, and that's the last time I saw him."

"What did you do after that?"

"My family was packing up at that point, so I helped them load up the cars and then they all left to head south. I felt bad about Brad, though, so I drove over to his apartment. But his car wasn't in the parking lot, so I went to the bar where he and his friends usually hung out."

"You see him there?"

I shook my head. "He had already been there and then left. I had a beer and hung out with one of his friends for a while, then I went back to the room where I'm staying and crashed. I slept until just before dawn, when I came out here to surf."

"Who was the friend you met at the bar?"

I gave him Ari's name. "I have his card back at my room," I said. "But his company's called something like North Shore Real Estate or North Shore Investments. It's probably in the phone book."

"He go back to your room with you?" Ruiz asked.

I shook my head. "Nope. I went home alone. And I didn't see anybody on my way home, or anybody I knew until I got here this morning."

I saw Ruiz write the words "no alibi" on his pad. That wasn't a surprise; I'd written the same note myself many times. What was a surprise was how bad it made me feel, even though I knew I hadn't killed Brad or the other man. I wondered if all suspects felt that way. This whole case was giving me a new perspective on how people view the police. "You have a number where we can reach you?"

I gave him my cell number. "Don't leave town, all right?" Ruiz asked. "I'm sure we'll want to talk to you again, once we figure out what's going on." He paused. "You know the other guy at all?"

I shook my head.

"How about anybody who didn't like your friend, anybody who might have reason to want to harm him?"

"He was a nice guy, lots of friends. But I got the feeling he had a tendency to pick up—guys who might not always be nice to him."

"Meaning?"

"When I met Brad, I was looking pretty scruffy. I hadn't showered or shaved in a while, that kind of thing. From things he said, and things his friends said, that was the kind of guy he often looked to pick up."

"And they weren't all as nice as you underneath?"

I shrugged. "I guess not. He said something to me right before we went to sleep, that first night." I struggled to remember how Brad had phrased it. "It was something like, 'I know you won't be here in the morning, but at least I know my wallet and my stereo will be.'" Remembering that, in Brad's voice, thick with sleep, made me want to cry, and I wanted so badly to get away from that beach.

"We'll check out his habits," Ruiz said. "For now, I think it would be best if you left the beach."

I was happy to comply. Even if he hadn't shooed me away, I couldn't have stayed there any longer, and I certainly couldn't have gone back in the water as if nothing had happened. I dragged my board back to my truck and headed toward Haleiwa. I swung past Hibiscus House and got my laptop, and then drove to The Next Wave. I needed a cup of coffee and an Internet connection.

Even though I wanted to curl up in bed and sleep until it stopped hurting, or pick up a six pack and drink myself into oblivion, I had to let Lieutenant Sampson know what had happened, and about my personal relationship with Brad. I was still a cop and I was still investigating the original three murders, so I would also need him to get me as much information as he could on the dead surfer, who I was willing to bet had been to Mexico recently, or at least had some connection to Mike Pratt, Lucie Zamora, or Ronald Chang.

It was going to be a lot more difficult for me to investigate now that the police knew me and knew I had a connection to the case, through Brad. I had to find out how Sampson felt about that. Maybe he would take me off the investigation, let me return to Honolulu, and reclaim my badge.

As I pulled up in front of The Next Wave, I realized I didn't want that to happen. I already felt connected to the three dead surfers, and wanted to know what had happened to them. And now with Brad, my personal sense of responsibility deepened. I couldn't give up the case so easily.

My first e-mail was to Lieutenant Sampson. I filled him in with everything I knew about the latest murders, including my personal connection. I squirmed a little writing it, trying to balance an honest recitation of the facts with my own personal reticence about spreading my sex life around the department. But in this case, it couldn't be helped.

I felt bad for Brad Jacobson, who had obviously been in the wrong place at the wrong time. If he'd only gone home and waited for me to show up and apologize, he'd be alive, I thought. Or if I hadn't let him leave the parking lot angry.

I finally finished the e-mail and hit send. Then I sent a couple of other messages and did some surfing. Just as I was closing up the computer to start nosing around The Next Wave, my cell phone rang.

I recognized the 529 prefix as originating from police headquarters before I answered. "Kanapa'aka."

"Sampson. I need to see you ASAP. How soon can you meet me?"

"I can leave now, and be in Honolulu in a little over an hour," I said.

"Traffic is tied up inbound on the Kam," Sampson said. "You'll be stuck around Wheeler for at least an hour while they clear it. How about if I meet you half way. Parking lot of the Dole Plantation, forty-five minutes."

"I'll be there." I hit end on my phone, and then sat there wondering why things had become so urgent that Sampson had to see me immediately. Was he going to be angry about my relationship with Brad? I hardly knew the man, so I couldn't say, but I knew he had taken a chance on hiring me when I wasn't exactly everybody's favorite cop. Would this give him a reason to change the deal we'd made, and cut me loose?

Chapter 21

AN EXPLOSIVE SITUATION

I SPUN GRAVEL in the parking lot of The Next Wave, heading out to the Kam. All the way south I alternated between guilt over Brad's death and worry over what Sampson would have to say to me. I made it to the plantation a few minutes before he did, and got out to look at the visitor's center, a long, hipped-roof building with a vaguely colonial feel to it. A big sign advertised the world's largest maze, as certified by the *Guinness Book of World Records.* I felt like this case was turning into a maze, and I was stuck somewhere inside it.

Sampson pulled up in a big silver Lexus. He had a folder in his hand when he got out of the car. "Hot off the press, just for you," he said, handing it to me. "As much as we have so far on the latest victims."

I stood there next to his car and flipped through a measly three pages. They'd gotten a quick ID on the guy with Brad. That was the good news. The bad news was that his name was Thomas Singer, and he was just a kid, twenty years old and a junior at UH. The worse news was that his father was a captain in the traffic division, which meant the pressure from inside the force to solve these murders was going to shoot through the roof.

We started walking, hoping to stretch both our legs and our cognitive powers. Sampson wore a gold short-sleeve polo shirt with khaki slacks, looking every inch the professional. I wore a pair of board shorts, flip-flops, and a T-shirt from the North Shore Cattle Company with an angry-looking black steer on it. No one would have made us for a pair of cops. "Any proof yet that they're related to the previous three?" I asked.

"Same caliber weapon was used as on Ronald Chang," he said. "We'll have to wait for ballistics tests to be sure, but my gut tells me they are."

The fields around us were laden with pineapple plants, and we walked around an exhibit showing the different varieties of pineapple and where they were grown.

"Any particular reason?"

"Too many coincidences. Pratt and Zamora killed with the same weapon. Zamora and Chang killed on the same day. Then two more surfers killed in the same general area, with the same type of weapon used on Chang. You do the math."

"Let me play devil's advocate," I said, stopping in front of a display of pineapples from Indonesia. "The first three were all involved somehow with professional surfing. I don't recognize this kid's name, so I'm willing to bet he wasn't professional grade, at least not yet. The first three victims were all killed individually; this one is part of a pair. And by the way, Brad Jacobson wasn't a surfer."

"So the alternative is two different killers, both in the same area, with similar weapons and similar targets. My coincidence meter rings on that."

Sampson toed the red ground with his black dress shoe. "Doc Takayama will do the autopsy tomorrow morning," he said, "and I'll get you the results as soon as I can. I already sent a detective over to the boy's dorm room at UH to see what we can find out about him, and I'm talking to the parents myself as soon as I get back to town."

"So this is a full-court press."

Sampson nodded. "I have a daughter," he said. "If anything happened to her, I'd want to see the force step up to do the same thing for me."

I understood. We began to walk back toward the parking lot and our cars. Around us, tourist families were oohing and aahing over the tiny pineapples, the oddly-colored ones, the very idea that their morning juice began in fields like these.

"I'll get online as soon as I get back to Haleiwa and see if I can find any record of the kid in any surfing competitions, and I'll keep my ear to the ground and see who's talking about him." I hesitated for a minute. "Am I going to be able to talk to the local detectives at all?"

Sampson shook his head. "If they want to talk to you, tell them what you know about your friend. But don't make any connections to the other murders, at least not yet. I'll send you copies of whatever they discover."

We stopped in front of his Lexus. "There is one thing I wanted to talk to you about," he said. "Unintentionally, you've developed a personal connection to this case."

Here it comes, I thought. He's going to call me on the carpet for sleeping with Brad. My heart rate started to accelerate.

"Each and every member of the force has a personal life, Kimo. I'm not here to tell you how to run yours. And I'm very sympathetic to your situation—I have gay friends, and I've watched them go through all kinds of problems, both internally and with the world around them." He leaned back against the car, crossing his arms in front of his polo shirt.

My throat was dry and all I could do was nod along.

"But you're going to have to find a way to balance your personal life with your investigation. I'm not telling you to become a monk, but I will tell you what I would tell any detective who worked for me, gay or straight. It's a bad idea to get personally involved with anyone you meet through a case, as long as the case is ongoing. Once a case is cleared, you want to reconnect with someone, that's fine. But you see where things can go wrong—if Jacobson's murder turns out to be connected to the first three, as I think it will be, your involvement with him only complicates matters."

"I understand," I said, struggling to get some moisture back in my mouth. "I know I made an error in judgment in starting a relationship with Brad. I guess I justified it at the time because he wasn't a suspect or even a victim in the case, just a source of information. But I promise you I will be more careful in the future."

I wanted to salute him, but out there in the parking lot, under the relentless sun, surrounded by red-skinned tourists and the hum of harvesting machinery, it didn't seem right. So I shook his hand instead.

My heart rate had returned to normal by the time I got back to my truck. I was impressed by how skillfully Sampson had handled the situation—I didn't feel that I'd been called on the carpet, though clearly he could have expressed a lot more anger with me. And I didn't feel that I'd been discriminated against because I was gay; I knew straight detectives who had gotten personally involved in cases, in many different ways, and knew that it was a dangerous road to tread.

If I was going to be gay, I thought, as I waited for traffic to open up a way onto the Kam for me, I was going to have to learn to keep my personal life separate from my job. I needed to practice some restraint; I needed to keep my pants zipped for a while. Not just for my job, but for my own sanity.

Despite the gentleness of the reprimand, I was pretty shaken up. It had been a tough day so far, probably one of my worst, beginning with seeing Brad's body on the beach. I won't say I had fallen in love with him, because I hadn't; I couldn't even really call him a friend, because I hadn't known him for long enough. But I had cared about him, and he had cared about me, and he was dead. Knowing that at least part of the responsibility for discovering who had killed him rested upon my shoulders was a heavy burden, and when it was added to the burdens I'd been accumulating and carrying for the past weeks, I started to feel like I was stumbling.

The only cure for that was to focus again on solving the murders. I knew even more clearly what was at stake: I wanted to find out who had killed the surfers, and who had killed Brad. And I wanted to earn the right to go back to Honolulu and pick up my career again.

I tuned in to the news radio station to see if there was anything about the bodies. Within minutes I heard, "Police announced the discovery of the nude bodies of two gay men, found on a North Shore beach just after sunrise," the announcer read. "Bradley Jacobson, 26, and Thomas Singer, 20, are alleged to have met at a gay bar in Haleiwa called Sugar's and then retreated to the beach to consummate a sexual relationship."

Sugar's, I thought. I wondered who had seen the two of them there, besides Ari, who had mentioned to me only that Brad had been at Sugar's and then left before I arrived.

"Jacobson, manager of an exclusive North Shore ladies' clothing boutique, is reputed to have frequently picked up strangers for sex. Sources close to the investigation hinted that a former lover may have been jealous of Jacobson's latest conquest."

That nearly caused me to drive off the road. Did Brad have jealous former lovers floating around? He'd never mentioned one, nor had any of his friends.

Suddenly I realized they might be talking about me. I was, after all, a "former lover" of Brad's, and though he was the one who had been jealous, people had seen us have an angry break-up at Waimea Bay Beach Park. It's a strange feeling to hear about yourself on the news, even in a veiled reference, and unfortunately a feeling I was quite familiar with.

"Singer, a student at UH's Mānoa campus, was a frequent visitor to the North Shore, an amateur surfer who liked to challenge the big waves at Pipeline, where the bodies were found. College friends indicated that they believed Singer to be heterosexual, and it is possible he was unaware of the nature of the gay bar before he entered it."

Unaware, my ass, I thought. If you're gay, and not yet out, you're hyper sensitive to places gay people congregate, and they exert a weird fascination over you, drawing you in even as you resist. Or at least, that had been the case with me.

Had Singer been straight, and simply stumbled into the wrong bar? If so, then why had he left with Brad? I'd have to find someone who was there to tell me how it had all looked. Given the jungle drum hotline of Brad's friends, who seemed to know where I was at all times, that shouldn't be hard. All I had to do was sit back and one of them would find me soon enough.

The news jumped on to the beaching of a killer whale off Lahaina, and I turned the radio off. My brain was still working on Brad and Tommy Singer by the time I turned into The Next Wave's parking lot.

It was noon by then and I desperately needed some caffeine. It had already been a long day, and I had a lot of work ahead of me. I got a grande cappuccino, set my laptop down on a wooden table, and connected to the Wi-Fi network. By the time two hours had passed, I'd assembled all there was to know about Tommy Singer's surfing career, and there wasn't much there.

I'd also done some checking on Brad Jacobson. No one had shut off my access to the police computer system, or perhaps it had been shut off and Sampson had reinstated me. I was able to get into the network remotely and surf a couple of databases. Brad had been arrested once, a misdemeanor charge involving offering a blow job to an undercover agent in Honolulu two years before. He was as fastidious in his financial life as he'd been in his dress; he had a number of credit cards, all up to date, and he was almost finished paying the loan on his Camry. He had a small nest egg in mutual funds.

Frank, the bartender at the Drainpipe, came over. "You hear about those two guys they found out at Pipeline?"

"I was there," I said. "Heard this girl screaming. I was the one who got somebody to call 911." I paused. "You know either of them?"

"I think I might have known the one dude," he said. "Brad. I think I met him once or twice with Lucie."

That made sense. "How about the other one, the surfer?"

Frank shook his head. "Don't think so."

It was the same with everyone I talked to at The Next Wave. I hung around for another hour or so, striking up conversations with people I recognized from the waves. It was an easy thing to do, and Brad and Tommy were on the tip of everyone's tongue. Though several people claimed at least a passing acquaintance with Brad, no one seemed to know anything about Tommy.

That made it certain to me that he wasn't a serious surfer. The world of the North Shore is a close one, as I'd already discovered, and everybody knew everybody else—or at least knew someone who did. Tommy Singer was an outsider, a college kid who made it up on weekends, and hadn't penetrated the inner circle of rhino chasers—the slang term for those who follow big water wherever they can.

It was frustrating, though. I knew there had to be a connection, but just couldn't figure out what it was. Just as I was finishing, KVOL's five o'clock news began playing from the TV by the cappuccino bar. I stood up as a bunch of other people gathered around to watch.

My brother's station, always first with any scandalous news, led with coverage of the murders, as I expected. They began with a pan around the beach, showing surfers out at Pipeline, then focusing in on the hollow in the sand where the bodies had been found. Ruiz and Kawamoto had set up plastic traffic cones around the area where the bodies had been, and roped it off with yellow police tape.

Ralph Kim, the guy who'd interviewed me, had been dispatched up to the North Shore for a stand up. He was all smarmy professionalism, his crisply pressed aloha shirt a poor attempt to seem like a North Shore kind of guy. He repeated what I'd heard on the radio, describing Brad and Tommy and how they'd met. "In a bizarre twist to the case," Kim continued, "police have identified a lover of one of the dead men as former Honolulu police detective Kimo Kanapa'aka, who left the department in disgrace over the revelation of his homo-sexuality, and who has recently been seen at numerous locations on the North Shore."

"Holy Shiite Muslim," I heard a voice next to me say. "They got you, brah."

I turned and saw Dario. He looked tired and drawn, and even the bright red aloha shirt he was wearing didn't bring up his natural color. Everyone in the area had swiveled around to look at me. So much for keeping a low profile.

Dario took my arm and hustled me back to his office. "What exactly are you doing up here?" he asked me. "Because you know, you're not a cop anymore, and you can't go around playing at being one."

"Excuse me?"

"You've been asking around about Lucie Zamora, haven't you?"

"What if I have?"

"But why? You didn't know her. What's it to you if she's dead?"

"I was a cop for six years, Dario. Even if they say I can't be a cop here anymore, it's still part of who I am. I guess I just can't let go of that yet."

"Well, you're going to have to. It's going to look pretty suspicious if you keep nosing around dead people. Especially if they're dead people you fucked."

He looked at me, an evil sort of grin twitching the edges of his lips. "You are a top, aren't you? Don't tell me under that macho man exterior there's a bottom just eager to spread his juicy hole for any guy who asks."

I crossed my arms in front of me and stared at him hard. "Are you asking, Dario? Because you could have fucked me that night, at your place. I was drunk enough."

Dario stalked around the room to the other side of his desk. "I knew I could get in your pants from the moment I saw you," he said. "It was just a matter of waiting for the right moment."

"Why didn't you just ask me? You didn't have to get me so drunk I was passed out, and then basically rape me."

"If I'd asked you, would you have said yes? Answer me honestly." He pointed his index finger at me and shook it.

For what seemed like the twentieth time that day, my heart rate zoomed and I felt flooded with adrenaline. My body was shaking, but not with fear. "Nope. I was scared shitless about being gay. And what you did only made it worse. I went running home, gave up all my dreams of surfing, and went to the police academy because it was the most macho thing I could think of to do."

I didn't realize I had so much anger in me toward Dario. I didn't think much about that night, because the consequences, the way I'd lied to myself and others for so many years, were too painful.

He pulled something out of one of the drawers, then came around to my side of the desk. "You were a lousy lay."

"I was drunk! Passed out!"

He moved closer to me. I could smell the beer on his breath and the perspiration mingling with a sharp lemon scent from his cologne. His whole body seemed to be twanging like a plucked guitar string. "Have you gotten any better?" he asked in a low voice, one tinged with sex.

"You'll never know." I moved a little away from him.

"Oh, yeah?" He came right up next to me again. "You want to show me, don't you?"

He was so close I could feel the heat radiating from him. But I was determined not to back down. He grabbed the back of my head and mashed his face against mine. It was so disorienting I closed my eyes, and then all I felt was his tongue forcing its way into my mouth, his crotch grinding against mine. I got hard immediately. So much for my resolution of the day before.

I kissed him back. I don't know why I have so little control over my hormones; maybe it's all those years of denying them. Or maybe I did want to show Dario something, take back something I felt he'd stolen from me all those years before.

"You wanted this," Dario said, through clenched teeth. I heard a ripping noise, and then felt a condom being thrust into my hand. "You want me." In a quick motion, he'd wriggled around so his back was to me, and he was facing the desk. He unzipped his pants and pulled them down, presenting his bare ass to me.

Then he reached back for my dick, groping it through my pants. "Come on," he said harshly. "Fuck me. I raped you all those years ago, you said it. Now do the same thing to me."

Chapter 22

CONFRONTING DARIO

MY GOD. My dick was straining to get out of my pants, but I knew if I took Dario there, like that, I'd hate myself for it. It was time for me to be a homicide detective again, and a professional one at that. I had promised Sampson, and myself, that I would learn to control these impulses, at least while I was investigating a case.

I put my hands down around his chest, leveraged him back up against me. I leaned down and kissed the back of his neck. "I won't do it like this," I said into his skin. "Not out of anger. I don't want to rape you."

He squirmed around and was facing me. We kissed again, this time both of us pressing against each other, and I felt his dick, hard as a rock, up against mine. He caught his breath and spasmed for a second, and I knew what had happened. "Was it good for you?" I asked dryly.

"Sorry." He smiled sheepishly and backed away from me. There was a big wet spot on my pants, but it hadn't come from the inside. "I guess you aren't the only one who remembers that night at my place."

I had a funny thought then. Suppose Dario had liked me, all those years ago, instead of trying to drag me out of the closet out of some misplaced anger. What if I'd hurt him almost as badly as he'd hurt me, by abandoning him after that night?

I didn't know what to think. All I knew was that I had a case to investigate, and this blast from the past was only going to get in my way. "You'd better get out of those pants," he said, tossing me a pair of board shorts from a pile behind the desk. "I can turn my back if you want."

"Don't bother," I said. I dropped my pants. His come had soaked through to my boxers, too, so I dropped them as well. My erection swung free as I bent down.

"I can take care of that for you," he said. He'd cleaned himself up, pulled his pants up.

"Another time," I said. I pulled the board shorts up, carefully tucking myself in, pulling the drawstring tight.

"You know the press is going to be after you," he said. "You can't go back to living at Hibiscus House."

"I'm not running back to Waikīkī," I said. "I came up here to surf, and I'm going to keep on surfing."

"I'd invite you to come stay with me, but my living situation is complicated. I've got a friend who rents out apartments," he said. "Let me see if I can get you a place that's a little more secure than that rat trap where you are." He looked at me. "Please? Let me do this for you?"

"That would be great, Dario. I appreciate it."

He dialed a number. "Hey, it's Dario. Listen, I need a favor."

As he talked, I realized I knew who it was. Aristotle Papageorgiou, also known as Ari, Brad's friend, Lucie's former landlord. It was true, the North Shore was a small world.

Dario hung up. "It's cool. He's going to meet you at this place." Dario scribbled an address on a piece of paper and handed it to me. "Give me your keys. I'll get your stuff and bring it over there."

I thought for a minute. The only incriminating thing I had was my laptop, with my notes about the murders, and I had that with me. All Dario would find at Hibiscus House was a pile of books, dirty laundry, and sports equipment. I dug the key to my room out of my pants pocket and handed it to him. "Thanks, Dario." I transferred everything else to the pockets of the new board shorts.

My erection had finally started to go down as Dario came back around the desk again. "I can't leave here until I close at nine," he said. "So you probably won't see me until ten." As he passed, he slid his hand under the drawstring and tried to cop a quick feel, but I grabbed his wrist.

"Uh-uh-uh," I said.

Dario smiled and shrugged. "Can't blame a boy for trying."

I struggled, as I left The Next Wave for my truck, to bring my focus back to the case, but I just couldn't. My brain was still buzzing from Dario's overture. I gave up the case for a moment and tried to figure out how I felt about Dario as I drove to meet Ari. Did I actually want to have sex with him? Or was my dick just responding to any old stimulus?

It was a complicated situation, all tied up with the past as well as my new sexual emancipation. Had I subconsciously wanted to have sex with Dario all those years ago, but kept pushing it below the surface until he finally made the move? He wasn't a bad-looking guy, and his figure was trim. I knew now that he had a shapely, smooth ass and an average-sized, uncircumcised dick. He was a passionate kisser, and his body made mine feel good.

I couldn't have done it at his office, even with him pushing his ass up against me, then ripping open the condom wrapper for me. The way the whole situation had played out was like some rape scenario from a porn movie, and I didn't like that.

He'd raped me, all those years ago, because I was powerless to resist, and trying to get me to act out the situation again, in reverse, wasn't going to make the past go away. And I couldn't do anything as long as I still had a case to investigate, and as long as there was any indication that The Next Wave, or possibly Dario himself, could be involved.

I wasn't opposed to a little power struggle as part of a sexual situation: a pair of tongues vying for dominance, a little wrestling, one person taking the lead. All that was good, it was part of the fun. But there was something weirder about our situation, and I would have to think about it for a while to figure it out.

The address Dario had given me was up in the hills above Haleiwa, and dusk had just begun to fall as I left the Kam for a narrow, climbing road. I had to stop before an iron gate and a big sign that welcomed me to Cane Landing. Through the bars I saw a winding street lined with tall royal palms and a series of big houses set back from the road in a swale of landscaping. Almost as soon as I arrived, Ari pulled up behind me. He left his car running behind my truck, got out, and walked up to my window.

"Here's the opener," he said, handing me a black remote control. "And here are the keys. It's the third house on the right and the code for the alarm is 2515."

"I don't know that I can afford to stay in some place so fancy."

"Don't worry about it," Ari said. "We'll make an arrangement about the utilities. Most of these places sit empty forty-eight weeks a year. The owners rent them out for a week or two at a time and make enough to cover their costs."

"Jesus."

"Nice to have money, isn't it?" he asked. "Anyway, make

yourself at home. You should be pretty safe from the press back there."

He turned away, but I got out of my truck and called, "Hey, Ari, can I ask you a question?" He turned back to me, framed in his own headlights. "You told me you saw Brad at Sugar's on Sunday night, before I got there."

"Yeah. He was pretty steamed."

"How'd he meet that kid—Tommy Singer?"

The night was quiet but for the low hum of our engines and the chirp of a cricket somewhere behind us. I saw Ari close his eyes, trying to remember. "I was sitting there with Jeremy when Brad came in. He didn't even stop for a drink first, just came right over to us. He told Jeremy something like, 'You were right. He really is a sleaze ball.'"

I felt an emptiness in the pit of my stomach. "That would be me."

"Yup."

"So Jeremy's the one who told George and Larry I was at the Drainpipe, and then he told Brad that I'd gone off with them."

"Jeremy's a sad guy," Ari said. He leaned back against his car. "Don't blame him too much. He gets off on manipulating people because he doesn't have much of a life of his own."

I shook my head. He'd manipulated Brad right into his grave. "So what happened after that?"

"Jeremy went up to the bar and got us all a round. When he came back, he told Brad he'd seen a cute guy up at the bar. We all looked around and we saw that boy, Tommy. He was wearing a motorcycle jacket, trying to look tough, but you just had to look in his eyes to see he was scared stiff."

I knew that feeling well.

Ari shifted around. "We talked for a couple of minutes, and

Jeremy encouraged Brad to pick the guy up. Not really Brad's usual type, as you know, but Jeremy kept insisting it would be good for him. That old get-back-on-the-horse routine after you've fallen off."

"So Brad took his advice?"

"Brad bought the next round. He chatted the boy up while he was at the bar, and after he brought Jeremy and me our drinks, he went back up there. Rik came in a little later, said hello to Brad and the boy, then came back to our table. He was telling us a story about something he saw at the park—some couple having sex in a tree, if I remember correctly—and the next time we looked up, Brad was gone. Jeremy and Rik left a little later, and then shortly after that you showed up."

He looked at his watch. "I've got to go," he said. "Take care, Kimo."

He got into his car and I pressed the remote to open the gate. I drove in and the gate closed behind me as Ari made a U-turn and headed back down the road.

I drove into the third driveway. The house was vaguely Mediterranean in style, white stucco with a sloping tile roof. I picked up my laptop and my come-stained pants and shorts and walked up to the front door. The big square key opened it and I immediately punched the four numbers Ari had given me into the keypad right inside. The system beeped softly and showed a green light.

I closed the door behind me and began to explore. I didn't get more than a few feet, though, before my cell phone rang. I checked the digital display and recognized my oldest brother's cell number.

"Hey, brah, must be real convenient for you having a source you can exploit right in your own family."

"Hey, Kimo."

"You could at least have called me, you know. Let me know I was hitting the news again."

"Things were crazy around here. It was just before air time when I saw a picture of the two victims and I recognized the guy you were talking to at the park."

"And let me guess. Now you're calling because you want to set me up with an exclusive interview with Ralph Kim."

"I always said you were the smartest of the three of us."

I walked over to a plush leather sofa and sat down. "No, you always said *you* were the smartest," I said. "What's in it for me? Why should I spill my guts for Ralphie?"

"Family loyalty?"

I laughed, stretched my legs out to the coffee table, and then made a buzzer sound. "Try again."

"What do you want?"

"How about a little respect," I said. "Family loyalty. Think of us before you think of KVOL."

"You're sounding like Mom."

"Jesus, insults upon insults," I said. "Listen, Lui, you're my brother, I love you, you've been there in the past when I needed you. Just try and be a little more considerate in the future?"

"I will. Can I give Ralph your cell number?"

"No. I don't want everybody in the world to have it." I looked outside, through sliding glass doors that led to a lanai edged with hibiscus and bougainvillea. It was already dark. I stalled for time, trying to think of a way to turn this situation to my advantage, to move forward my investigation. I knew that the press would hound me until I gave them something, and if I wanted to be able to investigate without having a re-porter trailing me looking for a story I would have to take con-trol of the situation.

"What time is your morning news tomorrow?"

"We go live at 5:30."

"Sunrise is about six," I said. "Have Ralph and a camera crew meet me at Pipeline at 6:30, and I'll give him an interview there. Scene of the crime and all."

"You're the best, Kimo."

"Yeah, I'll bet you say that to Haoa too. If there's any problem, all communications go through you, right?"

"Right." He hung up, and I figured I had better call my parents before they called me. My mother was worried, of course, but pleased that I had spoken to Lui.

"Of course, he could have called me, or you, before he put my face on TV," I said. That was a sore spot for Lui; in his zeal to put on the best news show he could, he had neglected to call and tell either me, or our parents, that his TV station was outing me after I had been suspended from the force on my last case.

"Your brother always has to be the best," my mother said. "He was born first, and he has been struggling to stay first ever since."

"And I was born third, so that means I always have to stay in third place?"

"You know what I mean. Kimo, your father and I have been talking. We think you should come home for a while, until everything settles down. You need your family around you at a time like this."

How could I tell my mother I couldn't come home until I had found out who killed Brad Jacobson and the four surfers, especially when she thought I was no longer a policeman? How could I keep lying to her and my father? The pressures just kept building on me, without any relief in sight. I ran a hand through my hair and thought about what I could say.

"I can't run away and hide," I said finally. "And that's how it would look if I came home now. I have to face whatever problems come up. And I'm going to do that by talking to Lui's reporter tomorrow morning."

"Al, you talk to him," I heard my mother say. "He's going back on TV."

My father got on the phone. "Don't you worry about Lui," he said. "You don't have to keep on talking on TV just because your brother asks you to."

"It's not that," I said. "I already have a public profile, Dad, you know that. If I don't take control of that, set my own interviews and my own agendas, the media will twist things around again. If there's one thing I've learned lately, it's that I need to manage the way the media treat me, as much as I can."

"What can we do to help you?"

"You just have to go on believing in me," I said, knowing as I said it that I was really asking them to believe a lie. "Just knowing that you're there and that you love me really helps."

My mother got back on the phone. "It was nice to see you yesterday," she said. "All the way home, all the kids wanted to talk about was how good you surf. They all want to be like you."

"Let's hope they can all stay out of the headlines," I said. "I love you guys. I'll see you soon, all right?"

My parents told me that they loved me, too, and I hung up. I knew that they would stand by me, no matter what—but when they finally learned that I had been lying to them, they would not be happy. That, I knew, was a problem I would eventually have to face.

Chapter 23

MOVING UP

I RESUMED MY EXPLORATION of the house. I was in a living room that was bigger than my apartment back on Waikīkī, with a flat-panel TV with VCR and DVD player. I could finally watch the video tapes Lui had brought me of Mexpipe.

The living room flowed into an expensively appointed kitchen, with European appliances and stone countertops. A rack of gleaming copper pans that I was sure had never been used hung over an island in the middle of the room.

There were a few staples in the cabinets but the refrigerator was empty. At least I'd have a chance to cook, I thought, happy to get away from the lonely restaurant meals I'd been eating since coming to the North Shore. There was a powder room on that level, too, and a curving staircase that led up to the second floor.

Up there, I found two small bedrooms and a nice bathroom, as well as a large master suite, with a king-sized bed and a bathroom with a glassed-in shower stall and a Roman tub. A balcony looked out to the dark ocean.

I opened the sliding door and stepped out. A necklace of streetlamps outlined the community's single, curving street. I looked up and down the street and saw lights in only a couple of the dozen houses, and only a few parked cars. Cane Landing felt like a protective cocoon, one I had spun around me to keep away horny ghosts from my past, inquisitive reporters, crazed murderers, and everybody else who wanted a piece of me.

My stomach grumbled and I realized I had hardly eaten all day. I made a quick trip down to Fujioka's for chicken breasts, vegetables and rice, and a big chocolate cake for dessert. I figured I deserved that much.

Back at Cane Landing, I turned on the TV, which had a satellite linkup, and used the Food Channel for background noise while I cooked. One program segued into the next as I ate and then slumped onto the couch. I was startled a little after ten when the house phone rang. I picked it up gingerly, not knowing who could be calling.

"Kimo, it's Dario. I'm at the front gate. Let me in."

I had no idea what to do. But I'm a detective, right? I can figure things out. I started randomly pressing buttons until I hit nine and heard a buzzing sound. When it ended I hung up and went out to the driveway.

Dario had packed my suitcase, which sat on his back seat, and my boards were lashed to his roof rack. He climbed up to untie them, then handed them down to me. "Wish I could stay," he said, "but I've got a situation at home."

He jumped down, gave me a quick and unexpected kiss on the lips, and then he was backing down the driveway, leaving me on the lawn surrounded by my belongings. I shook my head and started ferrying stuff inside.

Before I went to sleep, I opened up my laptop, plugged into the phone jack in the bedroom, and dialed up my Internet service provider. Hibiscus House hadn't bothered to install phone jacks in the guest rooms, so I'd had to stop by The

Next Wave every time I wanted to get my e-mail. It would be nice to be able to sit up in bed instead.

I fired off a message to Lieutenant Sampson letting him know I'd be on TV the next morning. I told him I hoped that once the media saw there was really no story about Brad and me, that it would free me up to continue my investigation without hindrance. There was a message from Terri Clark Gonsalves, asking me if I'd check on her uncle, Bishop Clark. Her father seemed to think that Bishop was acting stranger than usual.

I'd met Bishop once, years before, at a party at Terri's. He was her father's older brother, and his name came from a maternal connection to the Hawai'ian royal family rather than any religious affiliation. I wrote back to Terri and told her I'd check him out as soon as I could.

Harry had also sent me a message, telling me he was backed up between his course at UH, Arleen and Brandon, and some issues that had come up with one of his patents. He promised to research the bank accounts of the victims, and the mysterious Harry Pincus, as soon as he could.

E-mails finished, I turned to the issue of Ralph Kim. I knew from watching KVOL occasionally that Kim was a bulldog when it came to getting his stories, and specialized in ambushing subjects. I hadn't been worried when he talked to me on the beach, because I had been able to distract him with the idea of another series he could star in. But I thought it was just likely that Kim might have some embarrassing questions for me the next morning, and I wanted to be prepared.

I knew my brother wouldn't let me come off as a fool, but I thought if Ralph asked me an embarrassing question and I fumbled around for a while, Lui might just let that on the air, in the name of engaging television. I needed some fumble insurance, and I thought I remembered something about Ralph that would help.

I went to Google and typed in "Ralph Kim" as a phrase, with "mistress" after it. Sure enough, I came up with a couple of hits, the most promising from a blog written by an ex-staffer at the station. Ralph had married a demure Korean girl after he graduated from college and they had a son together, but these days he spent most of his time with his mistress, a blonde *haole* girl he'd met when she was a production assistant at KVOL.

That piece of information snugly nested in my brain, I stripped down, did my daily check for any new bumps and bruises, and then headed for the shower.

My dreams were restless and creepy, even though the bed was comfortable. In one, I walked alone down a darkened beach that I knew was Pipeline, knowing somehow that if I could just climb that ridge, I would be able to stop Brad's murder—but I couldn't. No amount of effort or willpower could get me over it.

I finally woke just before dawn, covered in sweat, and knew I couldn't go back to sleep. There was too much to do.

Pipeline wasn't as crowded as usual. I managed to get a little surfing in before I saw the KVOL truck pull up on Ke Nui Road. I walked up the beach in my shorts and rashguard as the cameraman was getting his B roll—shots of the beach that could play under Ralph's voice. I hoisted my board back onto the roof rack, uncertain of what I'd do after the interview, then walked over to Ralph who greeted me warmly, filling me in on how the interview would work. He positioned me so that the spot where the bodies had been found, still roped off with yellow police tape, was visible behind me.

Ralph listened to his earpiece, then said, "There's an overturned tanker truck on the H1, so they're giving the traffic guy an extra minute. After that, they go to a commercial, then they come to us. You OK?"

"Sure," I said. "After the last few weeks, I'm getting to be a pro at this."

"And you're doing a great job," he said. Then we stood, a little awkwardly, waiting for the voice in his ear to get us started. All at once, he looked alert, and I took a deep breath as the camera began to run. Ralph began with a little rundown on what had happened to me—how I'd been a championship surfer before attending the police academy, and then a decorated officer and detective in Waikīkī. All true, though a little exaggerated. He went on to describe how I'd come out of the closet, how the department had responded, and how I'd decided to give up my career, returning to my first love, surfing.

"But tragedy seemed to follow this dedicated officer all the way up here to the idyllic North Shore of O'ahu," Kim said. "Kimo's friend and recent romantic interest, Haleiwa retailer Brad Jacobson, was brutally murdered on this very beach late Sunday night."

He turned to me and the cameraman moved behind his shoulder, so that I'd be looking at the camera as I looked at Ralph. "Is it true that a stormy breakup with you Sunday evening led Jacobson to this stretch of beach, for a romantic rendezvous with a college surfer he'd met only moments before?"

"First of all, Ralph, I wouldn't call what happened between us a 'stormy breakup.' Brad and I were friends, and yes, we had a brief, intimate relationship, but we had a disagreement Sunday evening, nothing more than that. As to what led Brad to this beach, I couldn't say."

"And you didn't know the man he was killed with, Thomas Singer?"

I shook my head. "Not at all."

The cameraman stepped back, getting both of us in the shot, and Ralph said, "Eyewitness accounts indicate that Jacobson met Singer at Sugar's, a notorious gay bar here in Haleiwa, and the two retired to the beach for a sexual encounter."

To me, Ralph said, "How does it feel to know that if you hadn't cheated on Brad Jacobson with two of his male friends Saturday night, he might be alive today?"

It was the ambush I'd been waiting for, but it still hit me hard. My mouth went dry and my pulse raced. Years of police training, however, kicked in, and I said, swallowing carefully, "I don't know, Ralph. How would it feel if someone killed your wife while you were having sex with your mistress?"

For a moment, I saw Ralph Kim lose his composure. His eyes lit up, and if looks could kill I'd have died on that beach just as Brad did. But I saw his professionalism struggling to regain control, and he said, "This isn't about me, Kimo. It's about you and your behavior. What do you have to say for yourself?"

"If you have the right to drag my sex life across everybody's TV screen, Ralph, then I can do the same to you," I said.

Ralph turned toward the camera, ignoring me. "Contrary to police reports, however," he said, "this does not appear to be an isolated encounter. KVOL News has uncovered three other unsolved murders of surfers on the North Shore within the last three months."

Then he turned back to me, all professionalism. "Kimo, you're an experienced homicide detective. Do you think these murders are related? Should North Shore surfers be on the lookout for a homicidal maniac?"

"I wasn't involved in any investigations up here," I said, "so I really can't say anything. But I'm sure that the detectives from District 2 are doing everything they can to solve every open homicide on their books, and I have full confidence in their ability and in the ability of the Honolulu Police Department to protect the public."

The cameraman backed up, to include a wide shot of the surfers on the beach behind us. Ralph said, "This is Ralph Kim at Banzai Pipeline, with disturbing news about five violent deaths on the North Shore. Is someone shooting surfers? We'll have more on this story at noon. Back to you in the studio."

The cameraman gave him a signal and Ralph disconnected his ear piece. "Nice move, bringing up my girlfriend in a live interview, Kimo. I'll remember that."

"Yeah, and while you're at it, remember not to drag somebody else's dirty laundry out in the public unless yours is all clean."

He stalked off toward Ke Nui Road, followed by the cameraman, and I headed back to my truck.

Chapter 24

THE SHOOTER

JUST AS I REACHED KE NUI ROAD, my cell phone rang. It was Sampson.

"I saw your interview on KVOL," he said. "Seemed to go pretty well, until Ralphie tried to sabotage you. You've got balls, man, I'll tell you that."

"I'll take that as a compliment."

"I met with Singer's parents yesterday after I left you. They're both pretty broken up. The father had no clue the boy was gay, but the mother says she wasn't surprised."

I leaned back against my truck. "The mothers always know."

"They say there was never any evidence that the boy was into drugs, but the tox screens on the autopsy will tell us. I've got some witness interviews I can e-mail you about how Jacobson and Singer met at that bar, Sugar's. But you heard that from Ralph Kim."

"Yup. I've also spoken to an eyewitness myself."

"Good. What's your plan for today?"

"I'm going to hang around the beach for a while, make myself visible, talk to people, and see if anybody has information."

"Get back to me before the end of the day, Kimo. This investigation is getting a lot hotter very quickly and I want it resolved." He hung up and I stashed the phone in my glove compartment, then looked back at the beach.

Every time I saw that area of roped-off sand where Brad's body had been found, it made me want to turn right around and head back to Cane Landing. But I couldn't; I had a job to do.

I was pulling my board back off my truck as Mike Pratt's girlfriend Trish came by. Today her bikini was an electric green, just a couple of swatches of fabric tied together with matching green laces. "I need to talk to you," she said. "There's a guy you should know about."

"Who?"

"You heard about the surfers who got shot yesterday?"

I nodded. "I knew the one guy. Brad."

"Yeah, well, there's a guy who's been shooting at surfers. Somebody has to tell the cops about him."

I leaned my board up against my truck. "Who?"

"Mike found this great break near Kawailoa, and it was like, totally deserted," she said. "He took me there once and it was really amazing. But I went back one day by myself, and this crazy caretaker guy came running down the beach, yelling at me and waving a shotgun."

This sounded familiar, and I struggled to remember where I had heard a story like it. "Hold on," I said. "This caretaker, did he have a prosthetic leg?"

"That's him. His name's Rich; Mike used to row the outrigger canoe with him. I heard he's chased other surfers, too. Even shot at them."

"You know anybody he shot at?"

She shook her head. "Just stories I heard. The guy's a jerk.

I mean, I feel sorry for him because he can't surf anymore, but that's no reason to crack down on people who can."

"I heard Mike had a fight with him after he chased you away. He tell you anything about it?"

She shook her head. "Just that he told the guy, Rich, to lay off me. I remember I told him that was sweet, but I could take care of myself. He said something like, not if somebody's shooting at you." Her eyes widened. "Oh, my God," she said. "And then somebody shot him!"

"You think it could have been Rich?"

"I don't know, but when I heard more surfers got shot I thought you ought to know about him."

"Thanks. I'll look into him. I'll let you know if I find anything out."

"Actually, I won't be here," she said. "The other reason I wanted to see you today was to say good-bye."

"Where are you going?"

"Costa Rica. This guy I know runs a little hotel near a great surf beach, and he told me I can stay there if I help with the rooms." She wrapped her arms around her. "I don't want to stay here anymore. Not after what happened to Mike, and now those other two guys. It's just not safe anymore."

"I'm not sure I would go that far."

"Get real, Kimo. I mean, you, like, knew that one guy. Doesn't that freak you out?"

I thought about it. "It did at first," I finally said. "But I saw a lot of things when I was on the force, and so many times what happens to people is just random. If it's your time to go, you go, no matter where you are, or what you're doing."

"All due respect, I think that's bullshit," she said, pulling off the band around her ponytail and retying it. "I hope nothing bad happens to you, Kimo, and I hope you figure out who's killing all these people and the North Shore gets safe again." She stretched up and kissed my cheek. "Good luck."

"Yeah, good luck to you too," I said. I watched her cross the street and jump into the back of a pickup with a couple of other surfers. There were boards stacked along one side, and a pile of suitcases and plastic trash bags. I thought about surfing, but my heart just wasn't in it.

Ironic how when I was chasing cases full time, all I wanted was time to surf; now I just wanted to solve this case. I hung around the beach for a few hours, bringing up the shootings to see what anyone had to say, but the discovery of the bodies the day before had chased a lot of surfers away. I was sure the remaining police tape didn't help either. Everyone I talked to felt the same way Trish did. They were all leaving the North Shore, because they didn't feel safe there anymore.

I had tied my board back to the roof rack of my pickup and was just about to leave for The Next Wave and some Internet surfing when a dark blue Ford Taurus pulled up next to me.

Kawamoto was driving. Ruiz rolled down his window. "Saw you on TV," he said. "Nice of you to give us a plug."

"That's just the kind of ex-cop I am," I said. "Loyal to the force forever."

"Why don't you hop in," Ruiz said, "and take a ride with us."

"All the same to you, I'll come on my own," I said. "I'd rather not get stuck in Wahiawa."

Ruiz looked at Kawamoto, then back at me. "All right. Be there at three." Kawamoto floored it down the street, and I was left wondering what it was going to be like being on the other side of a homicide interrogation.

As I drove toward Haleiwa, I started thinking about Brad. If I'd gone directly from his apartment to Sugar's, I might have seen him before he picked up Tommy Singer and both of them might still be alive.

Jesus. I hadn't thought about it that way before. I didn't chase Brad that night because I didn't want him to think I was a stalker, and because I felt like I had the right to sleep with whoever I wanted. I hadn't made a commitment to him, exchanged rings or promised fidelity. We had some fun.

But what if I had tracked him down. Sure, we would have fought some more. He might have left the bar and gone home, alone, or we might have left together and gone back to his place.

There was a third choice, though. I might not have been able to reason with him, and I might have left the bar, leaving him open to meet Tommy. But why hadn't he just taken Tommy back to his place? Certainly they couldn't go to Tommy's dorm in Mānoa, but why go to the beach? Brad had brought me back to his place; why not Tommy?

When I reached The Next Wave the first thing I had to do, I realized, was find out Rich's last name. Duh. I could have asked Trish or Melody, but I hadn't. So I went to the Web site for the North Shore Canoe Club and searched until I found a set of pictures with team members identified. His last name was Sarkissian. That would make things a little easier; at least his name wasn't Smith or Jones—or in Hawai'i, Lee, Wong, Kim, or Young, the most common names in the phone book.

I googled for Rich Sarkissian and Richard Sarkissian, and found a few hits that I thought were good. A Rich Sarkissian belonged to the VFW chapter in Honolulu, and their Web site noted that he had served in Bosnia from January to September of 1993. That jibed with the Rich I'd met, who looked to be in his early thirties.

Then I found an article in an online magazine about people

with prosthetic limbs, dated two years before. Rich Sarkissian, 31, of Haleiwa, Hawai'i, had developed his own physical
therapy program, which involved rowing in outrigger canoes.
Another direct hit.

I logged into the police database, noting that my ID and
password still worked, and wondered idly who else had access to this data—who knew I was still working as a cop, besides Harry and Terri, and Sampson? Did it matter?

Rich Sarkissian had been the subject of two complaints,
both from surfers who said he had shot at them. Neither
ended up pressing charges, because they both had waves to
chase in other places. I e-mailed Lieutenant Sampson to ask
him to get hold of Rich's military records. It would be interesting to find out if he was a sharpshooter.

Chapter 25

WAHIAWA

I GAVE MYSELF PLENTY OF TIME to drive to Wahiawa, almost halfway down the Kam Highway toward Honolulu. District 2 headquarters was on North Cane Street, just off the North Fork of the Wahiawa Reservoir. I stopped at the front desk and gave the sergeant my name. "Here to see Detectives Ruiz and Kawamoto," I said.

He looked me up and down. "Have a seat."

Ruiz and Kawamoto kept me cooling my heels for about half an hour, but I was willing to give them the benefit of the doubt, thinking that they were just too busy to come get me. That had happened to me periodically as a detective. Sometimes I wanted a suspect to sweat; sometimes I was just swamped.

Finally Ruiz came out to claim me, wearing a white dress shirt and navy slacks. He was a good-looking guy, and I could see he cared about his appearance—every hair was combed neatly, his pants had a crease and his black loafers had a shine. I was getting a definite vibe from him and his partner; Ruiz was going to be the one who was sympathetic, who understood my situation. Kawamoto was going to be the asshole. That was fine; they were roles my own partner and I had played, trading back and forth as appropriate.

"Thanks for coming in," Ruiz said, as he led me to an interrogation room. "We're just trying to clean up a few details." As he opened the door to the room where Kawamoto was already sitting, he said, "You don't mind if we tape this interview, do you?"

"Not at all," I said. "I'm glad to help you in any way I can." I was about to say that I had nothing to hide, but in my experience people who say that usually do have something. And of course I did have something to hide from these detectives, who were only trying to do their job. What I had to hide was that I was trying to do their job, too. It wasn't an idea I thought they'd be too happy about.

"I know you told us how you and Brad Jacobson hooked up, but if you wouldn't mind telling us again, I'd really appreciate it," Ruiz said.

"Sure." I said that I was window-shopping at the North Shore Marketplace and Brad saw me, recognized me, and initiated a conversation. Which was all true. I took my time, explaining how I looked, and Brad's makeover. "It wasn't until I met up with his friends that I realized this was something he did often," I said.

"So you're saying you didn't have sex until after you'd been to the bar?" Kawamoto asked. He and Ruiz had a sort of *Odd Couple* vibe; Kawamoto wore those polyester pants that don't take a belt, and a light blue polo shirt with sweat stains under the arms. He was probably fifty pounds overweight, and I was willing to bet he had a nicotine habit he couldn't—or didn't want to—break. "Isn't that a little unusual—I mean, you were naked in the guy's apartment, weren't you?"

"Yup. And I wondered about it, too. I mean, the whole time I was in the shower I kept expecting him to come in and join me. I was pretty confused. I thought maybe he didn't find me attractive, that he was just being nice to me because of what had happened to me."

"Meaning the whole coming-out thing, then losing your job?" Ruiz asked.

I nodded. "It's a funny thing, being recognized on the street," I said. "Half the people want to say something nice, and the other half want to call you a name. And none of them actually know who you are, or anything about you other than what they saw on TV."

"I don't think I'd like that. Might even make me angry," Ruiz said.

I shrugged. "I didn't ask to be a role model, but that's the way some people look at me. I keep thinking there's a kid out there somewhere who feels bad or scared about being gay, and seeing me on TV helps. That's a real privilege, an honor almost. If I have to put up with some shit now and then, I guess it comes with the territory."

The look in Kawamoto's eyes told me he didn't believe anyone could see me as a role model. "Getting back to Brad Jacobson," he said. He stretched across the table for a piece of gum and his shirttail rode up out of his pants. Not an attractive sight. "You said he dressed you up and then took you to a bar to meet his friends."

"Yeah, I think it's the celebrity thing. He wanted to show me off." I named all five guys and passed on all the contact information I had on them. I didn't mention, though, that we had talked about Lucie Zamora's murder, or that I'd made plans to meet with each of them to talk further.

That information was bound to come out, though. I wondered what Ruiz and Kawamoto would make of it. For now, I wasn't volunteering anything beyond what they asked. Then if they challenged me in the future, I could simply say I'd answered all their questions.

I told them that I had gone back to Brad's place to pick up my truck, and that's when things had shifted between us. I repeated his comment, about his stereo being there in the morning. "You didn't make plans to get together again?" Ruiz asked.

"Nope. Honestly, I wasn't even sure if he liked me. You know, maybe that one night was a fluke, him feeling sorry for me, or wanting to be able to say he'd done it with me. But I went back to his place the next night."

I wasn't going to go into detail about Brad's sexual practices, because I didn't think they were relevant. He liked to pick up strays, according to his friends. I'd seen that, with me, and then with Tommy Singer. That was important; how he liked his sex wasn't.

"So on Thursday night, you still didn't make any plans?" Ruiz asked, putting down his pen. "Isn't that a little unusual?"

"You tell me," I said. "I haven't been dating guys for very long, so I don't know what's normal and what's not. I'm still figuring the whole thing out."

"But you didn't figure he'd be upset if you fucked his friends," Kawamoto said.

My pulse raced, but I tried to maintain control. "Nope, I didn't. Since we weren't exactly dating, I figured I was a free agent. His friends propositioned me, first on Thursday night, and I turned them down. Then again on Saturday night, when I finally said yes."

"What made you change your mind?" Ruiz asked. He looked genuinely curious, though I was sure it was all a front.

He was, after all, the good guy in this interrogation and he had to maintain his rapport with me.

"About six beers. If Brad had been there, I might have gone home with him again. But he wasn't, and they were. I was horny and curious and I didn't think through all the implications."

I figured if Ruiz and Kawamoto couldn't understand being drunk and horny, they both had to be neutered. But they seemed to accept how things had happened, and we went on to the confrontation on Sunday at Waimea Bay Beach Park. Then we went back over the whole thing again.

It was a long, draining experience. Even though the interrogation room was cool, I felt sweat pooling under my arms and at my brow. I was tired and felt a headache coming on. I could easily see how suspects might make mistakes; that's why we kept them for so long, asking the same questions over and over again.

"Is it possible," Ruiz said, talking somewhat slowly and softly, "that you actually did see Brad Jacobson at that bar, Sugar's, on Sunday night?" He lightly tapped his fingers on the table in front of him. "And you were upset that he was with someone else, maybe jealous? I know you've said you're not very experienced at this gay thing. Maybe you misread some signs, and you were actually way more interested in him than he was in you."

"Nope," I said. "Not possible. Didn't happen that way."

"Well, maybe it did," Ruiz continued. "And you were pretty upset seeing him leave the bar with this young boy, much younger than you. You were jealous, so you followed them down to the beach."

I wasn't frightened; I thought this was bush league interrogation, much more blatant than anything that had gone before. I was on comfortable ground here. "Nope. Ask Ari. He'll tell you I arrived at Sugar's after Brad had already left. Ari will tell you I stayed at the bar talking to him for some time. Even if I'd wanted to find Brad, I had no way of knowing where he was then."

"We will check this out, you know," Kawamoto said, drumming his fingers on the tabletop. "If anything doesn't jibe, you can be sure we'll be back at you."

"I've been honest with all your questions," I said. I looked from Ruiz to Kawamoto, and back. "Are we finished here yet? Because it's been a long day."

"We're finished," Ruiz said. "But you know the drill. Don't leave the island. We may need to talk to you again."

"I'll do anything I can to help," I said. "By the way, I had to move out of the place where I was staying after I was on TV again. A friend of mine arranged for me to stay at a rental property with security." I gave them the address and phone number at Cane Landing, and left. It felt good to get out of the police station—and that wasn't a feeling I wanted to contemplate too much.

Chapter 26

THE EXODUS

AFTER THE INTERROGATION, I was very much in need of caffeine. As I headed back to Haleiwa, I noticed that traffic heading away from the North Shore was much heavier than normal. Everybody seemed to be going down toward Honolulu. Cars and trucks I passed were loaded up with suitcases and surfboards.

The Kope Bean, on the other hand, was much emptier than usual. The barista, an older brunette woman in a colorful apron, was scared and wanted to leave, but she had a child in school and couldn't just pick up and walk away. Two other customers, both surfer types in their twenties, said they were leaving in the next day or two.

I went over to The Next Wave and the parking lot was nearly empty, which was very unusual. I walked in and the place was dead. Dario heard the door ring and came over immediately, looking disappointed that I wasn't an actual customer. He was wearing a polo shirt with the store's logo on it and a pair of khaki shorts. It was the first time I had seen him wearing a name tag.

"Two of my staff quit this morning," he said. "Look at this place." He waved his arm to encompass the empty aisles of clothing and the fact that no one was looking at surfboards or trying on sunglasses. "My business is going down the toilet."

"It's just a momentary panic," I said. "A couple of days will pass, and people will start filtering back up here."

"Yeah, a couple of days like this and I won't be able to pay my bills," he said. He stalked away toward his office, and I headed over to the café where I settled down with my laptop, still hoping to meet someone who knew something that could help my case. There were only about half a dozen other people in the entire building, most of them employees, so it was unnaturally quiet, the sound of Keola Beamer and his slack key guitar echoing off the surfboard displays.

I logged on to the *Advertiser's* Web site, and read their follow-up story on the shootings, which agreed with what I'd seen—that people were scared and leaving the North Shore. A police spokesman said people shouldn't worry, but obviously no one was listening.

The media reports, as usual, distorted things: Brad became a surfer, too, though I knew he'd never stepped on a board; Tommy became a budding champion, though he'd never actually entered a competition, no less won one.

I was getting ready to leave when Dario came over and sat down in the armchair catty-cornered to mine. We were the only people in the lounge area besides the barista, who was across the room cleaning the cappuccino machine. "Listen, I was out of line yesterday," he said. "I don't know what came over me."

"It's OK."

"I guess I always had a little crush on you, you know?" He crossed his legs and his khaki shorts rode up on his thighs. His legs were strong, slim, and tanned. He'd put some muscle on in the last ten years, but not much fat. If it wasn't for the worried look in his eyes or the bags underneath them, he'd be considered pretty handsome.

"I didn't know, but I'm flattered."

"Since that time, I've thought about what happened between us, at the beach. I think what I was trying to do was pull you out of the closet so that we could be together." He shrugged. "I guess it had the opposite effect. Instead, I pushed you even farther in, and then you left, and I lost any chance of a relationship with you."

Dario was starting to creep me out a little. Back when we were surfing, I always just considered him a friend. I knew he was gay, because he didn't try to hide it, but I wasn't particularly attracted to him. I had no idea he had had such feelings about me.

"Anyway, seeing you here again, I guess I just went a little crazy. I hope you can forgive me. I really want us to be friends."

I sat up a bit in my chair, pulling my legs in. "Sure, Dario. Friends are good. I've decided I'm going to be celibate for a while, you know? Just try and keep my zipper closed and stay out of any more trouble."

Until I solved these murders, I almost said, but I held back.

"I'll have to see if I can change your mind," he said, leaning forward a bit. "Gently, though. No more full frontal attacks."

"OK."

The front doorbell rang, and like one of Pavlov's dogs, Dario jumped up, hoping it was a customer. I used that opportunity to leave The Next Wave.

I must still be giving off some kind of closeted vibe, I thought. Some lost gay boy thing that attracted first Dario, then Brad, then George and Larry. I've always thought of myself as pretty ordinary, not movie-star handsome or anything.

Nothing that would attract all these guys who seemed to find me irresistible. I've been lucky enough to get the best features of my gene pool, starting with a tall, lean physique that I keep in reasonably good shape with surfing, roller-blading, swimming, and any other kind of exercise that strikes my fancy.

I have just enough of an Asiatic look to my eyes to make me a little exotic, skin just a shade darker than average, so I always look like I have a really good tan, and glossy black hair that I keep cut short. I think I give off a masculine vibe, which gay men seem to find attractive.

Whatever it was, I had never had trouble arousing sexual interest, either in girls, back when I was pretending to be straight, or now with guys. Sometimes it was more of a pain than it was worth. Like now, with Dario.

I drove around Haleiwa for a while, stopping wherever I saw people gathered, trying to make conversation, but I didn't learn anything new, just that these last murders, and the publicity that connected them to the first three, had people running scared.

I picked up some groceries and a six-pack of Kona Fire Rock Pale Ale at Fujioka's and retreated to my house in the hills. I popped the first of the Pipeline tapes Lui had brought into the VCR and settled back to watch some surfing.

They were pretty good quality, and the surfers were excellent. I saw Mike Pratt catch a couple of great waves, and a roving reporter actually interviewed Lucie Zamora. She was pretty and charming and both her skimpy bikini and the camera emphasized her physical attributes. Seeing both of them there was kind of spooky, knowing that they had been so alive and happy once.

It was almost dinnertime, so I went out to the small backyard and fired up the gleaming stainless steel barbecue out there—a huge, free-standing model I'd seen advertised for close to a thousand dollars. When the coals were glowing red, I put a steak on, along with some sliced peppers and a big Idaho potato I'd pre-baked in the microwave.

Pretty soon I had a great meal—just no one to share it with. I popped open another beer and went back to the TV. I watched the rest of the tapes, nearly four hours, until I'd gone through the last. I thought I saw Ronald Chang in the background a couple of times, but I couldn't be sure. Now that I'd gone through all those tapes, I wasn't sure what I'd hoped to learn from them. At least I had definite proof that both Mike and Lucie had been at Mexpipe, and I felt a little more connected to both of them after seeing them on tape.

I turned on my laptop and sent an e-mail to Sampson, filling him in on what I'd learned from the tapes as well as my interview with Ruiz and Kawamoto. "Can you let me know when ballistics comes in?" I wrote. "Obviously I want to know if there's a match to the gun used in the other cases. If it doesn't match I'm sure they're going to waste a lot more time looking at me."

I'd just finished sending the e-mail when my cell phone rang, a call from Terri. "I'm thinking of coming up to the North Shore tomorrow," she said. "I was hoping you'd have some time for me."

"You'll be heading in the wrong direction," I said. "Everybody up here is leaving town. Freaked out by the murders."

"I won't get on a board," she said dryly. "I'm sure I'll be safe, especially if I'm with you."

"I wouldn't count on that. Look what happened to Brad."

"Brad was in the wrong place at the wrong time," she said. "That's what the newspapers and the TV say. That is, when they don't say he was a surfer."

"My time is your time," I said. "I've just got surfing and investigating five murders on my agenda."

"I wouldn't be up there til noon," she said. "Want to meet me for lunch?"

We agreed to meet at Rosie's Cantina at noon, and hung up. I was pretty beat, but I had trouble getting to sleep. I kept thinking of Brad, wondering if it would have made a difference if I'd tracked him down at Sugar's. I must have dozed off eventually, because I woke to find a few rosy fingers of light coming in through the bedroom window. I got up, checked for bruises, and took a quick shower before heading down to Pipeline.

In the fifteen or more years I had been surfing there, I had never seen it so empty when the waves were high. It was almost spooky, sharing such a great beach with only a half dozen other surfers. The police had taken away the yellow cones around the hollow where the bodies had been, and I couldn't even identify that patch of sand again.

Maybe that was why my heart felt a little lighter; maybe it was that I thought I was making progress on the case. In any event, I was able to surf for a couple of hours. I was just dragging my board up the beach when I saw Kawamoto's blue Taurus on Ke Nui Road.

They were both out of the car, talking to a female surfer, though they finished up with her as soon as I got there.

"Morning, detectives," I said. I thought it was still morning, though noon was fast approaching.

"Need to speak to you, Kimo," Ruiz said. He was in full *Miami Vice* mode: beige sports jacket over navy shirt, knife-pressed black slacks, those spit-polished loafers again, all topped with mirrored sunglasses. "Come on, get in the car."

"I'm wet," I said. "And I've got a lunch date. What do you need?"

He motioned me with his head, and I followed him down the road a hundred feet. "Why are you so interested in Lucie Zamora?"

"Brad had this idea," I said. "He and Lucie were friends, and he had introduced her to most of his friends, too. He thought you guys weren't doing enough to find out who killed her."

I held up my hand to silence his immediate objection. "I know, I told him that a lot of police work goes on behind the scenes, that you guys might be just about to arrest somebody. . But he had this idea that since I had some investigative skills, maybe I could nose around and find some things out that might help you."

He looked down his nose at me, over the mirrored sunglasses. "We don't need the help."

"I know. Listen, I know how hard your job is. Remember, I used to do it, up til a couple weeks ago. Just to make Brad happy, I said I'd talk to each of his friends and see what they knew. If I found anything out I was going to bring it to whoever was in charge of the case."

Behind him, I saw Kawamoto, looking rumpled as ever, fiddling in his pocket and pulling out a crumpled pack of Marlboros. "Did you find anything?"

I shrugged. "Probably nothing you didn't already know. Lucie Zamora was dealing crystal meth, but nobody knew where she got the stuff. All three of the dead surfers had been to the Mexpipe surfing championships in Mexico in August."

Ruiz pulled a notepad out of his pocket and started to write. "How do you know that?"

"Brad told me Lucie had gone to Mexico, so I checked the competition listings on the Internet. That's when I saw all three of them were there."

"Why didn't you tell us all this yesterday?"

I tried my best to look casual. "You didn't ask."

Ruiz angled his jaw and the sunlight flashed off those mirrored lenses.

"Look, what was I supposed to say? Hey, Lucie's friends don't think you're doing a good job finding the person who killed her, so they asked me to help out. That's not something I wanted to volunteer. But you see, I'm happy to share anything I found out with you."

"Obviously, you've got some insight that we don't have," Ruiz said, putting away his pad. "I want to know everything you've discovered."

"Like I said, I've got a lunch date," I said. "After that I can write it up for you. Give me your card again. I'll fax something down to you by the end of the day."

"Complete," Ruiz said. He pulled out his wallet and handed me a card. "Everything you know. Otherwise we'll be having a little chat again, and you know my partner doesn't particularly care for you."

"That's OK," I said, glancing at Kawamoto, smoking and glaring in the background. "You can tell him he's not my type."

Chapter 27

BISHOP CLARK

ONCE IN MY TRUCK, I dialed Sampson's office. "I think my cover is in danger of being blown." I explained that Ruiz and Kawamoto had discovered I'd been asking questions about Lucie, and once I gave them a taste of what I'd discovered, they wanted more. "I can't withhold evidence," I said. "I have to tell them what I've found."

"I agree. What do you think of them?"

"Pretty decent interrogation," I said. "And they're doing a good job of digging information up now. Otherwise they wouldn't know anything about me."

"I think it may be time to let them in on your purpose up there. But only them. I don't want your cover compromised to the rest of the world." I didn't mention, though perhaps I should have, that Harry and Terri already knew. I didn't know how kindly Sampson would take to Harry's cyber-snooping, and I wasn't sure I wanted to find out.

"You're going to have to be the one who tells them," I said. "I'm still a suspect, so they won't believe anything I say."

"Of course. Let me check my calendar." He was off the phone for a minute, then back. "Tomorrow afternoon. I can be in Wahiawa by two."

"I'll be there." I hung up and looked at my watch. I had just enough time to run up to the house, shower and change, to meet Terri for lunch at noon.

Like the rest of the North Shore, Rosie's was nearly empty. It was as if some kind of disease had swept through, wiping out two-thirds of the population. Terri was right on time, despite the possibility of traffic or accidents on the hour-long trip up from Honolulu. But that was her; I've never known her to be late for anything. If you asked, she'd simply say it was the way she was raised; Clarks are not late.

"Thanks for meeting me," she said, after we'd kissed hello and sat down. She looked, as usual, casually elegant; a gray linen blouse, black slacks, black pumps. The dark circles were still there under her eyes, but she looked a little happier, a little healthier than she had on Sunday. "I want to say right up front I'm hoping I can drag you along to this meeting with my uncle."

"Why?"

"He's just getting nuttier every year," she said. The waitress came by and we ordered. "Not that I'm really frightened of him, but apparently he's walled himself in at this old place, with an electrified fence and a security guard. It sounds kind of creepy."

"Sure. I was supposed to spend today hanging out, asking people if they knew this last dead surfer, but as you can see, the North Shore has pretty much emptied out and there's hardly anybody left to ask."

"It's so sad, what happened," she said. "Were you dating that guy, Brad?"

I shrugged. "Honestly, I don't know what you'd call it." I explained about meeting him, how I'd spent most of the night with him twice, then how he'd come to the park on Sunday to yell at me.

"Well, can you blame him?" she asked, tilting her head toward me. "You shouldn't have slept with his friends."

"I guess not. I wasn't actually thinking much about him at the time."

Terri frowned. "No wonder he was upset."

"Yeah, you're right. I keep thinking, what if I'd gone to Sugar's first, to find him. I might have kept him from going off with that kid, and maybe they'd both be alive today."

Our food arrived, and as soon as the waitress left, Terri said, "You can't think like that. There are so many what if's. What's important is that you do what you can to find out who killed him."

"I'm trying, but it's not easy. I can't find a single connection between Tommy Singer and the other three surfers."

We talked as we ate, Terri throwing out ideas, almost all of which I'd tried myself. "Tommy never lived up here, so that cuts a lot of possibilities out," I said. "Of the other three, only Ronald Chang went to UH, and he dropped out while Tommy was still in high school. Tommy wasn't a good enough surfer to enter competitions, or even to hang out with older, better surfers like Mike Pratt or Lucie Zamora."

"No drugs, right?"

"His parents say no. The autopsy's today; I should get the report from Sampson sometime later. But I don't think any drugs will show up. So he couldn't have known Lucie that way."

"A computer connection to Ronald Chang?"

I shook my head. "Apparently Tommy had a computer, but just for school and e-mail and games. It's always possible he ran into one of the three on a beach and somehow they hooked up, but there's no evidence."

We finished, and Terri insisted on paying. "I'm on the Foundation dime," she said. Much of her family's money had been funneled into The Sandwich Islands Trust, a family foundation that did charitable works around the islands.

"How come? Does this land Bishop lives on actually belong to the Trust?"

"Not yet. The way the documents are written, it's his for life, and passes to his legitimate heirs. If he dies without children, then the property goes into the Trust."

"And he wants to change that."

She nodded. "Come on, I'll drive. I've already told him what kind of car I have, so his guard won't shoot me."

I must have looked dubious, because she said, "Don't doubt it. Apparently the guard has shot at trespassers before, but the police couldn't prove anything."

On our way up the coast, Terri continued to tell me about the land. "It belonged to my great-grandparents," she said. "My grandparents used to go up there in the summer. My father never liked it and Bishop did, so he was happy to let Bishop have it."

"Bishop never had kids?"

"Nope. He was married three times, always to much younger women, but they all left him—taking a chunk of his money with them, of course."

"Of course."

"He had a trust fund, but he hired an attorney from one of the big firms and broke it over some technicality. He drained it, and then started selling off other property that was in his name alone. He's finally run out of money and he wants to sell this land to a developer, who will give him cash and a new house on the property."

"Sounds like a good deal for Bishop."

"He and my father haven't spoken for years," she said, peering at the road ahead. There was very little traffic, but I could see she was looking for landmarks. "It's the ant and the grasshopper thing—my father worked his whole life, managing Clark's, building it up, and all Bishop did was have fun and spend money."

I leaned back against the door of the SUV so I could look at her. "Can you actually change the terms of the Trust?"

"It's not the Trust that needs changing, just the deed restrictions on the land. And my father, and my great aunt Emma, who's the chairman of the Trust, have the power to change those. My father wants to make sure that at least part of the land is preserved, though. That's where I come in."

I nodded. "The negotiator."

"Exactly. Now that I no longer have a husband to answer to, Aunt Emma is grooming me to take over the Trust from her. At least that's her attitude. She forgets I still have a son." She sighed. "Anyway, this is my first assignment."

"Is that something you want?"

Terri turned *makai,* or toward the ocean, off the Kam Highway at a barely visible driveway, narrow and rutted, between hibiscus hedges bright with platter-sized yellow blossoms. "The Trust gives away a half million a year in grants," she said. "Mostly to education and family issues. Do I want to control that? You bet."

"It's a shame your family sold the chain," I said. "You would have made a great CEO."

"Not me," she said, pulling up in front of a gate with a

crude speaker mounted next to it. "I saw how hard my father worked all those years. I want to have a family life, too."

She blew the horn and the speaker crackled. "Uncle Bishop, it's me, Terri," she said into it.

"Just a minute," a disembodied voice said.

We waited, and a man dressed in a camouflage T-shirt and khaki shorts appeared from behind a purple bougainvillea a few hundred feet ahead of us. As he walked toward us, I noticed his oddly stilted gait—and then recognized him. "I know that guy," I said. "His name's Rich, he rows for the North Shore Canoe Club." I remembered what I'd learned about Rich's habit of shooting surfers; that certainly tied in with what Terri had heard. I didn't want to tell her he was my only suspect in the shootings.

"We'll talk about him later," she said. Rich came up to the gate, unlocked the padlock, and swung it open. We continued up the driveway and turned the corner, to park at the back of the house. In the rear view mirror, I saw Rich swing the gate shut and connect the padlock again.

The house was long and low, plantation style, painted white with dark green shutters. A hipped roof sheltered the windows from the sun, and a gravel yard lay between us and a back door. Bishop Clark stood in the doorway.

He had aged a lot since I'd met him, which had probably been at Terri's and my high school graduation. "He used to be so handsome," she whispered to me. "Just devastating."

The man before us was skinny and stooped, with straggly white hair down to his shoulders. But he had good bones in his face, and if you looked closely you could see that indeed he had been very handsome.

We got out of the car and I stood to the side while Terri

hugged him. "Such a young lady," he said, holding her at arm's length for a good look. "Very Clark."

"It's the way I was raised," she said. "Uncle Bishop, this is my friend Kimo. I think you've met him before. We've known each other since Punahou. He's living up here now and I wanted to show him how wonderful this property is, and what a great development it could be."

Bishop stuck out his hand and I shook it. "Pleased to see you again," he said.

"The pleasure's mine, sir," I said. I did learn a few manners at Punahou.

"Well, come on inside," he said. "I've got some lemonade, if you're interested. I can show you the drawings." Out of the corner of my eye, I saw Rich come up the driveway, and Bishop waved him away.

Terri and I followed her uncle into the house. I guess I was expecting a rat trap—stained walls, the floor lined with piles of old newspaper—but the house was beautiful inside, with flagstone floors and the kind of antique furniture that would have had my mother salivating, all made out of *koa* wood and probably over a hundred years old.

In addition to a couple of sofas facing a wall of glass that viewed the ocean, there was a tall china cabinet filled with Chinese export porcelain, and next to that a gun cabinet with a display of old and new firearms. I recognized most of them, but some were such antiques that I'd only ever seen pictures of them.

I was naturally drawn over to the cabinet. I have a couple of guns myself, and though I believe that you shouldn't draw a weapon unless you intend to use it, I like having them around. "Interested in guns?" Bishop asked.

"Kimo is a . . . used to be a police detective," Terri said. Bishop showed no sign of having seen a newspaper or heard a TV broadcast for the last few years.

Bishop came over and opened the cabinet. "Let me show you a couple of pieces," he said. He opened the cabinet and pulled out a pistol. "This is the Colt Model 1860," he said. "The principal side arm used during the Civil War. It's the oldest one in my collection."

It looked it, too. Despite Bishop's best efforts to keep the pistol oiled and polished, it had seen hard service. I admired it, and he replaced it in the cabinet and pulled out a rifle. "The Sharps 'Big Fifty.' Used to kill buffalo. It's where the term sharpshooter comes from."

"Cool." I raised the gun up to my eye and sighted down the barrel toward the ocean.

"It can kill at a range of up to a thousand yards," Bishop said, as I handed it back to him. The next gun was a pistol. "This one's interesting," he said. "Japanese. Pistol type 94. One of the worst service pistols in history."

It was ugly and difficult to handle. "Doesn't look that great," I said.

"Supposedly it's capable of accidentally discharging rounds before they're fully seated in the firing chamber."

"Boys and their toys," Terri said, as I handed the pistol back to Bishop.

"Here's one you might recognize," Bishop said. "I promise you, Terri, it's the last one."

"A .38 Special," I said.

"You got it. Standard issue for most police departments in the U.S. at one time."

"They're still making these, but this looks like an old one," I said.

"At least seventy-five years old. I have some newer ones, too, but nothing all that interesting."

"Thanks for showing me."

"My pleasure. Don't get to take them out all that often. Rich helps me keep them cleaned and polished, but he's only interested in the new guns." Bells started going off in my head; Rich had access to a wide range of weapons, including the kind of rifle that had killed Mike Pratt and Lucie Zamora, and the type of handgun that had been used in the other murders. I had to know more about Rich, and soon.

The three of us walked over to the full-height glass windows of the living room. We were on a slight bluff and the land sloped down, toward the Pacific. Terri had told me the property spanned a hundred acres, most of it behind us and on the other side of the Kam Highway.

Bishop's land looked out at prime surfing area, but his fence ran down to the water's edge and kept surfers out. I saw that he probably kept Rich busy patrolling the waterfront—though today there were likely to be few surfers at any of the public beaches, no less trying to sneak onto Bishop's land.

The sky was a clear light blue, and there were no clouds in sight. There was mostly scrub, broken with the occasional splash of color, between us and the ocean, which rolled and frothed relentlessly against the shore. We watched the waves for a few minutes, then Bishop sat us down at a massive *koa* wood dining table, brought out lemonade in French crystal glasses, and spread out the plans for Bishop's Bluff Estate Homes.

"You'll see, it's going to be beautiful," he said, unrolling the first drawing. "Not some ticky-tacky little place like they put up nowadays." The plan showed a circular drive, much like the one at Cane Landing, with an entrance down on the Kam Highway and a guard house. The houses were situated on the bluff so that each one had at least a partial ocean view. He laid out a couple of other drawings, of each style of house. They looked much like where I was staying, and I had a feeling I was looking at the property Ari had talked to me about.

"This one's going to be mine," Bishop said, pointing proudly at a lot at one end. "I'll still be able to see all the way down to Haleiwa."

"What about all the land behind us?" Terri said, pointing to the area on the other side of the highway.

"Clubhouse and swimming pool," he said. "If we can get the zoning changed to multi-family, we'll put a couple of low-rise condo buildings up there. Max six stories, very high-end."

"I'm a little worried about developing all the land," Terri said carefully, "and I know my father and Aunt Emma are too. They might be willing to agree to change the deed restrictions if they knew part of the property would be preserved."

"The *mauka* part?" Bishop asked, meaning the area on the mountain side of the highway.

"I think I could get them to agree to that."

"I'd have to see what Ari says."

"Harry?" Terri asked, but I'd already recognized the name. A bell seemed to ring, but I figured I was thinking of Harry Ho.

"Ari. Short for Aristotle. Young Greek fella. He's the one put all the money together to buy the land and get the construction started."

"Can I take a copy of these plans with me?" Terri asked. "I'd love to be able to show my dad and Aunt Emma what you're considering."

"Sure. I've got more sets here somewhere." He rolled up the drawings for us, and then we sat and drank lemonade for a while. I watched the ocean while Terri talked about family stuff, and finally we all stood up and said our good-byes.

"I'll get Rich to open the gate for you," he said.

"What do you need a security guard for, Uncle Bishop?" Terri asked. "Has the North Shore gotten a lot more dangerous?"

"People today have no respect for private property," Bishop said. "Surfers used to traipse through here like it was a public beach. I put up the fence and the gate, but that hardly stopped anybody. So I hired Rich to keep an eye on things. He's had to fire a few warning shots, but people have started to get the message."

"I don't like the idea of anybody shooting up here, Uncle Bishop. Somebody could get hurt, and sue you, or sue the Trust. I don't think my father or Aunt Emma would like that."

"My brother and my aunt can jump in the Pacific and drown, for all I care," Bishop said, raising his voice. "Your father has looked down his nose at me since we were kids, and I'm sick and tired of it. And as for Aunt Emma, well, I never quite fit her idea of what a Clark should be, and the older I get, the less interested I am in that idea. And you can tell her I said that."

There was a knock on the back door, and it opened a moment later. "I heard some shouting. Everything OK in here, Mr. Clark?" Rich asked.

"These folks are just leaving," Bishop said. "You can open the gate for them."

Terri looked like she wanted to say more to her uncle, at least kiss him good-bye, but he turned and walked back toward the dining room. We got back into the Land Rover, and Terri turned around, then headed out the drive. Rich had already opened the gate, and as we headed toward the Kam Highway my last view was of him pushing the gate closed again.

Chapter 28

A PLACE LIKE THIS

"I'VE GOT A LOT TO TELL YOU," I said, as we reached the Kam Highway. "You in a hurry to get back?"

"Nope. My mother's picking up Danny at school, and she can even give him dinner if I call."

"Then you can follow me up to my new digs. I think you'll want to see it."

While we headed back to Rosie's so I could pick up my truck, I told her what I knew about Rich and the accident in Bosnia that had ruined him for surfing. "So he's pretty bitter," she said.

"You bet. There have been two complaints against Rich, so far, both for shooting, both dismissed."

"Lovely. That's a detail I think I'll leave out of my report to Aunt Emma."

"I don't blame you."

Terri followed me up to Cane Landing. I motioned her around me so that I could open the gate for her, and then open it again for myself, and then I jumped around her to lead her up to the third house.

"Boy, you're moving up in the world," she said, as we both got out in the driveway.

"Wait til you see the inside. And it's all courtesy of Aristotle Papageorgiou."

"Let me guess. The young Greek fella."

"You got it."

"Interesting."

I gave her the grand tour, and she oohed and aahed appropriately. There were still a couple of Konas left, and we sat down in the living room with them. "So this Aristotle must be some kind of North Shore real estate mogul," she said.

"Seems like it. He's a nice enough guy—I mean, it's certainly nice of him to put me up here. And he doesn't know that I know you, or Bishop, so it's not like he's doing it so I'll help him in some way."

She slipped off her pumps and slid her feet underneath her, relaxing on the leather sofa. "Speaking of Bishop, didn't you find all those guns kind of creepy?"

"It's a guy thing," I said. "My dad has a couple of guns, and so do my brothers. Almost every guy I know owns at least one gun."

"Not Harry."

"Um, actually, yes, Harry has a nine millimeter Glock. I helped him pick it out."

Terri shook her head. "Like I said before, boys and their toys."

I took a swig of my Kona. "Only your uncle has some toys that can do some serious harm. That buffalo gun that can shoot at one thousand yards, for starters."

"Could you shoot a surfer with a gun like that?"

"You're reading my mind. I think so. Maybe not that gun, because it's an antique, and there might be some rust or other damage inside. But a rifle like that, sure, you could shoot somebody off a board if you were a good enough shot."

She sat up and pulled her legs around to the floor again. "How about Rich? I didn't like him. Something about him gives me the creeps."

"Something like his prosthetic leg?" I kicked out with my right leg.

Terri frowned. "I can't say I like that, but no, it's not that. Something about his personality." She rubbed her upper arms.

"He's a security guard, Terri. I don't much like him, either, but I don't think a charming personality is a prerequisite for being a guard."

"You think he hates surfers enough to start killing them?" She shuddered. "I hope Uncle Bishop hasn't gone so far around the bend that he's behind these killings."

"I asked Lieutenant Sampson to look into Rich's war record," I said. "He's an ex-soldier, so he's probably a good marksman. I know he has a grudge against surfers, because he can't surf anymore, and because they piss him off when they trespass on your uncle's land."

I popped open my laptop and checked my e-mail while Terri went to the restroom. Still no word from Sampson on Rich Sarkissian's war record. There was an e-mail from Harry that he was looking into the dead surfers' bank records, and also trying to find Harold Pincus. I made a couple of notes about Bishop's guns, in case we ever needed to subpoena them for ballistics tests.

"This is some house," Terri said, when she came back. "I think Uncle Bishop would be happy with a place like this."

"You can't blame the man for trying to maximize his assets and secure his old age," I said.

Terri sat down again on the sofa. "You *can* blame him for squandering the money that was supposed to take care of him for the rest of his life," she said. "But I'll try and make some peace between him and rest of the family. I think I can convince Dad and Aunt Emma to let his plan go forward if we carve out some open space. And that will only make the houses more valuable."

"Assuming that the guy who's killing surfers gets caught, and people come back to the North Shore," I said.

"Oh, my," Terri said, and she sat quickly on the couch. "I just thought of something."

"What?" I was worried she'd remembered something about Evan, her late husband, that had upset her.

"Property values will go way down if people are frightened," she said. "Maybe some of the people who are opposed to Uncle Bishop's development will leave, or the government will ease up on restrictions in order to keep the economy moving."

"So you think your uncle might be directing Rich to kill surfers?"

"I don't know. But you saw him today—he's not the same man he used to be. He's getting crazier. And I can see a guy like Rich, wanting to prove he could be useful again, appreciating the chance Uncle Bishop has given him, wanting to help."

"And you don't know, Bishop could be paying him, or promising him money when the development gets going."

Terri shivered. "I don't want him to be involved. Please, I don't want him to be involved."

"I haven't really seen a connection between Bishop and any of the dead surfers," I said. "And it seems to me that Bishop would want land values to go up, not down, so he could get more money for the land."

"It's a question of short-term versus long-term," Terri said. "If Uncle Bishop trades his land for a piece of the equity, then the development company acquires the land cheaply. By the time the houses are built, everyone's forgotten about the killings, and house values go up. There's that much more profit to be made."

"You know who else has a motive there," I said, thought-fully, "Aristotle Papageorgiou. He's very determined to see this project succeed." I made a note to check him out further.

She looked at her watch. "I should go," she said. At the front door, she hugged me. "This was fun. I miss you. I want you to come back to Honolulu soon."

"I will."

I had barely gotten back in the door from seeing her off when my cell phone rang. "Yo, Harry, what's up, brah?"

"I'm thinking I need a little surfing in my life. You got some extra space at that hotel hell where you're staying?"

"Actually, I've upgraded," I said. I told him about the switch from Hibiscus House to Cane Landing. "Got room galore," I said. "But if you're going to surf the North Shore, you've got to be fearless."

"I have been surfing the North Shore with you since we were hitching rides on cane trucks."

"Yes, but no one was shooting surfers then." I told him how the whole North Shore seemed to have emptied out.

"More waves for us. I'm teaching until noon Friday. I can be up there a little after one and spend the weekend. And we'll find out what we can about all these folks you're interested in."

We made plans to meet and I hung up. I fired up my laptop and put together all the notes I wanted to share with Ruiz and

Kawamoto. Step by step, what I had learned about Lucie, Mike, and Ronnie, with as many names, places, and facts as I could put together. It took me almost two hours, but by the time I was done I was pretty impressed with myself. I e-mailed a copy to Ruiz, and then separately, a copy to Sampson.

When I was finished I sent a couple of other e-mails, fixed dinner, and then relaxed in front of the TV. It was definitely a different lifestyle from the one I'd enjoyed in Honolulu. There, I lived in a small studio apartment on Waikīkī. I tried to surf when I could, but most mornings found me at my desk rather than on the waves. I worked with a station full of cops, I had a partner to bounce ideas off, I had a badge and a gun and a sense of identity as a police detective. I spent a lot of time with my family, I read, I rode my bike, I roller-bladed, walked and ran. Here on the North Shore, all I seemed to do was eat, sleep, surf, and try to figure out who had killed five people.

Chapter 29

DARIO'S SURPRISE

AROUND NINE O'CLOCK THAT NIGHT, I started getting antsy. I knew I ought to just go to sleep, but I wanted to see if there was anyone hanging around at any of the bars. After all, people are more likely to talk when they're drunk, and I wasn't getting any leads sitting around the house staring out at the stars.

I decided to start at Sugar's, because I hadn't been there since Sunday night, when I'd gone there looking for Brad. I was still planning to keep my vow of celibacy—at least until I got this case behind me. Back in Waikīkī, who knew what would happen. But on the North Shore, I was keeping my pants zipped up. Then what was I doing going to a gay bar? Well, for one thing, I wanted somebody I could talk to Brad about. I was hoping his friends would be there.

Ari was there, surprisingly, at least to me, sitting with Dario at a table near the bar. Of course I knew that Dario was some kind of investor in Ari's project, and Dario had been the one to call Ari and get me the place at Cane Landing, but I still didn't picture them as the kind of friends who hung around together for a drink.

While I was at the bar getting a beer, Dario came up. He was wearing a Next Wave logo T-shirt and cargo shorts, looking like he'd spent a long day on the selling floor at the surf shop. "Got to drain the lizard," he said. "You gonna come join us?"

"Sure."

I took my beer over to their table. "Hey, Kimo, how's the house working out?" Ari asked. He was another tired-looking businessman, wearing a white dress shirt open at the neck with a loosely-knotted striped tie.

"It's great. I really appreciate your fixing it up for me." I held my glass up and clinked it against his.

"No problem. Any friend of Dario's, you know."

I realized, looking at Ari, that there was a question he could answer for me. "You know, I wanted to ask you something about Sunday night, something that's been bothering me."

"What?"

I put my beer down on the table. "I can't figure out why Brad took Tommy Singer out to the beach. He took me home; why not Tommy?"

"That would be thanks to Rik," Ari said. He folded up the papers he had in front of him and put them into his briefcase. "Rik stopped by Brad's to see if he wanted to come out, but Brad's car was already gone. Your truck, however, was there in the parking lot. When Rik showed up at Sugar's, while Brad was at the bar with the college guy, he told Brad you were out there."

"That's right. I wanted to apologize."

"Brad didn't know that. Just before he left, he told me he thought you were angry, that you were waiting for him to get home to make a scene. I told him he was crazy, you weren't like that, but that's probably why he didn't go back there."

"And with Tommy Singer being a closeted college student

sharing a dorm room, they couldn't go there," I said. "Beach was the next best thing."

"Guess so," Ari said.

Well, that made me feel like crap all over again. Everything I'd done with Brad had been the wrong thing, and everything seemed to have led inexorably to his death. But like Terri said, there were so many what if's. I couldn't focus on them.

Dario came back and sat down with us.

"How's The Next Wave doing?" I asked him. "Still slow?"

"Dead," Dario said. "I took in about a thousand dollars to-day. After I pay for the merchandise, I've got just about enough left to keep the doors open. Fortunately most of my staff quit, so I don't have much in the way of a payroll."

"The silver lining is that if this goes on much longer, the commission will get nervous and want to jump-start develop-ment up here. That puts Bishop's Bluff in a good situation," Ari said.

"If we can all hold out that long." Dario took a long drink from his beer. "But enough about my troubles. So, Kimo, how are you enjoying this forced retirement of yours?"

"It's not bad," I said. "Of course I'll have to get another job eventually, but it's nice to go back to a time when all I had to worry about was the surf conditions."

Of course that wasn't true, but I was playing a part—a part I felt I had to keep playing even around an old friend like Dario. We kept on talking, and drinking. We ordered a pitcher, and it was gone much too quickly so we ordered another. We talked about surfing and the North Shore, both as it was when Dario and I were younger, and now. Ari told us a couple of stories about growing up in Minnesota, and then we started talking about what had caused us to leave home and come to the North Shore in the first place.

"I was so damn glad to leave the Big Island I think I'd have been happy on a pig farm," Dario said.

"I forgot you came from the Big Island," Ari said. "Whereabouts?"

"Kamuela," Dario said. "Also known as Waimea. The whole town's pretty much run by the Parker Ranch. My dad was the real deal, a *paniolo* his whole life, just like his daddy and his granddaddy and his great-granddaddy before him." He drank some more beer. "You can just bet how happy he was when I told him I wanted to be a surfer, not a *paniolo*."

"Probably about as happy as my dad when I told him I was leaving Minnesota," Ari said. They both looked at me.

"Sorry, my dad was a surfer when he was young, and I'm the baby, so my folks didn't get too excited when I told them I wanted to surf. They just wanted me to wait until I finished college."

Ari drained the last of the pitcher. "Another?" All three of us nodded, and he signaled the waitress. "So tell us about growing up on the ranch," he said to Dario. "You learn to ride horses, rope cattle, all that stuff?"

"You bet. I'm a rootin' tootin' dang cowboy all right." He laughed. "It sounds pretty goofy to be a Hawai'ian cowboy, but the Parker Ranch is the largest privately owned ranch in the country. Over 225,000 acres, over 50,000 head of cattle, a hundred *paniolos* to take care of it all."

"Oh, those long, lonesome nights on the range," Ari said. "Just you and the other cowboys. No womenfolk around for miles."

"It wasn't exactly a porn film," Dario said dryly. "Most of the time you're just too damn tired to think about anything besides curling up in a bedroll or a bunk house and getting some sleep."

"Oh, come on, you must have a story to tell us," I said.

"My life is not the stuff of your late-night fantasies," Dario said.

"That's right, you're a married man," Ari said.

It's a good thing I didn't have any beer in my glass, or I'd have choked on it. "Married?" I asked. "What's his name?"

"Her name is Mary," Dario said. The waitress delivered the new pitcher, and I poured a glass full and took a good long drink from it. "I like a little variety in my diet. So shoot me."

"Don't say that so loud," Ari said. "Somebody's likely to take you up on it."

"OK, Dario," I said. "Explain to me how you got married. I'm dying to hear this one. It either has to involve parental pressure or a significant amount of alcohol."

"Neither. Well, maybe a little of the first. I went home a couple of years ago and saw Mary. Her dad's a *paniolo,* too, and I've known her all her life. She's five years younger than I am, and she was just wasting away there in Kamuela, dying to get out. The only way for a girl to get out of there is to get married, so I married her and brought her over here."

"But you don't actually sleep with her," I said.

"He has a child," Ari said, and I could see the mischief dancing in his eyes.

"This is surreal," I said. I leaned in close to Ari. "He sucked my dick," I said, and as I did I realized I was probably drunker than I had thought.

Ari laughed, a big guffaw that resounded around the room. "Mine, too," he said, when he finally stopped laughing.

"I'm a bisexual," Dario said, struggling to regain some dignity.

"You're an omnisexual," Ari said. "I've seen the way your dog runs away when you come in the house."

I laughed, and Dario said, "That was uncalled for, Aristotle."

"You must only fuck her from behind," I said. "Can you pretend she's a boy from that angle?"

"This conversation is on a vertical slide," Dario said. He drained his beer, then pulled out a few bills from his wallet and dropped them on the table. "Good night, gentlemen. And I use that term loosely."

He got up and stalked out of the bar. "I guess I hurt his feelings," I said. "But considering how much my tits hurt when he was done with them, I think we're even."

"Do tell," Ari said. He scooted his chair over closer to mine and I told him the whole sorry story. A funny thing, though; the more time I spent on the North Shore, the more times I told that story, the less power it seemed to have over me. I guess that was a good thing.

We left a little while later, both of us trying to make sure the other was sober enough to drive. I made it back to Cane Landing without incident—the roads were almost completely deserted, so I probably couldn't have hit another car if I'd tried.

I barely managed to punch in the security code and stumble to the bathroom, where I found a bottle of aspirin and took a couple, along with several glasses of water. Then I collapsed into bed.

When I awoke in the morning, just as the sun was rising, I barely had a hangover, just a vague headache that I treated with more aspirin. The yards at Cane Landing were fresh with dew and the promise of a new day. I got dressed and drove down to the outrigger *halau*, to see if their Thursday morning practice was still on.

Chapter 30

RICH SARKISSIAN

WHEN I GOT DOWN TO WAIMEA BAY, I found Rich sitting on the ground fiddling with the *iako* of one of the canoes. The basic design of an outrigger is that it's a long, narrow canoe with two wooden spars sticking off to one side. Those are the *iakos*. They are attached to a long narrow piece called the *ama*, which runs parallel to the body of the canoe and helps to stabilize it.

The lashing that held one *iako* to the *ama* seemed to have come undone. "Need a hand with that?" I asked.

"You know anything about it?" Rich asked. "'Cause I sure don't. Tepano's the one who knows about maintaining the canoes, but he told me he was heading to Honolulu until things get better up here."

"I helped build an outrigger when I was in high school," I said, sitting down across from him. "Not anything fancy, and we had the teacher telling us what to do, but I think I still remember."

I took over from Rich. "Are you a native Hawai'ian?" Rich asked, as I tied the *iako* to the *ama*. It was tricky, and I had to remember how it all went together, something I'd promptly forgotten as soon as the project was finished.

"Part," I said, trying to focus on what I was doing. "My father's father was full Hawai'ian, and his mother was *haole*. So that makes my dad fifty percent. My mom's father was Japanese, and her mother was Hawai'ian. So she's fifty percent too. That means my brothers and I end up at fifty percent too. Which is really interesting only because in order to be recognized as a native Hawai'ian, under state law, you have to be fifty percent."

I finished tying the *iako*. "That should do," I said. "How about you? What's your ethnic breakdown? Your name's what, Armenian?"

"Yup. All my grandparents came from Turkey, trying to get away from massacres. I grew up in this totally Armenian little town in New Jersey. Armenian church, all the old people speaking with funny accents. Almost every person in town had a name that ended in ian."

"Must be weird for you to be here, where it's such a melting pot." We both stood up and started carrying the canoe toward the water.

"I think it's cool. I hated everybody being the same back home." He shrugged. "I guess that's why I joined the army. To go someplace where people were different."

"Well, you certainly found a place here where people are different," I said. "Although there aren't a whole lot of people around at the moment." I looked around; where there had been twenty people at the *halau* the first day I'd shown up, now it was just Rich and me.

"How come you haven't gone back to Honolulu?" Rich asked me. "You're not scared?"

I shrugged. "I used to be a cop, remember. I've had people shoot at me before. I don't particularly like it, but you have to get philosophical after a while or you freak out. When it's my time to go, I'll go. Until then, I have to get up every morning, get dressed, and get on with my life." We picked up the canoe and started carrying it toward the water. "How about you?" I asked. "How come you're still here?"

"I'm the anti-surfer," he said, with a little laugh. "If anybody's killing off surfers, they aren't going to aim for me."

"You're assuming they were all killed because they were surfers," I said. "It could be some other reason altogether, just a coincidence that they all surfed. And as a matter of fact, Brad Jacobson didn't surf at all."

"But he was with someone who did," Rich said, as we lowered the canoe into the water. "You won't catch me making that mistake."

Melody showed up then, along with a couple of others, enough to fill one canoe. "This place is like a ghost town," Melody said. "I never thought I'd see all the surfers chased away."

"If it was up to me, I'd chase them all away," Rich said, as we were pushing the canoe into the water.

"You don't mean that," Melody said, jumping into the front of the boat. "You were a surfer once yourself. You can't hate surfers all that much."

"Try me," Rich said, and then we were all in the boat, paddling out past the breakers, and there was no more idle conversation. We did a couple of runs up and down the Anahulu River, and then we did a few in and outs, catching a wave and riding it back in, then paddling out and doing it all over.

It wasn't surfing, but it was pretty close. Riding atop a wave like that, the coastline rushing in toward you, the spray in your face and the sun above you. If something happened to me, like Rich, and I couldn't surf again, I'd definitely find myself in outriggers.

It was interesting, I thought, as I sat behind Rich and paddled, that I was starting to like him. Underneath the anti-surfer bluster was a real person.

Of course, I've learned over time that you can be a really nice person and still be a murderer, a rapist, an arsonist, or a child molester. But it always makes it harder for me to really hate a suspect if I start to feel like he (or she) is a human being.

We paddled for a while, but without another canoe to race against there wasn't a lot of fun in it, and eventually we beached the canoe. Rich and I volunteered to carry it in and hose it down before putting it in the storage shed.

"So why do you hate surfers so much?" I asked, as he unfurled the hose.

"I used to surf," he said. He pointed to his leg. "Can't anymore. Everybody thinks that's why I hate them."

"But that's not it."

He shook his head. "You saw where I work. Mr. Clark's property. I see the way the surfers treat the place. Like it's theirs to destroy." I turned the spigot on and Rich began spraying the canoe. I turned it as needed so we could get all the salt water off.

"What do you mean?"

"If the surf's up, surfers will drive right up on the beach, they'll drag their boards across the sand, tear up the vegetation. They don't care if they cross private property. All they care about is catching a wave. That's not right."

"I know a lot of surfers who do care about private property, who do respect the environment," I said. "You can't characterize all of us like that."

"All I know is that my job would be a lot easier, and the property a lot better off, if there were no surfers up here at all."

It felt good working out there in the sunshine, the sweat and salt water drying on my skin. I decided to push Rich a little, see what he had to say. "Somebody told me you used to work at The Next Wave," I said.

"Yeah."

"I just find it hard to picture you working in a surf shop."

"It was when I first moved up here," he said. He motioned to me and I turned the canoe upside down. "I used to know Dario, before I went into the army, and I looked him up when I got up here."

"Interesting," I said. "I used to know Dario a long time ago, too."

"I didn't know him that way," Rich said. "He tried, but I wasn't interested."

"Man," I said. "Who the hell hasn't Dario screwed, or tried to screw, on the North Shore?"

"There are a couple of chickens out back of Bishop Clark's place," Rich said, laughing. He swung his arm and I righted the canoe again. "But I think it's just that Dario hasn't gotten around to them yet."

I laughed too. "So what did you do there? Don't tell me you sold surfboards."

"No, I never sunk that low. I worked in the outdoor gear department. Until I let my temper get the best of me when this surfer asshole got on me about my leg."

"Wow."

I turned the hose off and began coiling it up as Rich stood the canoe on end to drain the water. "Dario was cool about it, and the guy decided not to press charges, but it was clear I couldn't work there anymore. Dario hooked me up with Bishop."

"Don't tell me Dario and Bishop . . ."

Rich laughed again. He looked like a whole different person when he laughed. "Not that I know of. They've got some real estate deal together."

"Oh, yeah, that's right. He showed us the plans." I'd forgotten for the moment that Dario was an investor in Ari's plan to develop Bishop's property. The whole North Shore seemed to be related in some way or another.

We stowed the boat away and Rich peeled off toward the other side of the lot. "See you around."

"Yeah, see you."

I was sure Dario would tell me the rest of the story about Rich and The Next Wave, so I headed down there, where Dario was sitting at the empty cappuccino bar. "Let me make you a latte," he said, when I walked in. "Put me out of my misery."

"When you phrase it like that," I said. "With extra whipped cream?"

"Only if I get to pick where I put it."

I smiled. "Do you ever stop thinking about sex, Dario?"

"It stops me thinking about bankruptcy."

"Surely you aren't going to go bankrupt after a couple of bad days," I said, sitting down at the counter across from where he was acting the barista. "What do you do when we get a stretch of bad weather?"

"Bad weather is my best friend," he said. "It pulls the surfers off the beach and into the store. This is like a month of blue skies and *mauka* trades."

He handed me the coffee. "You been out on the water yet today?"

"At the outrigger *halau*," I said. "I met a guy there used to work for you."

"Rich Sarkissian," he said. "Rich-punch-the-customer-in-the-kisser-ian."

"He really did that?"

"In front of my very eyes," Dario said. He leaned back against the cabinets behind him. Today he had a barista's apron on over his logo T-shirt. There was not a single customer in the store, and as far as I could see Dario was the only employee on duty.

"Not that the guy didn't have it coming," Dario continued. "Made a rude crack about Rich's leg. But still, I couldn't keep Rich here after that. Rich was damn lucky the customer didn't press charges. I had to go over and see him at the place where he was staying and have a little chat with him. I told him the case could drag on long beyond surfing season, and convinced him the judge wouldn't look too kindly on someone who made fun of the handicapped."

I wondered what else Dario had done to seal the deal, as I sipped the coffee. It was pretty good, better than what the regular barista made. "You referred Rich to Bishop?"

Dario nodded. "Bishop was going crazy with surfers traipsing all over his land, and we were worried that if he didn't enforce his property line somebody might claim an easement, the right to get to the water. Rich was low on cash and needed a job, and it seemed like a good match."

A good match indeed, I thought, since Bishop Clark had a collection of firearms, and Rich Sarkissian seemed like the kind of guy who could use most, if not all, of them. The only real question was, how good a shot would he be—good enough to shoot a surfer off his board? The doorbell rang and Dario pounced on a potential customer, leaving me to my latte, and my thoughts.

Chapter 31

BACK TO WAHIAWA

WHILE I WAS AT THE NEXT WAVE, I figured I might as well fire up my laptop and check for e-mail. There was a message from Sampson with a reminder about our meeting in Wahiawa at two, as well as a copy of the ballistics results.

Brad Jacobson and Tommy Singer had been killed with a rapid-fire pistol, probably a Beretta. Crime scene investigation had revealed that they had both been fully clothed when shot, though very close to each other, and both had been dispatched with multiple bullets to the brain. Quick, relatively painless deaths. The killer had then stripped them down, posed them, and quickly rinsed their clothes in the ocean.

It was definitely the work of an unstable mind, and it bothered me. The first three murders had been cold and efficient; the motivation here was a lot murkier. There was no clear connection between the murders I'd been sent to the North Shore to investigate and these two; virtually everything was different. The only links were the location—Brad's and Tommy's bodies had been found at Pipeline, and Mike had been shot there—and the fact that like the first three, Tommy was a surfer, although in an entirely different class.

But I had some gut feeling, similar to the one Sampson had, that these murders were all related. It was possible that the first three killings had been steps in a process that un-hinged the killer—with each death, he or she became progres-sively unstable, leading to the weirdness surrounding Brad's and Tommy's deaths.

That was very spooky, because it meant that a killer whose brain was increasingly deteriorating was loose on the North Shore with a wide selection of weapons at his or her disposal.

Along with the ballistics results, Sampson had included some basic information on Rich Sarkissian, including his ad-dress, which I had been unable to find myself—his phone was unlisted, and as a renter, he wasn't listed in any of the prop-erty records I could search. I didn't know how Sampson had found the address, but I was glad he had.

I went out to my truck and got my street map of the North Shore; Rich's address seemed to be on a rise overlooking Kawailoa Beach, not far from Bishop Clark's place. I decided I'd swing past on my way to Wahiawa. Maybe I could peek through the windows, see the murder weapon lying out on a table, and solve the whole case before lunch. Unlikely, but a boy can dream.

I figured that Rich would already be at Bishop's, but I still tried to be careful as I cruised past his place. It was a cute little cottage, perched on a bluff with what I figured was a fabulous view of the ocean and the few surfers who were already out on the waves, daring both the Pacific and the possibility of get-ting shot off their boards.

It was kind of ironic that, hating surfers as he did, Rich's front windows had a perfect view of them. As I looked around, I wondered idly how Rich could afford to live in such a place. Sampson's notes had indicated that Rich was a renter, and I knew from the signs up at Fujioka's that a place like his was pretty expensive. It was possible, of course, that he had some kind of deal, the way I did at Cane Landing. Perhaps Bishop Clark owned the property and it was part of Rich's salary.

But I remembered Terri saying that Bishop had pretty much run through his inheritance and sold off everything he owned except that beachfront property. So it was unlikely that he owned the cottage. I made a note to check the property records myself.

Where could Rich get the money to afford a place like that, I kept wondering, as I drove down to the beach. The first answer that sprung to my mind was the same place Lucie Zamora got the money to afford her designer clothing—crystal meth. I wondered if Rich knew Lucie.

Perhaps Rich had been killing off his competition. Maybe Mike, Lucie, and Ronnie had all been crystal meth dealers, and Rich had killed them off to corner the market?

The flip side to that was that someone else had been doing the killings, and Rich himself might be a target.

But Tommy Singer didn't connect to any of them—Mike, Lucie, Ronnie, or Rich. How did he fit in? I felt sure that there was some connection I was still missing, and that was the one that would point me in the right direction.

I headed toward the Kam Highway for the trip south. I tried not to think about what was going to happen, but by the time I arrived at the station I couldn't avoid it. Most likely, Ruiz and Kawamoto wouldn't be happy about getting outside help. I know if I was in their position, I wouldn't want anyone else butting in on my case.

It was one thing to get help from an outside source, an expert, say. And if I'd been undercover on this case from day one, the way you might be on a drug case, then no one would have any cause for resentment. But now it would be clear to Ruiz and Kawamoto that Sampson wasn't happy with their progress, didn't trust them, and felt they needed somebody else.

Me. That was the second part of the equation. I wasn't exactly everybody's favorite person around the station. My sexuality and my notoriety combined to make me an outcast. Sampson would not have an easy time bringing me back inside; but that's why he was the lieutenant.

The best thing would be for the detectives to accept me and leave me on my own. I'd be happy to report in, pass along whatever I found out. I didn't need to be on the inside, looking over their shoulders, questioning everything they did. I just had to make them understand that.

Though I knew it was the coward's way out, I waited in the parking lot for Sampson, so we were able to go inside together and meet with Ruiz and Kawamoto immediately. He was wearing what I had come to realize was one of his trademark polo shirts, this one black, with gray slacks. He did not look happy.

"I don't like to do this, Kimo," he said to me in the parking lot, looking around to make sure no one could hear us. "But I'm going to ask you to keep an eye on these guys. If you pass on information, I want to know that they have run with it as necessary. Any time you feel they're ignoring you, I want to hear about it."

"I need to know what I'm walking into, Lieutenant. Do you suspect something is going on?"

He frowned. "I just don't know. But I looked at the evidence you came up with, and I don't see why Kevin and Al didn't find out at least some of it. I mean, you just looked the three surfers up on the Internet and found they'd all been in Mexico, right?"

I nodded.

"So why couldn't they? Jesus, they've got computers, and they've both been to training classes. They aren't stupid guys—they've got a damned good clearance rate. Which makes me think there's something fishy going on." He looked at his watch. "I've got to be back at headquarters in an hour, so we're going to have to make this quick. Come on."

Sampson led me inside, and once we met with Kevin Ruiz and Al Kawamoto, he got right to the point. "You guys told me you were having trouble getting information," he said. "You thought that the surfers up here didn't trust cops and wouldn't tell you what you needed to know. Am I right?"

Kawamoto's posture, slouched back in his chair, accentuated his fat belly and made him seem even more like a dumb country boy. That was reinforced when he started to argue, and Sampson cut him off. "Am I right?"

"Yes," Ruiz said. Ruiz, on the other hand, was still looking slick, as if he'd visited some fancy men's clothing store on his way to work.

"So I brought somebody in who could talk to the surfers for you. Contrary to popular belief, Detective Kanapa'aka did not turn in his badge. Instead, he has been working undercover to supplement your efforts."

Kawamoto started to speak, but Sampson held up his hand. "Notice I said supplement, not replace," he said. "Kanapa'aka has been reporting directly to me. He's now prepared to share everything he has found with you, with the idea that you will remain the primaries on this case, and he will remain undercover. But from now on, he will pass his information directly to you. Are we understood?"

"Yes, sir," Ruiz said. "I spoke to Detective Kanapa'aka yesterday and I was impressed with the information he had gathered. He e-mailed some materials to me yesterday evening that I think can help us move along our investigation. I'm sure we will all be able to work together." He shot a look at his partner that I'm pretty sure Sampson missed, one that said, 'keep your mouth shut.'

"Good. I'll leave you to it, then." He got up and walked out of the room.

"I've only worked for him for a couple of weeks," I said. "He always like this?"

"He wants results," Ruiz said. "We haven't delivered. You have."

I pulled out my notes, really just a rehash of what I had e-mailed the evening before. "OK, I'm ready if you are."

Kawamoto was largely silent the whole time Ruiz and I talked. I went over every step of my investigation with them, beginning with the lucky break of running into Brad Jacobson at the North Shore Marketplace.

"I thought there was something fishy about your story, but I figured it had to do with sex," Ruiz said. "Like you met him in a chat room or an X-rated bookstore."

"You were right, I was holding out," I said. "But not anymore." I walked them through Brad's makeover one more time, then meeting up at the bar with all his friends.

"Like a gay grapevine," Ruiz said, nodding. "We could never have tapped into that."

"He tapped into it with his dick," Kawamoto snorted.

I stood up. Though my heart was racing, I tried to keep my voice calm. "I'm only going to say this once," I said. "I know you don't like me, and that's OK. We aren't going to come out of this as drinking buddies. But I earned my badge just like you did, and I expect you to respect me. If you can't do that, I have nothing more to say."

"I don't have to like you or respect you," Kawamoto said.

"But I do have to work with your faggot ass, so sit back down and stop throwing a hissy fit."

"I'll throw your fat ass through that door if you call me a faggot one more time." I paused. "And I won't bother to open it first."

"Ladies, ladies," Ruiz said. "Let's all be friends here, all right? Kimo, you work for Lieutenant Sampson, and Al, you do too. Let's agree not to talk stink about each other, at least for as long as this investigation goes on? Please?"

He looked at Kawamoto, who didn't say anything for a long beat. Finally he said, "All right."

"Kimo?"

"Fine by me." I sat down again, and laid out for them what I had learned from each one of Brad's friends.

"Let's talk about this guy you say hates surfers," Ruiz said. "What's his name?"

"Rich Sarkissian." I showed them what Sampson had dug up on Rich. "I haven't had a chance to go through it all, but I will. For now, he's the only strong lead I have."

"You have a connection to The Next Wave, too," Ruiz said. "Lucie worked there, and your guy said that's where he thought her drugs came from. Why don't we see if we can do anything with that information."

"We can cross-reference with Vice," Kawamoto said, finally contributing something useful to the conversation. "See if any other known dealers have connections there."

We agreed that they would continue the up-front investigation, as well as looking into The Next Wave. I would keep looking into Rich Sarkissian, and keep surfing, hoping somebody would swim along who had the clue we were looking for.

Chapter 32

INVESTIGATING RICH

DRIVING BACK UP TO HALEIWA, I felt a surprising sense of relief. I hadn't liked working behind the backs of fellow detectives, even if I didn't particularly care for them, like Al Kawamoto. And it was good to know that I was no longer alone on this investigation, that I had Ruiz and Kawamoto to back me up if I needed them.

I stopped off at The Next Wave for a cappuccino and to go over my notes and see what I was missing. The only employee on the floor of the store was Ellie, an older woman whom I'd most recently seen as a barista at the Kope Bean. "Had to close down," she said, making me a mochachino. "No more customers. Luckily Dario hired me."

"Where is he?"

"In the office," she said, nodding toward the rear of the store. "Been there ever since opening. Even when I call back there and tell him I need help with customers, he doesn't budge."

I took my coffee back to his office and knocked on the closed door. There was no answer, so I tried the handle. The door was locked. "Dario?" I called. "It's Kimo."

"I'm busy," he called from behind the door. "Go away."

I considered saying, "I'll let you suck my dick if you open

the door," but decided that probably wasn't my wisest move. Instead I went back to the coffee bar, which Ellie had abandoned to ring up a pair of sunglasses for a *haole* tourist at the front register.

Dario's business was going downhill fast, as were a lot of businesses on the North Shore. If I didn't find the killer soon, the economy of the whole area might crumple, leaving a lot of people out of work and in dire financial straits. Not to mention Dario's sanity, which seemed to be evaporating as fast as his business.

I recapped what I had learned, trying to put it all into perspective. The chain of events seemed to begin with Lucie Zamora, a girl with dreams who needed money. She had begun selling ice, getting her supply from someone at The Next Wave. Ruiz and Kawamoto were going to check with Vice on that. I entertained the thought briefly that her contact could be Dario himself, but I decided that was wishful thinking on my part. If I still felt threatened by him in some way, I couldn't depend on the law to lock him up. He was my problem to deal with.

Lucie had probably recruited Mike Pratt and Ronnie Chang to bring back crystal meth after attending the Mexpipe competition. I would see Harry the next day and find out if his snooping into their bank accounts revealed anything, but I already had anecdotal evidence, from Trish and Will Wong, that both had extra cash on hand after their trip.

Something had gone wrong after they returned from Mexico. Mike had been upset about the damage to his board, and his experience with the Christian surfers in Mexico might have given him bad feelings on moral grounds, too. Either way, he had been complaining and somebody might have seen the need to shut him up.

Lucie and Ronnie had been killed a few days later. Had Lucie figured something out about Mike's murder and challenged the killer? She was just ballsy enough, and cash-hungry enough, to have tried a blackmail scheme. Perhaps she had implicated Ronnie, relying on his computer experience to track her supplier's funds.

If that was the case, it was a wrong move on her part, because it had gotten them both killed. But I still stumbled when I came to a connection between those three murders, and the killing of Brad Jacobson and Tommy Singer. I closed my eyes and tried to let my mind run free. Where was that elusive connection?

Suddenly, with an electric jolt, my eyes popped open. Could it be that I was the connection? I had been sent to the North Shore to investigate the three murders. Suppose the killer knew that, and wanted to throw me off the track. So he or she killed Brad, knowing of my relationship with him? That was bound to put a whole new spin on things—maybe even to remove me from the investigation.

It was a strange idea, but not the strangest. There were many cases on record where a killer had attacked someone close to an investigator, either as a warning, a tease, or a distraction. Who knew I was investigating these murders? Who could have been threatened?

I started making a list. I had talked to Trish, Melody, Rich Sarkissian, Palani Anderson, and Tepano about Mike Pratt. Frank, Lucie's old boyfriend, the bartender at the Drainpipe, had filled me in on her life and directed me toward Butterfly. Brad and his circle of friends—Jeremy, Ari, Rik, George, and Larry—all knew I was looking into her death. Since Ari was in business with both Dario and Bishop Clark, I had to assume that they might have heard from him, at least in passing. I had talked to Ronnie's parents, his high school teacher Victor Texeira, and his old friend Will Wong, as well as his boss, Pierre Lewin. I'd spoken with Lucie's mother, too.

The only people, besides Lieutenant Sampson, who knew I was officially undercover were Terri and Harry, but both of them were so far removed from the case I couldn't imagine them having an impact. Anyone on the first list, though, could have been the killer, or could have passed the word on to the killer that I was nosing around.

My cappuccino had gone cold. I threw it away and drove back up to Cane Landing, where I spent the next couple of hours going through all the material Sampson had sent, searching for something that would be a clear implication of Rich Sarkissian. He knew I was nosing around, asking questions about Mike, and it was certainly possible that he could have heard I was looking into Lucie, too, either from Bishop Clark, his employer, or Dario Fonseca, his previous employer.

I let my mind wander on Rich Sarkissian. I knew he was jealous of surfers, that he hated the way they trespassed over Bishop Clark's land. Could the case be as simple as that—despite everything else I'd discovered, perhaps Rich had simply killed Mike, Lucie, Ronnie, and Tommy because they'd all trespassed. Brad had just been in the wrong place at the wrong time.

Or maybe Rich was dealing ice, too. Those prosthetics had to be expensive, and he lived in a lovely cottage that he certainly couldn't afford on a security guard's salary. Maybe he had killed the first three as part of a turf war. He certainly had access to a lot of weaponry in Bishop's cabinet.

But it was a far cry from anger over trespassing to murder,

and there was nothing that tied Rich to either Brad or Tommy. Unless, as I reminded myself, Brad and Tommy had been killed to put me off the scent.

It was incredibly frustrating. I felt that the solution was there, just beyond my reach. A storm swept in from the center of the island, rain lashing at the French doors, and the upset in the weather seemed to mirror the turmoil in my brain. I spent a couple more hours going over the material on Rich, reading it again and again and getting nothing new. After dark I tried to read a novel, and then to watch TV, but I couldn't focus on anything.

Friday morning I surfed, hoping I could accomplish two things. First, that being out on the water would help clear my brain. And second, that some random surfer would come up to me with the solution to the mystery. Neither happened. I finally quit around noon, stopped at Fujioka's for some weekend food supplies, and was on my way back to Cane Landing when Harry called my cell phone to say he was passing Matsumoto's and needed further directions.

I met Harry at the entrance to Cane Landing and buzzed him through the gate. "Your surf killer is all over the news in Honolulu," he said, as I helped him carry his stuff into the house. "They say people have left the North Shore in droves."

"You'll see when we get out to Pipeline," I said. "The place is deserted."

I showed Harry to the guest room. "Your mother called me this morning and she sounded pretty frantic," he said. "She really wants you back home."

"She called you?"

"She wanted me to persuade you to give up and come home. I told her you wouldn't leave until you were ready." He paused. "I got that information we discussed. But I don't think it's anything you didn't already know."

"Then we can look it over later. Right now I think we should just go surf."

We grabbed our boards and headed for Pipeline, where we got in a couple of hours of heavenly surfing, the beach almost totally to ourselves.

"Man, I've never seen it this empty," Harry said, when we finally took a break and collapsed on the sand. "I don't think I've ever caught so many big waves in one day in my life."

"And you have a serial killer to thank for it."

We rested in the warm sun, then surfed for a little longer. Around four o'clock we dragged ourselves and our boards back up to Cane Landing, where after showers and a couple of Kona lagers we were ready to tackle dinner. I'd bought steaks, which we fixed on the fancy grill in the house's backyard, accompanied by grilled peppers and baked potatoes. Finally, we sat down at Harry's laptop a little after eight.

He brought up some spreadsheets he'd created after looking at bank records for Mike Pratt, Lucie Zamora, and Ronnie Chang. Lucie's was the most interesting, because there was almost no activity there. She made the occasional cash deposit, and wrote checks for things like the HECO bill—Hawai'i Electric Company—and the phone bill, to Verizon. No checks to Butterfly, no checks that resembled rent or car payments. Like Brad had said, Lucie was a cash basis customer.

Both Mike and Ronnie had made large cash deposits shortly after they returned from Mexico. Mike had made two deposits, about a week apart, for $5,000 each. "The government requires the bank to fill out forms for amounts larger than ten grand," Harry said. "That's probably why he split it up."

Ronnie had made one deposit, for nearly $7,000. We figured he'd spent the rest on gifts for Lucie and his new board.

"What do you think Lucie did with her ten grand?" Harry asked.

I shrugged. "No clue. But she might not have had the money yet—remember all that crystal meth that I found in her apartment. Maybe she was holding out for a higher price, or waiting for demand to go up.

"This is all interesting, but there's another guy I'm interested in now," I said. I told him what I knew about Rich, what I'd learned from Sampson's reports, my own searches, and my conversations with Dario and with Rich himself.

Harry logged on to the Internet. "What do you want to know?"

"For starters, I'm curious now to know who owns that house where Rich lives, and if there's any way to find out if he pays rent, and how much he pays."

"You can't start out with something simple, like where he went to school?" Harry grumbled. But he applied himself to the laptop, and not too much later he said, "The house is owned by the Sandwich Islands Trust. Isn't that Terri's family foundation?"

"Yup." I frowned. "So it's probably a Bishop deal, like Dario said. So much for my theory that Rich is living off drug money."

"Nobody says he isn't. It's just that if the Clarks own the house where he lives, he's probably not paying much rent."

Harry applied himself to the computer again. When he looked up, he said, "You aren't going to be able to use this information in court. I just want to let you know before you see it."

I shrugged. "If I get some real evidence, I can always get subpoenas."

"Well, you can't tell anyone you've seen this."

"Come on, Harry. What did you find? Pornographic pictures?"

"Nope. His bank statement." He swiveled the screen around toward me.

"Jesus, Harry! I didn't know you could crack the bank's computer system right in front of me!"

"Uh-huh. Well, now you know. I'm getting good at this stuff—this is my fourth break-in in the last couple of weeks." He pointed at the screen. "Unfortunately, if Mr. Sarkissian is raking in drug money, he's keeping it under his mattress, not in his checking account."

Rich's balance looked like mine, right after I've paid all my bills. A five-figure number—if you counted the numbers after the period. "I don't even want to know how you got in there," I said. "But you'd better get out quickly."

Chapter 33

BANKING WITH DARIO

HARRY HIT A KEY and the screen disappeared.

"Umm . . . Harry . . ." I said. "How about we try Dario Fonseca's account?" I knew I was stepping over a line there, but I had been ignoring Dario, in the face of mounting evidence, for a long time. At first I'd been reluctant to consider that he was involved because I had such strong feelings about him—I worried that they were coloring my judgment. Then I had waited for Ruiz and Kawamoto to come up with a link to The Next Wave through the District 2 vice cops, but nothing had been forthcoming. It was time for me to get over my personal feelings and do the digging I had to.

I rationalized it a little by the nature of being undercover. If I was in Ruiz's position, or Kawamoto's, I could get a subpoena for these records. And I certainly could ask them, and then wait. And wait. Or I could get over those scruples and set Harry loose.

"With pleasure." He leaned over the keyboard again. I noticed that his dark hair, which usually fell into his eyes, didn't anymore; probably Arleen's influence. Harry had met Dario a few times in the past, and they'd never gotten along. He had always suspected that Dario had something to do with my decision to quit surfing and go to the police academy.

His dislike of Dario had been cemented when I had finally confessed, not too long before, the story of what had happened between Dario and me. "I can't believe you're still willing to be friends with that guy," he said, as he tapped the keys. "I've been telling you for years there's something not quite right about him."

"He has his good points," I said. "He got me this house, didn't he?"

"Actually, your friend Ari is the one who arranged the house. Dario only made a phone call."

"But he didn't have to make it. And he stuck up for Rich Sarkissian over that punching incident."

"Saving his own neck," Harry said, continuing to talk while he hunched over his laptop. "Protecting his store from a lawsuit. Hello!"

I looked over his shoulder. We were looking at Dario's bank account, and the balance wasn't that much bigger than Rich's. "He must have more accounts," I said. "How about the store?"

"All his accounts are linked," Harry said. He pulled up a summary page. There was an account for the store, and then a joint account with America Fonseca. "Who's that, his mom?"

"Probably his wife," I said. Harry looked up, and his mouth was open like a fish's. "Yeah, that's the way I reacted the first time I heard he was married."

"But I thought he was . . . you know."

"Gay. Turns out he's bi. Or, as Ari says, omnisexual. That Dario will fuck anything that doesn't run away."

"Jesus." Harry shook his head.

"Him, too, probably," I said. "Hard to run when you're nailed to a cross."

"That's just sacrilegious," Harry said.

"You're a Buddhist."

"Yeah, a Buddhist with good manners."

"Back to Dario," I said. "How can he be so short of cash?"

"Give me Ari's full name," Harry said. I spelled it for him.

"Hold on a minute," he said. "I recognize that name. Remember that guy you asked me to look up, Harry Pincus?"

I nodded. Harry applied himself to the laptop again. "I think it's the same guy," he said. "In 1999 Harry Pincus was arrested in Minneapolis on federal charges—basically a bunch of financial crimes relating to the viatical business." He looked up at me. "You know what that is?"

I shook my head. "Basically, it's the selling of insurance policy death benefits, at less than face value, by a terminally ill person to a third party. Now, that's not illegal—but there are lots of scams. Our Mr. Pincus was accused of recruiting AIDS patients in Minneapolis, getting them to sign up for life insurance with companies that didn't require a physical exam, then buying their benefits."

"That's creepy. And illegal?"

"Well, signing up for insurance under false pretenses is. But see what happened is that these patients weren't dying, and Pincus couldn't cash in. He couldn't pay his investors— the people who put up the cash to buy those benefits—because the patients weren't dying. That's when he started fiddling with the money, and attracted the attention of the Feds. Eventually, though, he filed for bankruptcy and the Feds realized they couldn't make a case, so they dropped the charges." He took a final swig from his beer. "He changed his name and moved to Hawaii three years ago."

"Somehow Lucie found out about Ari's past," I said. "She did some work for him, and we know she was nosy. But was she blackmailing him? Or was she just holding the information for future use?"

"Perhaps his bank account will tell us."

Ari, at least, had some money in his account, although there was a lot of money flowing in and out. "He's trying to put together a deal for Bishop Clark's land," I said. "So he's probably paying architects and lawyers. I know Dario is one of his investors."

"If that's the case, then we should be able to match the transactions," Harry said. I went to the kitchen and got us another couple of beers while Harry went back and forth between the two accounts. While I drank and occasionally peered over his shoulder, he punched keys and made notes on a pad. Finally he was done.

"OK, I was able to see a pattern here," he said, showing me the pad. "Starting about six months ago, Ari started getting deposits into this account from what looks like three different sources. Each source puts in $25,000 at a time."

"That's a nice chunk of change."

"Especially because each source has put in about $225,000 so far. I can match up Dario's withdrawals with Ari's deposits in each case. Now, every month for the last six months, Dario has transferred $25,000 to Ari. And each time, he makes five cash deposits of $5,000 each just before the transfer."

"Why not just one deposit in the right amount?"

"Remember what I said earlier? Because the bank has to report transactions greater than or equal to $10,000. And by the way, making small deposits like this is also illegal. It's called structuring."

"Who ever expected you'd be the one telling me what's illegal."

"Since Dario probably doesn't want to show where he got that cash, he makes deposits into his account that go under the radar." He showed me a number of other big deposits Dario had made in cash, all of them under $10,000. "Now where do you think he gets all that cash from? Selling surfboards and cappuccinos?"

The wheels were turning in my head, and I didn't like the direction they were going. "Back at the station, when we see somebody making large cash deposits, we figure that money usually comes from drugs."

"It's hard for me to imagine Dario standing out in the parking lot of The Next Wave peddling nickel bags."

"Dario doesn't do retail," I said. "He must be the middleman. The contact Lucie had at The Next Wave who supplied her with merchandise. He may even be the one who commissioned her to go to Mexpipe and bring drugs back. I'll bet he's got a whole lot of Lucie Zamoras out selling."

"Selling what? Dope? Heroin?"

"Ice," I said. "That's what Rik said Lucie was selling. And I know they make crystal meth in Mexico, which is where the first three victims all went a little while before they died. There's probably a lab somewhere here on the North Shore that converts the crystal into ice."

"There's no way the cash just comes from the store?" Harry asked.

I shook my head. "I've been in and out of that store a lot over the last couple of weeks, and most of the big transactions I've seen are on credit cards. Sure, people buy lattes for cash, but I'm guessing most of his sales are plastic."

I sat back and thought. "Rik said Lucie's source was at the store. I suppose it could be Dario. But I just don't like it."

"You don't like it because Dario's your friend," Harry said.

"No, I don't like it because I don't like Dario," I said. "I'm scared that I'm trying to pin something on him just because he raped me ten years ago."

Harry shook his head. "I think the numbers show it's got to be him."

"What are these numbers over here?" I asked, pointing to a different column of figures.

"About four months ago, Dario took out an equity line against the store. He's already drawn down nearly a hundred thousand on that line."

"Wow."

"Yeah. And it's all going into Ari's account. Have they been running up extra expenses?"

"I know they've run into zoning problems and deed restrictions on Bishop's land. Maybe that's why they've needed extra cash."

"Dario's about to run into a big problem," Harry said. "See here, these are the store revenues. With business taking such a steep dive, there's no way he'll be able to afford the expense of running the store, paying for merchandise, paying his help, and paying the debt service on this equity loan. He must be sweating bullets right now."

I got up and started walking around the living room. "I'm trying to get my head around this," I said. "If Dario's selling ice out of The Next Wave, why isn't he rolling in cash?"

"Because he's pumping it all into Ari's real estate deal."

"Why would he do that, though? Ice's a profitable business. Why risk all his capital?"

"To make himself legit?" Harry asked. "Nobody arrests you for building condos these days."

"Or it's a place to put a lot of spare cash," I said. "Until the deal with Bishop started running into trouble, and then suddenly Dario's business dried up."

"The ice business is probably sucking now, too," Harry said, "with everybody leaving the North Shore."

"Both his businesses are going south, to coin a phrase."

I sat down on the sofa. Harry turned toward me and we both just sat there looking at each other for a long time.

Chapter 34

SHARPSHOOTER

THE IDEA THAT DARIO WAS DEALING ICE out of The Next Wave, and had been doing so literally under my nose for the last couple of weeks, threw me for a loop, and I was having trouble processing the information. Or maybe it was the beer. Either way, the best I could do was suggest we get some sleep and try to think more about the problem in the morning.

Harry was suitably impressed with the guest room, and he was still asleep when I woke at first light on Saturday. I didn't feel rested at all; I had spent most of the evening rolling around in bed, trying to get comfortable, thoughts about Dario moving back and forth across my brain.

"There's something I think is really scary about Dario as a suspect," I said, as I made pancakes for us for breakfast. "I had this weird idea the other day—which isn't seeming so weird anymore—that whoever killed the first three got scared when he or she found out I was investigating these murders."

"Kimo, do you really think it's possible a woman is the killer?"

I shrugged. "Probably not."

"Then stopping being so English major on me. You don't have to be politically and grammatically correct all the time."

"Point taken. So I had this idea that maybe the killer shot Brad and Tommy Singer to throw me off the track."

"Not such a weird idea."

"No, I guess not. But suppose it gets weirder. Dario told me the other day that he likes me."

"Yo, dude, the guy got you drunk and had sex with you ten years ago, and he's been coming on to you ever since you got up here. I'd say he likes you."

"Suppose he was jealous, though. Suppose he killed Brad and Tommy, and stripped them down and all, out of some weird jealous rage?"

Harry shook his head. "I don't know why anybody does anything, brah. You want the touchy-feely, you've got to talk to Terri. You have any more hacking, you ask me."

"How 'bout we just go surf, then," I said, and we did. Since it was Saturday I knew it wouldn't be easy to get hold of Ruiz or Kawamoto, so I thought I'd let my ideas about Dario gestate for a few days. He'd been around the North Shore for a long time, and he wasn't going anywhere. Plus I had to practice restraining myself from telling the world about my long history with Dario Fonseca—or even about what had happened between us in his office a few days before. I didn't want it to start looking like I'd had sex with every victim and villain on the North Shore.

The beaches were less empty than they'd been. Human beings have short memories, and surfers are only human. I could see from the number of cars on Ke Nui Road and the number of boards out in the water that people were starting to come back, even if there was a crazed killer out there. Good for business, if nothing else; The Next Wave would be buzzing again like it had before.

We surfed, with breaks, for a couple of hours. I saw people

I knew—my cousin Ben; Frank, the bartender from the Drain-pipe; even Tepano, the Hawai'ian guy from the outrigger club. Everybody was delighted that the beach was so un-crowded, and nobody was particularly worried about a crazed killer on the loose. Harry and I went to Rosie's Cantina for lunch, stopped at The Next Wave for our caffeine fixes, and then went back to Pipeline to surf some more.

From the top of a wave, you can often get a clear view of the shore, if you're not too busy struggling to maintain your bal-ance or place your next turn. I was surfing smoothly, so I had a chance to look up at the beach. I just had enough time to make out the barrel of a rifle pointing out at me before the wave dipped unexpectedly and I went down.

I'd like to say I heard the rifle, but since I was tumbling head over heels into the center of a wave, there's no way I could have. But as soon as I surfaced, I walked the last couple of feet in to shore dragging my board, trying to figure out if what I'd seen was an optical illusion.

There are a number of palm trees up along Ke Nui Road, and some have various kinds of underbrush around them. I'd seen the rifle barrel protruding from a stand of *pili* grass, which grows naturally in two or three foot lengths—thick enough and tall enough to hide someone lying flat.

I stuck my board in the sand and trudged up to the road. I could smell the cordite in the air, so I knew a weapon had been fired nearby. The *pili* grass had been broken and pushed flat in one area, big enough for a person to lie down. The kicker was finding a spent shell, and then another and an-other, in the sand just in front of the grass.

I didn't have anything resembling an evidence bag, but I did have an empty water bottle. I waved Harry in, and yelled for him to bring me the bottle.

"What did you find?" he asked, as he came up with it.

"Shell casings," I said. I pointed down. "Somebody's been shooting at us, brah."

Neither of us had much interest in going back in the water at that point, even though the waves were running high and the beach was still mostly empty. The idea of somebody pointing a rifle at you can wreck even the simplest pleasures, I guess. So we packed up and went back to Cane Landing around three o'clock, where I looked up Kevin Ruiz's card. No beeper or cell number on it, which wasn't surprising. After all, he'd given me the card when he considered me an informant.

I called the Wahiawa station to try to track him down. But because I couldn't say I was still an on-duty officer, I got a runaround, the opportunity to leave a message on his voice mail. I did, though I didn't expect him to check it until Monday morning.

I e-mailed Sampson and told him I was holding the shells for ballistics. I knew, though, that they would match the gun that had shot Mike Pratt off his board, the one that had killed Lucie Zamora as she exited Club Zinc. Even if they didn't match, I knew it had to be the same shooter.

"So what do we do now, brah?" Harry asked, as we lounged on the leather sofas in the living room at Cane Landing.

"Damned if I know," I said. "But I'm sure a beer would help me think." I'd stocked up on Konas in anticipation of Harry's visit, and we each had one and sipped in silence. We ended up grilling steaks on the major-league barbecue in the yard, and if we hadn't been worried that the shooter might somehow find his way into Cane Landing, it would have been a near-perfect evening.

Sunday morning my cell phone rang as I was making

chocolate chip pancakes for Harry and we were debating whether to risk surfing again. It was Sampson. "I got your e-mail," he said. "I want to see you at nine tomorrow morning in my office. Let's go over what you've got and regroup. I want to know everything about this surf shop owner. And bring those casings you found—you can run them downstairs to ballistics while you're here."

I agreed and hung up the phone, then repeated the gist of the conversation to Harry. "He didn't tell you not to go surfing, did he?" Harry asked.

I shook my head.

"So you want to?"

I thought about it for almost a minute. "I do," I said. "But not Pipeline. And I don't want to go anywhere near Bishop Clark's place and risk Rich Sarkissian taking pot shots at us there. How about Sunset?"

Sunset was another great break, one I hadn't patronized much because so much of the case seemed to revolve around Pipeline. Harry agreed that was a good compromise; it was unlikely that the killer would be driving up and down the North Shore with a pair of binoculars. Just to be on the safe side, we left my truck at Cane Landing and drove in Harry's BMW, our two boards strapped to the roof. It was almost like being in high school again, only with a much better car.

We surfed until mid-afternoon. We were sitting on our boards beyond the breakers, looking for waves, when Harry said, "This is my last wave, brah. Then I have to start packing up for the trip back to Honolulu. Arleen's mom is babysitting Brandon so she and I can have dinner on our own." He smiled. "That's a big event in my life," he said. "I really like Brandon a lot, he's a great kid, but sometimes I want Arleen all to myself."

"Hey, I won't stand in your way," I said. I saw a wave coming and grabbed it, leaving Harry behind. I got a couple of turns out of it, and then started dragging my board up the beach. Then I saw Al Kawamoto sitting in the blue Taurus up on Ke Nui Road. My first instinct was to turn around and get back in the water, even though I was exhausted and every muscle in my body ached. I was just tired of dealing with him; he was a homophobic asshole, and I just didn't have the energy for his bullshit.

"Gotta talk to you," he said, rolling down his window as I approached.

I didn't want to tell him about someone shooting at me. Frankly, I didn't think he'd believe me, even with the shell casings as evidence. "I'm exhausted, Al. Can't it wait until tomorrow?" I kept moving past him.

"It can't."

There was something in his tone of voice, a note of resignation, even despair, which I had never heard from him. I turned around. "What's up?"

"I don't want to talk about it here. Come on, get in."

"Al, I'm full of salt and sweat. You don't want me in your car." I looked at my watch. "Meet me at the Surfrider in half an hour. There are some tables beyond the *tiki* huts in the back. Nobody will see us there."

He rolled up his window and drove off. "Nice talking to you, too," I said.

Harry came out of the water then, and I waited at his car for him. "Who were you talking to?"

"Homophobic asshole," I said. "I have to meet him for a drink in half an hour."

"Then we'd better hustle," Harry said.

Chapter 35

MY DINNER WITH AL

HARRY HAD TO LOAD UP HIS CAR HIMSELF, because though I didn't want to, I had to jump in the shower then throw on an aloha shirt and khaki shorts. We told each other to take care and I promised to call him the next day after my meeting with Sampson. It was probably forty-five minutes before I made it to the Surfrider, and Al Kawamoto was just starting his third beer.

I sat down across from him. "So what's so important?"

"I didn't know who else to go to," he said.

I'd been getting attitude from Kawamoto for days, and I was in the mood to give him some back. "Al. Don't tell me you're really gay and you've been in the closet all this time."

He gave me the dirtiest of dirty looks. "All right," I said. "I'm here. I'm listening. Talk."

"Me and Kevin, we've been partners for six years," he said. "He's a stand-up guy. Jesus, I hate this."

My sensors started to go off. "Hate what, Al?"

"Maybe I'm just crazy. But I don't want to jam Kevin up if I'm wrong."

Al Kawamoto looked genuinely anguished. I had to figure he wasn't happy about having to come to me—from day one, he hadn't exactly been my biggest fan.

So what he had to say had to be that much more important, for him to overcome his dislike of me. "You're a cop, Al. You know you can't make accusations like that without evidence. So lay the evidence out for me."

He took a long sip of his beer—Dutch courage, my father called it. "We caught that first murder, the guy, Pratt. One of his buddies told me he thought Pratt had gotten mixed up in some kind of drug deal. I brought it to Kevin, he pooh-poohed it. 'The guy's a straight arrow,' he said." He looked up at me. "No offense."

"None taken," I said. "Your partner was right. Pratt was a good guy. Everybody liked him. Didn't fit the profile of a guy mixed up in drugs."

"Nope."

I took a sip of my beer and considered. "Except for the fact that surfing's an expensive hobby. If you don't win tournaments you don't get sponsors and you've got to come up with all the cash yourself for equipment, entry fees, travel, all that stuff. Pratt taught surfing on the side, but you've got to give a lot of lessons to make any real money."

"That was what I thought, but Kevin, he wouldn't listen. Finally I gave up."

"OK. What else?"

"Same thing with the girl. We started hearing rumors she was a dealer. Even connected her to that surf shop where she used to work, The Next Wave."

"I heard those same rumors, you know."

He nodded. "We couldn't connect Pratt to the girl except through ballistics. Some reason, Kevin didn't want to explore the drug angle. And I have to say I didn't push as hard as I could have."

"Hey, I've had partners," I said. "It's a give and take."

He finished his beer. "You ready for another round?"

"I'm still working on this one. And why don't you get a burger or something, Al? You don't want to let the beer get too far ahead of you."

He called a waiter over and we both ordered burgers. He ordered another beer, too, but I noticed he started taking that one more slowly.

"So far, Al, you haven't got much to worry about. Kevin didn't want to follow a couple of leads, well, maybe he thought they were a waste of time. Can't argue with a judgment call."

I looked at him. "Do you think he's using something himself?"

He looked up at the thatched roof above us. We were in a glorified *tiki* hut, a couple of big poles holding up the sloping roof, only a few other high-topped tables around us. A pretty private area, even when the rest of the place was busy. That night, only about half the tables were filled.

It was clear he didn't really want to answer that question, but I waited. Finally he said, "I think so." That admission seemed to take something out of him, and his whole body sagged.

"Why?" I asked gently.

"His moods have been all over the place, and he's always complaining about money. And lately he's been cagey sometimes, about where he's going or where he's been."

Nothing was damning, but Al was a good detective. He'd been assembling small clues for a while. "Anything else?" I asked.

"He wouldn't let me talk to Vice," he said. "Got all angry. Said he'd handle it. Like he didn't trust me. That's not like the old Kevin. Jesus, I was best man at his wedding."

"You talk to Vice anyway?"

He looked down at the table. "Nope. I didn't want them to get suspicious. I was thinking maybe you could."

"Al, I'm undercover. Nobody's supposed to know I'm working these cases. Not even you guys, until a couple days ago."

His head popped up suddenly. "You think Sampson suspected something?"

I shrugged. "I know he was suspicious that you guys couldn't come up with anything. Not surprising if it turns out Kevin was hiding stuff."

"What can we do?" Al asked.

The waitress appeared with our burgers. "We can eat," I said.

We ate in silence, and then finally I said, "I got called down to headquarters tomorrow for a meeting with Sampson."

Fear immediately jumped into Al's eyes. "You think he knows something?"

I shook my head. "I had the same suspicions about The Next Wave that you did, only I tried to ignore them because I know the guy who owns the place. We used to surf together years ago." I figured that was all Al Kawamoto really needed to know about my relationship with Dario. "I finally e-mailed Sampson what I was thinking." I took a drink of my beer. "Plus somebody shot at me yesterday at Pipeline."

"Jesus!" Al said. He dropped his fork on the laminated table.

"Probably wasn't him shooting at me," I said. "I'm sure he could use thunderbolts or a plague of frogs or something. I found a couple of shell casings on the beach; I'm taking them with me."

"Are you going to tell Sampson about Kevin?"

"What do you want me to do? He's your partner."

Al Kawamoto didn't say anything for a while. I could only imagine how he was feeling; a partnership is like a marriage in many ways, and you cover for each other, you support each other . . . but that only goes so far, and I could see Al knew it. "You gotta tell him," he said. He reached down to the floor and picked up a briefcase he'd brought in with him. Opening it, he pulled out a file folder. "Copies of everything we found," he said. "You can read between the lines, you'll see what Kevin didn't want to follow up. You can point that out to Sampson."

That must have been really hard for him, photocopying that file on Sunday afternoon, knowing exactly what he was going to have to do with it, even if he was trying not to consciously think it through. I was actually starting to feel sorry for Al—and I hate it when somebody I don't like starts to get me on their side.

We finished dinner and Al picked up the check. "No arguments," he said.

"All right." I took the file back home with me to Cane Landing and read it over, and then read it through a second time, taking notes. I already knew almost everything in it; what I was interested in was what Ruiz knew when, and what he chose to ignore.

It was almost eleven when I finally closed the folder and went to sleep.

Chapter 36

ROAD TRIP

By the time I got out of the shower the next morning, the sun was up, and the air was bright and fresh. Perfect surfing weather, and the North Shore beaches were still unusually empty. A siren song, but I had to ignore it.

Traffic really picked up when I connected to the H2 around Wheeler Army Field. At least the traffic kept moving, and I made it to police headquarters on South Beretania Street in downtown Honolulu with a few minutes to spare.

As I sat for a minute in my truck with the radio playing the Hapa version of the *Hawaii Five-O* theme, I couldn't help remembering the last time I had been to headquarters, just three weeks before. At the time I'd been nervous, reporting to a new boss for a new job. I'd had no idea that the job would be undercover, and that I'd be immediately plunged into such a difficult case.

I fed the meter and walked up to the front door, past the memorial to officers killed in the line of duty. It was a place I never wanted to see a familiar name, but I stopped, like I often do, to scan it, letting all that sacrifice sink in. Another cop bumped into me as I turned to go in, and he started to excuse himself, but stopped when he saw who I was.

I didn't recognize him, but I smiled and said, "Sorry." He

bowed his head a bit and continued inside without saying a word. The aide at the metal detector was joking with everyone who came in, but didn't say a word to me. Everywhere I went, it seemed like people stopped talking as I approached. I'm sure it was just my paranoia, though I worried what it would be like to deal with people like that every day, if I ever solved this case and got off the North Shore, and returned to work at headquarters.

Sampson had somebody in his office with the door closed, so I had to hang around outside waiting for him to finish. I saw a couple of detectives I knew and said hello, and they were all pleasant enough. Still, I felt very conspicuous standing out there and was glad when Sampson opened the door. I was quite surprised, though, to see my old boss from Waikīkī, Lieutenant Yumuri, come out.

He was just as surprised to see me. "Lieutenant," I said, nodding.

"Kanapa'aka." He turned back to Sampson. "I'll call you later," he said, and walked past me.

"Come on in, Kimo," Sampson said. I wanted to ask him what Yumuri had been doing there, but I reminded myself the world didn't revolve around me, and they probably had some other business. Still, the reception I'd gotten downstairs, and seeing Yumuri again, didn't put me in the best mood.

I sat down across from Sampson, noticing again the crowd of personal photographs on his desk, the miniature cannon on the shelf above. "Sounds like you're getting close," he said, leaning back in his chair. "But I want you to be careful. I don't like the idea of anybody shooting at my detectives."

"I'm not that fond of it myself," I said. I pulled out the folder Al Kawamoto had given me and explained how I'd gotten hold of it.

A shadow passed over Sampson's face. "I was afraid of something like this. Let me take a look."

I handed him the folder and he skimmed through it. While I waited, I thought about what it would be like to work at headquarters, to report to Sampson on a daily basis. I liked him and thought I could work for him, but the rest of the force . . . I wasn't so sure.

Could I work in an environment where people didn't like me, where they talked behind my back and went silent when I walked in the room? Maybe the force wasn't the right place for me after all. I could move to the mainland, become a cop in a place like L.A. Or I could stay in Honolulu and become a private eye.

What would that be like, I wondered. How would I get clients? Would I be stuck on the sleazy underbelly of the law, chasing deadbeat dads, photographing illicit trysts?

"What's your take on all this?" Sampson asked, startling me out of my reverie.

I'd been thinking all the way from Haleiwa to Honolulu about how I'd answer that very question. "I like Kevin Ruiz," I said, choosing my words carefully. "He seems like a stand-up guy. And after what I've been through myself, I hesitate to put the finger on anyone, to make them go through what I did. But I have to listen to my gut, and to his own partner. I think he merits some investigation. His case leads the same place mine does—to The Next Wave. He wouldn't follow that lead, and when you couple that with Al Kawamoto's suspicion that Kevin might be using himself, you've got a bad situation."

"I'll have to read this over carefully," he said, closing the folder.

"Somebody has to talk to Vice," I said. "I told Al Kawamoto I thought that had to be him. We have to know what they have on The Next Wave. They may have their own investigation going, and we don't want to step into it."

"I agree. I'll get hold of Al and make sure he knows I'm behind him." He made a note on his Palm Pilot. "I want you to keep a low profile for the next couple of days," he said. He motioned to the folder on his desk. "Let me get this stuff squared away, and let's try not to give this shooter the chance to take any more pot shots, for your sake and for the sake of the general population on the North Shore." He looked up at me. "Anything you think you can do?"

"I'm going to take these shell casings downstairs to the SIS lab and see if they can match the markings to the gun that shot Mike Pratt and Lucie Zamora," I said. "Then I figured I'd head back to the North Shore."

"Hold off a day or so," he said. "Go back to your own apartment. Check with me tomorrow morning."

I left the casings with a technician in the Scientific Investigation Section, so they could be run through the Integrated Ballistics Identification System, an automated tracing system that allows the police to track bullets and their casings the same way investigators run fingerprint checks. Then I left the building, avoiding any further confrontations with officers who didn't like me.

It was strange to pull up in my own parking lot, walk up the outside steps to my own little studio apartment. My whole place would have fit into the living room of the house Ari was lending to me, but it was home, and I was glad to see it. The place had a musty, closed-in smell, and I opened the windows and turned on the fan to air it out.

I hadn't been home for more than a few minutes when my cell phone rang. It was Harry, with a plan for the evening. He would pick me up around six, we'd get some takeout Chinese and a six pack of beer, and head to Terri's house in Wailupe. I'd get to see her son, Danny, who was still pretty traumatized from his father's death, and then the three of us could hang out and talk.

I made one change in the plan. I had to swing past my parents' house late in the afternoon to see them, so I said I'd get the beer, and leave Harry in charge of takeout, meeting him out at Terri's house.

Due to the way the buildings stack up between me and the beach, I've got a decent view of the ocean from the big picture window in my living room, and after I hung up on Harry I walked over and looked out toward the Pacific.

A lot had happened to me during the past couple of months, and I hadn't had much time to process it. Watching the surf dash itself against the shore gave me a minute to stop and think. The pace of my life seemed to have accelerated lately; I had moved much further in the last few weeks, in many ways, than I had in several of the years before. It was enough to make a guy dizzy.

I imagined running into a friend who'd been off island for a couple of months. "Hey, what's new, Kimo," he'd say.

"Well, I caught a really tough case and nearly got killed solving it," I'd say. "Came out of the closet, nearly lost my job, saw my life splashed all over the media, fought with my brothers and my parents, saw a friend die and killed a man myself, then went undercover and had to be nice to a guy who basically raped me ten years ago. I've been pretty busy."

It was a wonder I hadn't started knocking back shots, or popping pills or smoking Maui Wowie. I stared at the water for a while, trying to think of what else I had to do. I had my laptop with me, so I plugged it in, got online, and looked for information on The Next Wave. There had been a few police reports to the property, including the time Rich Sarkissian punched out that customer, but nothing in the police system about drug connections there.

I read about the store's involvement in the community, sponsoring a softball team, collecting funds for an injured surfer, and donating merchandise for charity auctions and raffles. Dario had been a good citizen. I read about Ari and his meetings before the zoning boards. Finally, around noon, I ran out of research. It reminded me of a page Harry Ho had referred me to once. It read "You have reached the end of the Internet. Go out and have a life."

So I went surfing. I didn't want to go to Kuhio Beach Park because of its proximity to the Waikīkī station, so I drove out to Black Point. I surfed for a couple of hours, trying to clear my head enough so that everything about the case would come together—but I didn't have much luck. Eventually I gave up, went home, showered, changed, and drove up to my parents' house.

My mother did not kiss or hug me when she opened the door, before I had a chance to fish out a key or even ring the bell. "Tell your father he is a silly old man with a heart condition," she demanded.

"No," I said. I leaned down and kissed her cheek. "Nice to see you, Mother."

"Maybe he will listen to you, since he won't listen to me."

"Quiet, old woman," my father said. He enveloped me in a big bear hug. "You been gone too long, Keechee."

My father has nicknames for all three of us boys. Lui is Lulu, Haoa is Howgow, and I'm Keechee, unless he's angry, in which case I'm James Kimo Kanapa'aka, my full legal name. I have an English first name and a Hawai'ian middle name, because until 1962 it wasn't legal to give a child a Hawai'ian first name. Paperwork is complicated in my family, as you can imagine.

"Tell your son what you did today, Al," my mother said. We were standing in the foyer of our house, a modified ranch with a single story set on a sloping piece of land.

"Can we go into the living room?" I asked. "Or at least the kitchen?"

"Your mother no happy," my father said.

"Duh. I got that part. Why?"

"I told you no tell Kimo, Lokelani. But you insist." My mother's name means Heavenly Rose, and at the moment she was definitely showing her thorns.

"Tell me about what? Will you two stop arguing long enough to let me in?"

"A man at doctor's office talk stink about you," my father said. "So I hit him."

I put my head in my hands. "Ai yi yi," I said. "Did he call the police?"

"He wasn't really hurt," my mother said. "The nurse took him into the examining room, cleaned him up, and put a bandage on him. She was very nice. She put us into another room right away."

"Probably to keep Dad from beating up the rest of the patients," I said. I turned to him. "Don't I remember you saying, 'Violence is the never the answer' when one of us wanted to beat somebody up?"

"I was wrong. Violence answer sometimes."

"Did they take your blood pressure at the doctor's office?"

"Two hundred over one-twenty!" my mother trumpeted. "We have to go back again tomorrow for another reading, but your father had to promise the nurse he wouldn't hit anyone else."

I sat down on the sofa. "This is all my fault," I said. "I should move to the mainland. I heard the LAPD is hiring."

"No!" my parents both chorused at the same time.

"No one chase you away from your home," my father said. "Not while I your father."

"Dad, give it a rest," I said. "You're sixty-three years old, you have high blood pressure and high cholesterol. If I hear about you punching anybody else, whether you're sticking up for me or Lui or Haoa or some neighbor down the street, I'm going to call in favors and get you locked up. You understand me?"

"See?" my mother said. "Your son talks sense. You should listen to him."

The whole encounter was surreal. Usually my mother rules our household with an iron fist inside a velvet glove. My father might raise his voice occasionally, but all it takes is a look from my mother and he turns into a penitent schoolboy. Now, though, he was looking sullen and openly defiant. "Don't make me call my brothers," I said. "You don't want all three of us ganging up on you."

"I am your father," he said. "I have to protect you."

"No you don't," I said. "I am younger than you are, stronger than you are, I have self-defense training, weapons training, and I know a little kung fu. If you really want to protect me, you'll take care of yourself and protect me from ever having to bail you out of jail or visit you in the emergency room."

"How about some lemonade?" my mother asked, satisfied now that my father had been suitably chastened.

"One glass," I said. "I can't stay long, but I couldn't come to town without seeing you."

When my mother went into the kitchen, I leaned over and

kissed my father's grizzled cheek. "Thank you for standing up for me," I said.

"You're my boy."

My mother came out with the lemonade, and I knew I had to tell them. It wasn't fair to keep them in the dark any longer. "I have a confession to make," I said, running my finger through the condensation on the side of my glass. "I haven't been completely honest with you."

I saw my parents exchange a look. I could only imagine what fresh horrors they were imagining. "Dad, remember when I told you Lieutenant Sampson wanted me to do something for him, something that would make me lie?"

My father nodded. "I did it. I lied." I took a deep breath. "I've been working undercover on the North Shore, trying to solve a series of homicides."

"The surfers who were killed?" my father asked.

"Yes. Sampson didn't want me to tell you, because he didn't trust Lui. He was afraid that if you knew I was still a cop, eventually you would tell Lui, and he would make news out of it."

My mother opened her mouth to protest, but very quickly stopped herself. I guess she knows her oldest son well. "I think the case is going to break open soon, and my cover will be blown. I wanted you to know before that happens."

"I know it!" my father trumpeted. "I know you no quit."

"What your father means is that we both know how much being a detective means to you," my mother said. "What will happen when this case is solved?"

"I don't know. I will probably go back to headquarters, though I know there are people there who don't like me."

"Which people?" my father demanded.

"You don't need to go down there and start smacking people around, Dad, though I appreciate the thought. Whatever happens, I'll work it out."

"I don't like what is happening here," my mother said. "You lying to us to keep information from your brother. We are family, Kimo. You must remember that. When the police suspended you, who was on your side? Your family."

An acid taste began creeping up my throat from my stomach. "I know, Mom, and I appreciate it."

"Do we have to prove something to you, Kimo? How do we know when to believe you now?"

"We accept what he say," my father said. "Kimo grown man, with his own secrets. Not child who answer to his parents."

"We all must answer for our actions." My mother glared at both of us.

"Look, I've got to go," I said, getting out of my chair. "I'm going out to Terri's tonight. She's still very shaky."

"You give her our love," my mother said, standing so I could kiss her cheek. It was obvious, though, that this topic had only been tabled temporarily.

Chapter 37

WAILUPE

DARKNESS HAD JUST SETTLED on the Wailupe peninsula as I drove down Terri's street, my headlights illuminating the well-manicured lawns, the stately royal palms, the expensive cars and boats on trailers in driveways. "Danny insisted he had to wait up for you," Terri said, holding him in her arms as she answered the door.

Her son was barely keeping his eyes open, but he mumbled, "Uncle Kimo," and I took him in my arms and gave him a kiss on the forehead and a big hug.

"Will you go to bed now that I'm here?"

"OK. If you tuck me in."

"I can do that." I waved hello to Harry in the living room as I carried Danny to his bedroom.

I had to be introduced to all his stuffed animal friends and begin reading him a story, but within minutes he was snoring softly. I turned the lights out and went back to the living room, where Harry had a beer waiting for me.

"Man, I need this," I said, taking a grateful drink. "You'll never guess what my father did today."

I told them the story. "Poor thing," Terri said. "It's sweet the way he stood up for you."

"It's stupid," I said. "I can't tell you how many cases I've seen where people do dumb things like that and the outcome is a lot worse." I took another long swallow. "I also told them that I've been working undercover."

"How did they take it?" Harry asked.

I tore at the label on the beer bottle. "I shifted all the blame to Lui—said Lieutenant Sampson didn't trust him not to make news out of me, so I couldn't tell anyone. My mother wasn't real happy. Even so, it feels great not to have to lie to them anymore. Though God knows if they'll believe anything I say for a while."

"Your parents love you," Terri said. "They'll believe whatever you tell them."

We caught up on Danny's school, Harry's girlfriend Arleen and her son Brandon, and life in general. Finally, Harry said, "So any chance of you getting back to Honolulu in this lifetime?"

"I think I'm getting close." I drained the last of my beer and got another, and we moved to the kitchen table, where we dug into the Chinese takeout. "I've been assuming that the target was Tommy Singer, because he surfed, and that Brad Jacobson was in the wrong place at the wrong time. Suppose it was the opposite?"

"Somebody wanted to kill your friend?" Harry asked. "Why?"

"I think the killer knew I was getting close to him, and he killed Brad and Tommy to throw me off the scent and confuse me, and maybe even make me into a suspect."

"Because of your personal relationship with Brad?"

I nodded. "It could have been a warning to me. Or maybe somebody's who so homophobic that he wanted to make sure the gay ex-cop would get blamed. There's no ballistics match to the previous crimes, but I still think they're related."

"And don't forget the idea that someone wants to clean out the North Shore," Terri said. "Remember how we talked about land values. Somebody like your friend Ari, that 'nice Greek fella,' could buy up more property at a discount, or push through the approvals he needs, if business on the North Shore goes way down."

"He's not exactly a nice Greek fella," Harry said. "He was actually born Harold Pincus, but changed his name after dodging a fraud conviction."

We filled Terri in on Ari's background and then I told them both everything I had learned about Dario, The Next Wave, and the possibility that Dario, Kevin Ruiz, and the ice trade on the North Shore were all connected.

"That's a lot of material," Terri said.

"You bet. I've been trying to get my mind around it for days now."

Harry opened his laptop and started creating a matrix for all the information. Terri chimed in occasionally with ideas, and by the time we were done, at least I had everything organized—a sequence of events, possible perpetrators and motives, and additional details for me to track down.

Our last suspect was Rich Sarkissian. "That guy gives me the creeps," Terri said.

Remembering how we had worked together at the outrigger *halau*, I said, "He's actually not that creepy, except for the fact that he hates surfers."

Harry made a snorting noise, which I ignored.

"Aunt Emma gave me the papers today for Uncle Bishop to sign," Terri continued. "But I can't let this deal go through until I know that he's not involved in these people getting killed. Especially with what you've told me about Ari, the whole thing makes me very uncomfortable. Uncle Bishop is expecting me to bring the papers up to him tomorrow but I don't know what to tell him."

"Don't say anything yet," I said. "Just stall for a few more days. Can you cancel your meeting tomorrow?"

"Let me call him now. He should know that there's something fishy in Ari's background."

She left the room, and Harry and I went back to his matrix. She returned in a few minutes, though. "Bad news. I told Uncle Bishop I'd done some checking into Ari's background and wasn't sure he could be trusted, and he went ballistic. He insisted that I come up tomorrow and give Ari a chance to defend himself."

"I'll go with you. I'm the one who found the evidence, after all."

Her meeting was at two, so I decided I'd head up in the morning, meet her for lunch, and then we'd go over to Bishop Clark's together.

We finished dinner and I drove back to Waikīkī. I had trouble falling asleep with so many ideas ricocheting around in my brain—my parents, the surf killer, real estate values on the North Shore, my brothers, Brad, Ari, Dario. Harry's matrix kept recurring in my dreams, as I struggled to catch the killer before he could strike again.

≈

I COULDN'T GET HOLD of Sampson before I left Honolulu, but I left him a voice mail. Driving up the Kam, I wondered if I would ever get back to Honolulu, to the life I had once lived. Would I be transferred permanently to someplace like Wahiawa—if I was ever able to go back to official detective work? I had not been with anyone since Brad, and I worried that any guy I dated might become a target. How could I risk loving someone knowing he could be killed?

I pulled up at Cane Landing and unloaded. I couldn't go surfing, because I had promised Sampson I'd keep a low profile. I didn't want to go to The Next Wave, because I didn't know how the store, or Dario himself, might figure in the case. I pulled out Harry's matrix and studied it, turning the pieces over in my head.

I gave up just before noon and hurried down into Haleiwa to meet Terri at Jameson's for lunch. The roads were empty, and many businesses along the way were closed and shuttered, as if a hurricane was approaching. There was only a single car in the parking lot of The Next Wave as I passed.

Terri and I sat by the window and looked out at the ocean. There was hardly any traffic and only a few brave surfers out on the waves. "There is such a fragile balance," she said. "Between success and failure, between nature and development, between life and death. Look at how quickly things have fallen apart up here."

I knew she was also talking about how fast her life had changed when her husband died. "I know, sweetie," I said, reaching out to take her hand.

"Tell me you don't think my uncle is involved in this business."

"I just don't know. There's a link that ties all this together, and I can almost see it. But it's like a name that's on the tip of your tongue, just one brain cell away from connecting."

Neither of us had much appetite and the dismal atmosphere inside Jameson's and outside the window didn't help. Finally we gave up and drove my truck up to Bishop's house. Rich let us in the gate, though he showed no sign of the friendliness I'd seen at the outrigger *halau*.

Ari was already there when we arrived, drinking lemonade out of those same French crystal glasses, talking to Bishop about how beautiful his new home was going to be. "I hope you'll let me explain," Ari said. "I think you owe me that much."

"Nobody's here to accuse anyone of anything," I said. "Terri just has some concerns about your background and how that impacts the deal."

"None of Terri's goddamn business," Bishop muttered.

"It's OK, Bishop," Ari said. "I welcome the chance to get this all on the table." He described the viatical corporation he'd begun in Minnesota, to help some friends with AIDS who were desperately in need of money for medicine and living expenses. How the financial assumptions had been knocked out when the new drugs gave AIDS patients the chance to return to work and health.

"I finally had to file for bankruptcy," he said. "My investors ended up holding the policies, and they'll cash in eventually. No one was ruined, and a lot of guys got the cash they needed. I'm sorry the business folded, but I believe I acted morally."

"Then why'd you change your name?" I asked.

"I wanted a fresh start. You can understand that, can't you, Kimo? Don't you wish sometimes you could move to a new place where no one knew you, start over again? Growing up, we had Greek neighbors, and I loved their culture. I always hated my name—when I was a kid, the bullies used to call me

Pincushion and stick me with pins and needles. One day I'd just had enough, and I decided to start over."

"See!" Bishop said. "Everything's fine. Terri, you worry too much."

Terri opened her portfolio and pulled some papers out. "There are just a couple of little changes Aunt Emma wanted to make," she said.

"No more changes," Bishop said. "I want to get this deal signed."

"I agree with Bishop," Ari said. "My partners and I are very anxious to get something going, and we've been approached by the owner of another parcel out in Mokuleia that we might be able to find just as suitable."

"See, Terri, we've got to get this deal signed," Bishop said. "Otherwise we might lose it, and then where would I be?"

"You'd be right where you are, Uncle Bishop. You've run through your inheritance and your trust fund, and all you've got left is this property. But you forget, it's not completely yours. The Trust and the rest of the family still have a say, and I'm here to make sure that at least a part of this land is protected in a way that our family can be proud of."

Bishop started yelling, demanding that she agree to the terms as already spelled out. Terri wasn't yelling back, because that's not what Great-Aunt Emma would expect of her, but she wasn't backing down either.

Then Ari started talking, trying to mediate between the two of them, but frankly, they were all giving me a headache. I walked over to the windows to look out at the water, and that's when I heard the shots.

Chapter 38

SHOTS FIRED

No one else seemed to have heard anything—at least, none of them stopped talking. I was worried that Rich was out there taking pot shots at surfers again, so I slipped out the side door, taking care not to let it slam.

It was in the low eighties, and there was a nice breeze coming up from the ocean. I stood there for a long moment, listening, but all I heard was the low susurrus of the waves and the sound of the occasional truck grinding through its gears out on the steep part of the Kam.

I started down toward the beach, stepping carefully through the scrub and sand, trying not to make any noise. I walked along one side of the property, under the shelter of a long row of *kukui* trees, so I wasn't easily visible. I realized, as I moved slowly, that my pistol was up at my truck; the only thing I had to defend myself with was a cell phone, which would probably go off at just the wrong moment.

I reached down to my belt and flipped the phone off. Strike one for the well-prepared cop. After about ten minutes of a slow, steep descent, I finally came to a rise that gave me a panoramic view of the beach, only to find it completely deserted.

By then, sweat had begun beading on my forehead and dripping under my arms and down my back. I felt foolish, and yet I knew I had heard shots. Rich couldn't have passed me going back up toward the house, I thought. I would have seen or heard him. So maybe the shots had come from the other side of the property, by the road.

I looked back up the hill at the house and through the big windows I saw Terri, Bishop, and Ari still arguing. I swung around to the side of the property and climbed back up the hill, staying close to the property line and the row of *kukui* trees. In order to get back to the house, I'd have to go out in the open again and I didn't want to do that, so I just stopped for a minute to listen again, a few hundred yards from the side door. I heard yelling coming from the house, but the only thing I knew was that it wasn't Terri's voice. I heard nothing else out of place except a creaking sound.

Staying under the line of *kukui* trees, I continued to climb toward the street. This area was much more heavily vegetated than the land between the house and the beach. The soil had to be richer up here, and I could barely make out the contours of the twisting driveway, overgrown as the whole area was with hibiscus, succulent, white-flowered *hinahina,* and the papery flowers of red and purple bougainvillea. If you looked down from the Kam, you'd hardly even know there was a house back there, the land looked so natural and unspoiled. It wouldn't be that way for long, I thought, once those papers got signed.

Once I'd moved a few yards toward the street, I even lost sight of the house itself due to all the vegetation around me. Because the underbrush rustled, I had to move even more slowly. I pulled out the tail of my shirt and kept wiping the sweat from my forehead. Finally I was able to peer through the underbrush and see that the gate to the street was open. I distinctly remembered seeing Rich swing it closed behind us, moving with his loping gait.

I didn't see him anywhere, but if he was wandering around with a gun I didn't want to surprise him, so I called "Rich?" softly. "You out here somewhere?"

I heard something like a moan, and quickened my pace, forgetting about the noise I was making crashing through the underbrush. Jesus, had Rich shot some surfer who was trying to get on to the property? "I'm coming," I called. "Hold on. Where are you?"

I followed the sounds of the moans, and when I burst through the underbrush up at the highway's edge I was startled to come upon Rich Sarkissian, lying on the ground next to the open gate. He was holding onto his mid-section and when he pulled a hand away to wave at me, it was covered in blood.

"Jesus, Rich, what happened?" I asked, dropping to the ground. I pulled off my shirt and started ripping it into strips.

"That asshole," he gasped.

"What asshole?" I asked, as I pulled away his own shirt to expose the wound. "Who shot you? Some surfer?"

He nodded. "Fuh-fuh," he said. I was busy stuffing strips into the open wound in his chest.

"I know, a real fucker," I said.

He shook his head violently. "Fuh-fuh," he said.

"Is that someone's name? You know the guy?"

He nodded weakly. I pulled my cell phone off my belt and turned it back on again, waiting impatiently for it to catch a signal. As soon as it did, I dialed 911. "I need an ambulance," I said. "A man's been shot." I gave them Bishop's address. "He's already lost a lot of blood," I said. "You need to be here now."

The dispatcher wanted me to stay on the line, but I had to see to Rich. "Fun . . ." he said.

"No, I know it's not much fun getting shot, Rich, but you've been through this before, buddy. You're tough. You already know that. Looks like I got the bleeding stopped, so you just have to hold on until the ambulance gets here."

"Fonseca," he said, though his voice was hoarse and barely above a whisper.

"Fonseca? Dario Fonseca? Dario shot you?" He nodded weakly. "Where did he go? Up to the house?"

"Go," he said. He pushed at me, very lightly. "Bishop."

I positioned Rich at the gate to the property, where anybody coming down the highway could see him easily. "You hold out, buddy," I said. "I called an ambulance for you and they're going to be here any minute. I'm going up to the house and as soon as I see what's what, I'm coming back down here."

He nodded again. He looked like he was about to pass out, but there was nothing more I could do for him. If I was right, Dario had killed five people already, shot at me, and just shot Rich. And he was up at the house with Terri, Ari, and Bishop, and he had a gun.

Oh, and Bishop had an arsenal himself, which could be all at Dario's disposal.

Before I started making my way back up to the house, I pulled my cell phone out again and called Sampson's office phone. The call went immediately to voice mail.

"Shit," I said. Frantically I paged through my call log, finding his cell number and dialing it.

He picked up on the second ring.

"I need backup," I said. "ASAP, and you're the only one who can get it for me fast." I explained, as quickly as I could, that the suspect he and I had discussed was armed and at Bishop's address, and that one man had already been shot.

"Right," he said, and hung up.

Thinking that Dario was already at the house, I didn't bother staying undercover as I hurried up the twisting driveway. I made it to my truck without seeing anything or anyone except a lean brown horse that appeared to be wandering and grazing the open land near the highway.

Dario's truck had pulled up next to mine. My old hand-me-down pickup still bore faint traces of the logo of my father's business. Dario had seen me in it at Cane Landing, at Sugar's, and at The Next Wave. So he knew I was somewhere around—if he was thinking rationally.

You could see the parking area from the house, so I dropped to my knees and crawled to my truck, using Dario's as cover. I opened the passenger door as slowly and carefully as I could, and unlocked the glove compartment. The 9 millimeter Glock my father had given me was nestled in the back, wrapped in a chamois. I pulled it out and slid it into my pocket. I had a spare pair of handcuffs in there, too, and I clipped them to my belt.

I didn't bother to close the door, but slunk around the side of the truck and then the side of the house. I heard raised voices as I came to the back, and dropped flat to the ground. From the cover of some *pili* grass, I could see up into the tall windows.

Ari, Terri, and Bishop were clustered together, at one end of the room. Across from them stood Dario Fonseca, with a pistol trained at them. As I crept closer, I could hear him yelling at them, "Where the fuck is my wife?"

That was so different from what I expected to hear that I had to pull back and regroup. Terri had called Bishop the night before to tell him there might be a problem with the deal. He had obviously called Ari. Ari must have spoken to Dario, who was already in deep financial trouble. He couldn't afford to lose his investment in Bishop's Bluff. He might have come to force Terri to agree to the deal.

But his wife? What could she have to do with anything?

I closed my eyes and racked my brain for anything I could remember about her. Her name was America. She was younger than Dario, and had grown up near him on the Big Island, the daughter of another *paniolo*.

Suddenly connections started zinging through my brain. That night at Sugar's, Dario had said he was a rootin' tootin' cowboy, able to ride, rope, and shoot. Did that mean America could, too? Was that America's horse I'd passed before? Was she somewhere at the house? What could she have to do with anything? Why would Dario be looking for her?

I lay there flat on the ground, surrounded by the *pili* grass, and out of the corner of my eye I caught a tiny movement to my left, just the waving of another stand of *pili* grass. I shifted ever so slightly, moving my head so I had a clearer view.

I saw the outline of a woman's body, and black hair in a ponytail that hung over one shoulder. While I could not see her face, something about her was familiar. Could that be Dario's wife? I thought it was possible that I had seen her at The Next Wave, though we had never been introduced. Then she shifted again and I saw the outline of her face, and recognized her. I had seen her at the outrigger practices and kissing Melody at Kahuna's; she had been called Mary.

It was an easy leap; if my name was America I'd want a nickname, too. Mary lay there, her eyes fixed on the tall windows of Bishop Clark's house. The air around us was so still and quiet, I could hear the waves down at the beach and an occasional gentle whinny from her horse, out toward the road. Where was the ambulance, I wondered. I hoped Rich Sarkissian was holding on.

Mary shifted and raised the barrel of a rifle. Was it the same M4 carbine that had shot Mike Pratt and Lucie Zamora? I had to reevaluate everything I had been thinking about the case—but I couldn't do that until the people in the house were safe.

I did have to think about the situation, I realized. If Mary had shot Mike Pratt off his board at Pipeline, that meant she was an expert marksman, and that meant I was in big danger if she realized I was watching her. If I could see her, camouflaged as she was in the *pili* grass, she could certainly see me.

Up at the house, I saw Ari lunge for Dario through the big windows. I held my breath as they wrestled for the gun. I wanted so much to rush up there and save them all, but couldn't do anything as long as America Fonseca had her rifle trained on the windows.

Finally, I heard a siren. Was it an ambulance? The police? There was no way I could get in contact, warn anyone. As soon as I tried to use my cell phone Mary would hear me and that rifle would swing my way.

I heard a shot fired up at the house and saw both Dario and Ari fall. Mary rose to one knee, sighted her rifle, and released the safety. I pulled my pistol up and sighted her myself.

I was a fraction of a second too late. She got a shot off toward the house just as I shot her. I caught her in the chest and knocked her backward. She dropped the rifle and I ran toward her. It appeared I'd only winged her shoulder; she reared up from the *pili* grass and shakily pointed the rifle at me, but by then it was too late for me to stop charging. I took a big jump and landed on her.

We wrestled back and forth, and she was a tough opponent. The rifle was kicked away, but I still clutched my pistol in my hand. Finally I was on top of her, and I took that opportunity to knock her on the head with the pistol. She went out cold, and I quickly popped the cuffs on her.

I couldn't tell what was going on up at the house, and couldn't wait any longer. I heard more sirens in the distance, but knew I had to get up there as soon as possible. I jumped up and ran for the side of the house; fortunately, no one seemed to be firing at me. I ran around to the side door and found it locked, then ran around to the *makai* side, the one facing the ocean.

Terri was leaning over her uncle, who lay on the floor. I didn't see any blood coming from him, but that didn't really mean anything. Ari was sitting cross-legged on the floor next to them. Dario was sitting on the floor a few feet away, shakily training his pistol on them.

"Kimo," he said. "Nice of you to join us. I knew you had to be around somewhere." He nodded toward his leg. "Your aim sucks, you know."

"I didn't shoot you, Dario. Your wife did."

Blood was leaking out of a wound in his leg, spilling all over Bishop's hardwood floor. There was a hole in the window where Mary's bullet had come through. Looking around quickly, I saw other bullet holes in the walls. I tried to count, to see how much ammunition Dario had left, but I couldn't take my eyes off him for too long.

I didn't want Dario to realize that there was a cabinet full of weapons and ammunition, so the only thing I could think to do was keep him talking until reinforcements arrived.

"Mary wouldn't shoot me," he said. "Mary loves me. My little piece of America." He laughed bitterly.

"She's outside," I said. "She had a rifle. Are the ballistics on that rifle going to match the gun that killed Mike Pratt and Lucie Zamora?"

Dario burst into tears. "I could never make enough money to make her happy," he said.

"Who? Lucie?"

"No!" Dario said angrily. "Mary!"

"Is that why you started dealing ice out of The Next Wave?"

"I never did," he said. His hold on the gun wavered. "It was always Mary. She got the idea, get surfers to smuggle the drugs in for us, and use surfers as dealers. They were hungry for cash, just like she was."

He looked up at me. "I was trying to get us legit," he said. "I was taking the money Mary made from dealing and putting it into this project." He aimed at Bishop again. "This stupid project, which never seemed to take off, and just needed more money, more money. Until there wasn't any more money left to put in."

I heard Terri whispering to her uncle. "Hold on, Uncle Bishop," she said. "Everything's going to be OK."

"Everything's not going to be OK!" Dario shouted.

"Calm down, Dario, we can work things out," I said. "How did everything get so bad?"

"That idiot Pratt couldn't keep his mouth shut," he said. "Mary heard him bitching at the outrigger club. She came home and told me. But shit, I didn't know what to do. I said I'd talk to him. Mary said no, she'd take care of it."

He looked at me. "She used to sit right in front of him in the canoe," he said. "I thought she'd talk to him, convince him it was better to shut up." Tears dripped down his cheeks. "The next time I heard his name it was somebody at the store saying he'd been shot."

He waved the gun a little. "I swear, I didn't know she was going to shoot him. But what could I do?"

"Did Lucie find out?"

"Stupid little bitch. She tried to shake Mary down. Wanted enough to finance a year around the world, going to surf competitions. Mary told her she was a dumb cunt."

"How did her friend Ronnie get involved?"

He snorted. "The idiot hacked into the store's accounts, thinking he could find the money in an account and take it out. But there wasn't any money anymore—we'd given it all to Ari."

Ari finally spoke. "You should have told me, Dario. We could have worked something out. You didn't have to do . . . this."

"I didn't have a choice," he said. "Shit, I haven't had a choice about anything for eleven years."

Oh, Jesus, I thought. I knew what was coming.

"It was almost eleven years ago, you know that, Kimo?" he asked. "I still remember the first time I saw you."

I had to keep him talking. At least he wasn't shooting. "Yeah, Dario? Where was that?"

"At the Surfrider," he said. "You had just come home from college and moved up here. You were with Dickie Yamassa, remember him?"

I did. Dickie had gone to Punahou with Terri, Harry, and me, but instead of going to college on the mainland the way we all did, he had stayed at UH, surfing the North Shore every chance he had. He was an amazing surfer by then—he had dropped out of UH the year before, started entering tournaments, and started winning.

I stayed on Dickie's floor the first three months I was on the North Shore. He had a girlfriend he stayed with most nights anyway, but we often surfed together during the day, then cruised bars together at night.

"The Surfrider has a lot of memories for us," I said.

"Jesus, Kimo, I thought the sun rose and set on you, and you hardly knew I was alive. For months—months—I knew where you were all the time, I followed you around, just waiting for you to notice me."

"I noticed you, Dario. We used to surf together all the time."

"But you ignored every hint I gave you."

"I was scared, Dario. I didn't want to be gay, and the way you kept coming on to me, touching me, saying stuff—what did you expect me to do?"

"I expected you to tell me you loved me, that you wanted to be with me," Dario said. "Then I finally got the chance to show you how I felt, and you ran away."

"I'm sorry if I hurt you, Dario," I said. I started inching closer to him. "I never wanted to. Honestly, I didn't know how you felt. But maybe things can be better now."

The noise he made in his throat sounded oddly like the one my father did, when he didn't believe what I was saying. "I'm serious, Dario. Things can be different. I'm out of the closet now. I'm here on the North Shore." I inched closer to him. "Give me the gun, and I'll look after you," I said. "Mary is going to have to go to jail, but then you and I can be together."

"Mary!" he said. "Where's Mary? I have to talk to Mary!" He tried to stand up, but he fell back to the floor.

I was close enough that I could tackle him. "Give me the gun, Dario," I said. We wrestled on the floor, and then another rifle blast shattered one of Bishop's big glass windows. Dario's attention was distracted enough that I got my body on top of his, got my hand on his gun hand. I had a knee in his crotch and I was close enough to smell the raw scent of fear and perspiration coming off him.

I mustered up a final burst of strength and wrenched the gun from him, pushing myself back. Another rifle burst split the air. "Everybody OK?" I called. "Terri?"

"OK," she said shakily.

"How's Bishop?"

"Dario shot him, and he's going in and out of consciousness. Kimo, I'm scared. Who's shooting at us?"

"I thought I knocked Mary Fonseca out and handcuffed her, but either she's gotten up or somebody else has gotten her rifle. See if you can drag Bishop under the table. Ari, can you help?"

I kept one eye on Dario, who was crying on the floor in front of me, and the other focused on the window. Mary Fonseca was a damned good riflewoman if she was able to shoot with her hands cuffed together.

"What about Brad, Dario? Who killed him, and that college kid? Why?"

"I couldn't stand to see somebody else have what I couldn't," he said, and he was crying full blast by then. "I know I shouldn't have done it. I just went crazy."

"And me? Did you shoot at me when I was out at Pipeline?"

"I'd never shoot you, Kimo. That must have been Mary. I think she knew how much I cared about you and she was jealous."

I heard another blast of gunfire, but this one wasn't aimed inside. There was a volley back and forth, and then I heard a voice call out, "Hello the house. Anybody there? Police!"

"Officer on the scene," I called back. "Scene secured."

Chapter 39

AFTER

AL KAWAMOTO WAS THE FIRST in the door, his gun held out ahead of him. In short order he was followed by uniforms who took custody of Dario, and an ambulance crew that took Bishop Clark away, with Terri by his side.

I sat at the table with Ari and we reconstructed everything that had happened for Al. When we were finally done, I drove down to Wahiawa General, where Bishop was in critical condition. Terri's parents had driven up from Honolulu by then, and her father sat holding his older brother's hand and talking gently to him.

"I'm so sorry things worked out the way they did," I said to Terri, when we had walked out together. "If I had known there was any danger I never would have let you go to Bishop's in the first place."

"You didn't know what was going to happen," Terri said.

"Yeah, that's been the theme of my life lately. Everything happens and I don't have a clue about it. Hell of a detective, huh?"

"You knew there was a connection between Dario's store and the deaths of the surfers," she said.

"I should have figured it out sooner. The first time I heard that Dario had a wife, I knew something was funny. I should have looked at him a lot more closely, but I was afraid I was trying to make him the killer because I was scared of him."

"You weren't scared of him," she said, taking my hand. "What you were scared of is inside of you, but you're working on that."

≈

BISHOP'S DEATH WAS BIG NEWS because of the family's prominence. And of course they had to note that there had been another Clark death, just a few weeks before. This time, though, I went to the funeral, with my parents. We sat at the Kawaiahao Church in downtown Honolulu, across from Honolulu Hale. The Clarks were descended from early missionaries to the islands and had ancestors buried in the graveyard behind the church. After a brief service, Bishop took his place among them.

I was in the news again, as Sampson told reporters that I had been working undercover to bring both Fonsecas to justice. Mary was being held for trial for her drug activities, as well as for the murders of Mike Pratt, Lucie Zamora, and Ronald Chang. Dario was being held as her accessory for all that, as well as for the murders of Brad Jacobson and Thomas Singer.

I closed up the house at Cane Landing and moved back to my apartment in Waikīkī. After a couple of days off, and evaluations by both the department physician and psychiatrist, I drove my battered pickup into downtown Honolulu once more, parked at a meter a block away from the main station, and prepared to start the job I'd thought I was getting all along, as a detective in District 1. I sat in the truck for a minute, though, listening to Keali'i Kaneali'i ask where all the beach boys of Waikīkī had gone. This boy, I knew, had gone away, but was back. Secure in that thought, I locked my truck and headed inside.